KIM TANAKA: *and I do. I love family life and he wants to live on the road. So how do we compromise? We'll have a dog instead of children and a home for part of the year? He'll try not to be afraid of stability and I'll try to be more of a vagabond? And what about our families? His grandmother hates me and mine doesn't think he'll make a good husband. With all that against us, how can we possibly expect to be happy together, no matter how great we are in bed?*

TODD McALLISTER: *I'm crazy about her, but can I live my life her way? She wants kids and she'd be a terrific mother. I'd be a lousy father. My own parents certainly didn't set a good example. I never knew who my father was. My mother couldn't tell me...she didn't know. And she never developed any feelings for me at all. Kim thinks if we have a baby my parenting instincts will kick in. Is it fair to the kid to risk it?*

Dear Reader,

I was happy to be included in the Class of '78 project, along
with three such wonderfully talented authors, and to be
allowed to write the story designated as a family drama.

As a writer I have always been interested in family, in all its
variations. Nobody can deny that the traditional family is in
trouble and under severe pressure. One need only watch a
few television talk shows to understand the problems. Most
of us cherish a dream of the ideal family, but we are still
forced to cope with the reality of our own situations, which
can fall woefully short of that ideal. But I remain optimistic.
I believe that families come in all shapes and sizes, wherever
people care deeply about one another.

In fact, I feel much the same way about my readers. Getting a
bundle of letters from you and sitting down to answer them is
one of the nicest and most rewarding parts of my life. If I ever
met you, it would feel like the most natural thing in the world
to give you a big hug and start chatting. We share so many
things through these books that all of you feel just like...family!

Margot Dalton

Margot Dalton

Kim & the Cowboy

Harlequin Books

TORONTO • NEW YORK • LONDON
AMSTERDAM • PARIS • SYDNEY • HAMBURG
STOCKHOLM • ATHENS • TOKYO • MILAN
MADRID • WARSAW • BUDAPEST • AUCKLAND

ISBN 0-373-70622-7

KIM & THE COWBOY

Copyright © 1994 by Margot Dalton

Kim & the Cowboy

PROLOGUE

IT WAS FINALLY over.

Four years at the Berkeley School for Girls had finally come to an end. The graduation ceremony, on the other hand, seemed to take forever, with all those droning speeches and earnest lectures. Kim wondered if any of her friends would remember a single word.

Maybe Sandra, who never forgot anything once she heard it, in case she'd need it for a story sometime in the future.

But Meg looked bored and restless, as if she longed to be out running on the track instead of sitting here in a cap and gown. And Laurel was staring into space with a maddening private smile, the way she did when her mind was somewhere else.

Kim felt a touch of sadness, wondering what the future held for all of them. They'd shared so many dreams over the years, so many plans and secret yearnings. Now it was time to part and travel their separate ways.

"Every encounter is the beginning of a parting." Her grandmother's words popped into Kim's mind. "Your family are the only ones who stay with you to the end of your life, *chérie*. Family are the most important people of all. You must choose them very wisely," Masako had told her that morning, her wise face full of gentleness and love.

"But how can you choose your family, Grandmother?" Kim had asked. "It seems to me one hasn't much choice in the matter."

"You have a great deal of choice. You have the power, my darling, to choose the father of your children. What more important decision can a woman make?"

"Maybe I won't have children," Kim had said.

Masako had smiled. "Yes, you will. Not soon, Kimiko, because today you are only graduating from high school. You must go to college and become a well-educated woman. And when you have sharpened your mind and nourished your spirit, the day will come when you will look for a man to father your children. I hope you will choose him very carefully."

"I still don't know why you're so sure," Kim had said with a touch of adolescent rebellion. "There are so many things I want to do, Grandmother. I don't want to be tied down with a bunch of noisy kids."

"You will," Masako had repeated, stroking her granddaughter's hair and smiling tenderly. "Within you, my dear, are fine souls waiting to born. I can see them in your eyes."

Kim shivered in the afternoon warmth. She turned in her chair to look at her grandmother, who sat with hands calmly folded, small and erect in her best Chanel suit.

Suddenly, Kim had a powerful sense of continuity. She saw a vivid picture—almost a vision—of generations stretching endlessly through time. And Kim recognized herself as one of the links in that chain of strength, producing the children who would carry the human race into the generations to come.

I'll be careful, she promised her grandmother silently. *When it's time to pick a man, Grandmother, I'll be very, very careful.*

"Come on, you guys," Meg whispered, once the speeches had finally come to an end. "Let's sneak away and grab a few minutes to ourselves before we get trapped in that stuffy banquet hall."

The four girls slipped out of their chairs and headed for the edge of the crowd, giggling together. Kim's moment of prophecy was set aside for the moment.

But, though the years grew crowded and busy after that brief glimpse of the future, she never forgot her silent promise to her grandmother.

CHAPTER ONE

A COLD SPRING RAIN hammered against the window-panes, driven by a gusty wind that came sweeping down from the icy mountains and forests of Canada. The sky darkened and night fell early. All over the northwestern city of Spokane, lights glowed warmly behind curtains drawn against the storm, and wood fires flickered in thousands of hearths.

Barbara McAllister let herself in the front door and moved through the foyer to the sitting room. She stood in the archway looking thoughtfully at her fireplace, where an aging brown-and-white basset hound lay in his padded basket next to the leaping flames.

Barbara McAllister was an erect and handsome woman, although, like her beloved dog, she was also getting on in years. She had turned seventy-six this past winter, and her hair was now snow-white, rolled into a heavy chignon at the nape of her neck. Tonight she wore tan flannel slacks, a long camel-hair coat and a rust-colored paisley scarf of soft wool that comple-mented her almost-flawless complexion. She was car-rying something in her hands, a container similar in design to the padded basket in which Homer slept, but much smaller.

"You look so cozy, Homer," she murmured fondly. "I love watching you sleep by the fire."

Homer, too, liked the fire, both the warmth and the brightness of it. These days, sleeping next to the fireplace was one of his greatest pleasures, although mealtimes still engaged his interest, as well, and if the weather was nice, he enjoyed going out for slow dignified walks.

Homer was extremely old, almost fifteen. His muzzle was white with age, and one of his eyes was clouded by a smoky blue cataract. He moved stiffly and spent most of his time sleeping, but he still managed to observe the comings and goings of the household to a degree that would have surprised its members.

Barbara smiled at the old dog, who was stolidly ignoring her. It was not Homer's style to wag his tail in greeting, or bark a welcome, or leap out of his basket to lick anyone's ankles. Homer was a dog who maintained an attitude of inscrutable dignity. He seldom showed emotion, and he never suffered fools gladly. Even those he adored, like Barbara, were not accustomed to displays of affection from him.

His mistress appreciated this reserve, because she had much the same kind of personality. Her fine-boned face was narrow and aristocratic, her breeding as impeccable as Homer's. She seemed perfectly matched to this setting, standing among the polished wood, antique stained glass and gleaming brassware of the gracious home she'd lived in almost all her life.

Barbara chuckled when she saw Homer's gradual awareness of the basket she carried, and his struggle not to show any interest. He peered at her with rising alarm and a look of annoyance, then let his eyes slide back to the soft glow of the fire.

Barbara came into the room and set the basket carefully down on the other side of the hearth, kneeling to look inside.

Curiosity finally overcame Homer's lethargy. He climbed from his bed, padding heavily across the Persian rug to stand next to her. Barbara rested an arm on his broad back and tickled one of his long silky ears.

"See," she whispered. "See this, Homer?"

He peered into the basket, then stiffened in horror. A pair of bright tearful eyes gazed back at him, from a face that was a tiny replica of his own. Appalled, Homer stood gazing at the brown-and-white creature who squirmed and cowered on a pad of bright red tartan identical to the lining of Homer's larger basket.

The puppy was very small, with a blunt pink muzzle and a distinct white marking that ran up his forehead. He was a messy tangle of ears and feet, exuding a lonely milky smell as he wriggled in the basket, tumbling and squealing, searching for his mother's warmth and the noisy scuffle of his brothers and sisters in this vast alien world.

Homer stared at the newcomer in shocked disbelief, then looked up at his mistress, his good eye icy with disapproval.

"Isn't he adorable?" Barbara murmured, touching the puppy's soft pink belly with a gentle forefinger.

"His name is Hugo. I want you to help me take care of him, dear."

Homer snorted contemptuously, gave a last cold glance at the squirming creature in the basket and plodded back to his bed, climbing up with much effort and turning his back on the world with heavy finality. He remained unmoving when Barbara crossed the room to kneel beside him, caressing him with the long slow strokes that he most enjoyed. "Oh, Homer," she whispered with a break in her voice. "I do love you, my old darling. I love you so much."

Homer ignored her, resting his muzzle on his front paws and gazing impassively at the inside of his basket. Barbara looked down at him, then turned and started up the stairs to her room, feeling suddenly old and tired.

For a long time, the old dog lay in silence, trying not to hear the plaintive whimpers that rose from the small basket opposite him. He watched while a shy, dark-haired woman came softy into the room and began setting the big oak table for dinner. She wore a white apron over a gray servant's uniform, and her actions were spare and brisk, with a gentle silence and an economy of movement that Homer found deeply soothing.

After she left, he tried to drowse, but the doleful sounds emanating from the other side of the hearth were too annoying. He glared at the intruder, then stiffened in his basket, the hair rising on the back of his neck, his ears lifting briefly like silky flags as he tuned in to another sound. For a moment, he looked like a much younger dog.

The front door had opened just beyond the archway. A pair of suitcases appeared in the hall, followed by a bulging duffel bag and a couple of damp cardboard boxes tightly bound with twine.

Homer's good eye brightened and his heavy body became rigid with excitement, though only the slight lifting of the ears gave visible evidence of his emotion. He forced himself to keep his chin on his paws and his eyes half-closed as a man appeared in the entry and glanced at him.

The man was of medium height, broad and sturdy, with a warm, crooked smile, a curly tumble of light brown hair and eyes so blue in his tanned face that they shone vividly even in the soft glow of the firelight. He wore boots, jeans and a long, wet topcoat. Raindrops glittered in his hair like a sprinkle of diamonds.

Homer gazed at the man hungrily, trying not to wag his tail.

The old dog was able to discern the essence of people, to see the emotions and feelings that surrounded them like an aura. Many people were darkened by cruelty and harshness, or heavy with sadness. But this young man had always been bathed in a glow of cheerful well-being and kindness that warmed and pleased Homer, made him feel safe and happy. Homer could tell that Todd McAllister was still the same, though it had been a long time since they'd last seen each other.

"Hey, Homer," Todd murmured softly, coming a few steps into the room and looking affectionately at the old dog by the hearth.

Ignoring him with great effort, Homer let his eyes drop shut and pretended to be asleep. Todd hesitated for a moment, then gathered his bags and boxes and disappeared up the stairs with a noisy clatter of boots on the polished wood.

When the room was silent again, Homer lay in his basket pondering this new development. Todd hadn't been home for almost a year, except for a brief visit last Christmas. But all those suitcases and boxes looked promising, as if he might stay a little longer this time. The old dog felt a surge of wistful hope, and a warm glow of love.

Homer had arrived in the house when he was no bigger than that forlorn creature in the other basket, and Todd was finished high school, just starting college here in the city. The two of them had been virtually inseparable for those early years.

Homer had dim recollections of exuberant play on the wide sloping lawns of the big house, of long rambles in the nearby woods and cozy evenings up in Todd's room when the latter lay studying his textbooks and Homer rested contentedly on the boy's stomach.

But, of course, all that was long ago, lost in the mists of the past. Todd had grown up and left his grandmother's home more than ten years ago, and Homer had grown accustomed to being alone with Barbara and a succession of domestic help.

He frowned and moved his old body to a more comfortable position on the tartan padding, still trying to ignore the sounds coming from the other basket. But they were growing increasingly desperate, a series of squeaks and howls so mournful that they hurt the old dog's head.

At last, with an impatient sigh, Homer again heaved himself from his bed and padded across the room to glare at the newcomer. The puppy huddled in his basket, his eyes tightly closed and mouth open, crying miserably in his loneliness and bewilderment. Gradually, he became aware of Homer's presence and tumbled onto his back, eager to get closer to the big dog. Then he began climbing and scrabbling against the sides of the basket, his efforts to escape ineffectual.

Homer eyed the wriggling pup with cold disapproval. The old dog's paws were firmly planted on the carpet, his ears limp and drooping as he stood gazing into the depths of the basket. Finally, he edged closer, reached in and closed his powerful jaws over the puppy's fragile neck.

With infinite care, Homer mouthed the puppy, lifted him and carried the fat little body across the room. The puppy dangled in midair, startled into silence.

Homer dropped the warm squirming thing into his own basket, then climbed in behind it. The puppy rolled onto the soft padding and gathered himself up, shaking his tiny blunt head. Then, aware of Homer's presence, he gave a soft whimper of joy and burrowed close to the big dog, wriggling between Homer's massive front paws.

Homer sighed wearily, nosed the puppy out of the way so he could rest his muzzle on his paws and allowed the body to wedge itself between Homer's body and the side of the basket, where it let out a couple of contented gurgles and promptly fell asleep.

Homer kept his eyes open, fearful of drifting into sleep and crushing the puppy against the basket. He turned around with rare gentleness to push the soft body farther back into the warmth, then returned to his gloomy contemplation of the firelit room.

"WHERE'S THE PUPPY?" Barbara asked, coming into the room and nodding briskly at her grandson, who sat at the table reading the paper.

Todd smiled up at her, thinking how elegant she looked in her navy blue silk and pearls. Barbara always dressed for dinner, though she had long since given up insisting that Todd do the same.

"He's with Homer. He must have gotten lonely and climbed into Homer's basket."

"Don't be ridiculous. That puppy couldn't climb out of his own basket, let alone get into Homer's."

Barbara crossed the room to stand by the hearth, gazing down thoughtfully at the two sleeping dogs in the basket.

Todd lowered the paper and looked with interest at his grandmother. "So how'd he get in there?"

"Homer must have brought him there. He probably felt sorry for the poor little thing."

"That's hard to picture, Nana. Homer hardly stirs himself anymore. I can't really see him baby-sitting."

"There's always been more to Homer than meets the eye," Barbara said, returning to seat herself at the table. "Put that paper down," she added sternly, shaking out her linen napkin and smoothing it on her lap. "You know I can't abide reading at the table."

"I haven't even been back an hour," Todd complained to nobody in particular, "and already she's barking out orders."

But his voice was cheerful, and he smiled fondly at his grandmother while he spoke. As long as Todd McAllister could remember, this woman had been the center of his life, a rock and fortress when the rest of the world seemed treacherously unreliable. He'd come to her house as a baby, dumped here like an abandoned kitten by an eighteen-year-old mother who was Barbara's daughter, but who had never resembled Barbara in any way that Todd could discern.

His face clouded briefly when he thought about his mother, then brightened when he noticed the crystal salad bowl that his grandmother was passing to him. "It's Waldorf salad," he said with pleasure. "My favorite, Nana."

"I knew you were coming," she told him with a rare glance of affection. "Although," she added, her smile fading, "why any adult human being would want to eat something made from raw apples, walnuts and mayonnaise, is certainly beyond me."

Todd helped himself liberally to the salad. "You're such a harsh woman," he commented. "Such rigid judgments. Loosen up a bit, Nana. Go with the flow."

Barbara's mouth twitched as she glanced over at her grandson. "How was Hawaii?" she asked.

"Beautiful. You should have seen the ranch I was staying at, Nana. They have some of the biggest ranches in the world in Hawaii, you know. And the light is wonderful for painting. I could have stayed there another year."

"So why have you come back to Washington, and left all that tropical splendor?"

"Because I've been offered a huge commission. Some representatives from Standard Oil came down to see me on the island, and offered me a contract to do a series of paintings for their head office. The money and the publicity are both really impressive, so I packed up and came home. The paintings will take me at least a couple of years, and I'll be more comfortable working here in Spokane."

"Will you be working up in the attic again?"

Todd smiled. "Oh, I don't think so, Nana. I'm considerably past that stage, I'm afraid. Besides, I know how much you're bothered by the smell of paint and turpentine."

"It's all right in the summer," Barbara said, "when I can open the windows and air the place out."

Todd gazed lovingly at his grandmother. "You don't have to make sacrifices for me anymore, Nana," he said. "I'm a grown-up man now. I can look after myself."

Barbara gave him a scornful glance that told him just how grown-up she considered him. "I can never quite believe that you've turned out to be an artist," she commented absently. "It's so strange."

"It is? Why?"

"You don't look like an artist. Especially with blue jeans and a plaid shirt and that tan you've got now. You look more like a cowboy."

"Well, that's what I am, a 'cowboy artist.' That's what the reviewers call me. . . . Among other things," Todd added with a grin, helping himself to more salad.

A small woman in a gray uniform entered the room on silent feet, carrying a tray heaped with roast chicken, mashed potatoes and vegetables. She appeared to be in her mid-thirties, quiet and quick-moving, her hands rough and callused. Todd smiled at her, thinking that although she was too thin and severe to be conventionally attractive, the housemaid would probably be pleasant-looking if someone could get her to smile. But she kept her head down, serving the food and vanishing with noiseless efficiency.

"She's new, isn't she?" Todd asked, looking with a blissful sigh at the plates heaped with food.

"Yes, she is. Her name's Julia Adolpho, and she's very, very good. I'm pleased with her."

"She looks Oriental. Is she Japanese?"

Barbara lifted her chin sharply and stared at her grandson. "Of course not. She's Filipino. Why would you ask me such a thing?"

Todd felt a brief stab of impatience with this strong-willed old woman who'd raised him.

"I guess I keep forgetting," he said with a careful lack of expression, "that you're the only living American who's still fighting the Second World War."

"My husband died in a Japanese prisoner-of-war camp. Am I supposed to forget that?"

"No, Nana," Todd said, willing himself to be gentle with her. "You're not supposed to forget that. But you are supposed to put it behind you and live in the present, and evaluate people on their own merits, not their racial or ethnic backgrounds."

"The Japanese stole my entire life. They probably ruined my daughter's life, too. I'll never forgive that, not as long as I live."

"Your daughter's life?" Todd echoed in disbelief. "Nana, do you honestly think you can blame another culture and a war that happened fifty years ago for the way my mother behaves?"

Barbara's face took on a dangerous hint of color. "Lillian would have been different if her father had lived. He died without even getting a chance to see her, and I had to raise her all alone in this house. I'm sure it made a difference in her life, growing up without a father."

Todd thought about the handsome young soldier who lived in a silver frame on his grandmother's dressing table. He wondered if that gentle-looking man really could have done something with the willful daughter who'd resulted from the soldier's brief marriage to Barbara McAllister.

"Do you think so? It never made much difference in my life. At least not that I'm aware of, and you raised me all alone in this house, too."

"So," Barbara asked, changing the subject with her usual firmness, "will you be living at home?"

"I don't think so, Nana. You know I'd drive you crazy before long if I moved back in here. I'll find an apartment somewhere in the city."

"You can't work in an apartment."

"I know. I'm going to look for studio space to rent, because I'll need a lot of room for these paintings. They're huge canvases."

"Can you rent studio space?"

"Sure. Most artists do. As a matter of fact, I already found an ad in the paper from somebody looking to sublet half a studio."

Barbara glanced up at him. "Half a studio? You mean you'd have to share your work space?"

Todd shrugged and poured gravy over his mashed potatoes. "If it's the place I think it is, there's lots of room for two artists to work. It's right downtown, on the second floor of the old Commercial Bank."

"And who's renting it? Who's this other artist?"

Todd cut his meat carefully, keeping his head lowered. "Not a name I recognize. Somebody called Kim Tanaka," he said.

He felt Barbara's eyes resting on him with disapproval, but he wasn't in the mood for any more sparring or arguing.

"This chicken is just great, Nana," he said with forced heartiness. "And you should taste the stuffing. What's that spicy flavoring, do you know? It's really delicious."

Gradually, Barbara softened and allowed herself to be drawn into a discussion of the cooking prowess of her new Filipino housemaid, who had immigrated to the United States only a few months earlier and already knew how to prepare many recipes exactly to Barbara's taste. Todd ate and listened to his grandmother, glancing covertly at his watch from time to time. He loved his grandmother, and he was happy to be back in this gracious old house that would always feel like home to him. But more than anything, he longed for the smell of oil paints, the breathless promise of a fresh white canvas and the throbbing, almost sexual pleasure of a favorite brush in his hand and a strong, clear light falling over his shoulder.

He could hardly wait to call Kim Tanaka—whoever she was—and make arrangements for some studio space.

AT THE SAME time that Todd McAllister was looking at his watch and making polite conversation with his grandmother, Kim Tanaka was in her bedroom in her father's sprawling bungalow on the other side of the city, staring gloomily into the mirror at her hair.

She lifted the long shining mass with her hand and twisted it against the back of her head, then grimaced at her reflection.

It was hopeless. No matter what Kim did with her hair, she still looked like a porcelain doll. She might as well dress up in one of her grandmother's old silk

kimonos and cover her face with rice powder. Why not
strive for the whole effect? Kim looked unhappily at
the severe black dress lying on her bed, the dramatic
silver necklace and earrings she'd selected to help her
make a statement for this important gallery opening.
What good were they going to be if her hairstyle made
her look like one of the chorus girls in *The Mikado?*

Over the years, Kim had tried many things with her
hair. One summer during high school, she'd dyed it
red, a color so horribly unflattering that she'd burst
into tears and refused to go anywhere until it grew out.
She could still remember Meg's teasing, and Sandra's
gentle sympathy.

Later in the same year, Laurel had persuaded her to
get a perm, hoping that Kim would emerge with a
dramatic cloud of hair that would make her look like
Diana Ross. But Kim's black mane was so straight and
heavy that no perm, regardless of strength, had any
appreciable effect on it for more than a week.

In college, Kim had gotten her hair cut in a bouncy
wedge, striving for a sophisticated, modern-woman
appearance. But with her small body and delicate face,
she'd looked more like a solemn little page boy in the
Imperial Court. People had tended to stand close to
her and give her fond pats on the head. Not at all the
effect she'd hoped to achieve.

At last, defeated, she'd let her hair grow long again
and now she usually wore it in a casual ponytail that
suited her well enough for everyday. But there were
times when she wanted to dress up and look like what
she was, a thirty-three-year-old woman with an im-

portant, responsible position. And at those times, her hair was always a source of concern. Finally, Kim let the shining mass fall loosely around her face, pulled on a pair of jogging pants and an old UCLA sweatshirt and padded through the wide hallways to her grandmother's room.

The luxurious house was an interesting blend of Japanese and Western architecture. It was built solidly enough to withstand the grim northwestern winters, yet there was an airy spaciousness that was both subtle and pleasing.

One of the hallways that Kim traversed had an entire wall of glass, beyond which lay a central courtyard planted with shrubs and covered with clean gravel raked into patterns in the Japanese style. Now that Kim's brother and sister were married, she and her parents lived alone in the big house, except for Kim's grandmother, who had lived with them for as long as Kim could remember. Since earliest childhood, Kim had loved to visit her grandmother in the rooms beyond the courtyard.

She paused by the familiar, lacquered door, then raised her hand and knocked softly.

"Entrez!" a voice called from within. Kim edged the door open and slipped inside, smiling at the old lady who sat by the window with a book in her lap.

Masako Tanaka was well over eighty, and her small body was beginning to look frail, but her sparkling black eyes still showed an indomitable spirit. Her hair was beautifully cut and styled, and she dressed with the same care Kim remembered from childhood—in

tailored silk dresses cut in the Western style, fine jewelry and expensive shoes.

Kim looked around the room and sighed with
pleasure. When she was little, she'd thought of her
grandmother's suite as a magic place. Being here was
like being inside one of the fragile, multicolored soap
bubbles that drifted across the courtyard, blown from
Kim's bubble wand. She used to look at those fragile
shimmering globes and think of this place, with its
silvery walls and sparse lovely furnishings, its single
branch of cherry blossoms in a corner alcove and long
silken scrolls on the wall opposite the windows.

Like the rest of the house, Madame Tanaka's rooms
were a combination of Japanese and Western elements. The spareness and lack of adornment were
purely Oriental, but the big bed with its carved ebony
frame and solid, comfortable mattress was more
American in style, as were the long dresser and painted
cabinet filled with books and curios.

Still, nothing in the room seemed incongruous. Like
Madame Tanaka herself, the various elements united
in a single entity that was harmonious and appealing.

Still smiling, Kim crossed the room and bent to kiss
the old lady's soft cheek, enjoying her grandmother's
fragrance. Kim had always loved the way her grandmother smelled.

"You spoke French just now, Grandmother," Kim
said.

"I did?"

"When you told me to come in."

Madame Tanaka waved at the book of French poetry in her lap. "I was reading."

Kim bent to look at the small leather-bound volume, then crossed the room to peer into the wooden jewelry case on her grandmother's dressing table.

"Grandmother, do you have some combs for my hair? Something that would go with black and silver?"

"Combs?"

"You know," Kim turned, sweeping her hair up and holding it against her head. "I want something kind of... different. More sophisticated," she concluded lamely.

"Less Oriental," Madame Tanaka said with a shrewd glance at the young woman.

"Maybe," Kim admitted, turning restlessly to frown at herself in the mirror. "I get a little tired of looking like somebody called Tiny Spring Flower, you know?"

"I know, my darling. What occasion are you dressing for?"

"It's my first gallery opening in my new job. We're featuring a collection by a Chicago photographer, and I want to look like a curator who knows something about art. The mayor's going to be there tonight, and several of the aldermen, and maybe even the senator..."

"None of whom knows a great deal about art," Madame Tanaka said with a dry smile.

Kim grinned fondly at the old lady. "I know. But they pay my salary, Grandmother. It's a public gallery, and it's a really good job."

"Come here, then, my dear. I'll do you up in a French braid."

Kim brightened. "Oh, would you? Your fingers aren't hurting today?"

"Not to speak of. Part of aging is learning to live gracefully with pain. Come, bring a comb and sit here in front of me. We can talk while I work."

Obediently, Kim settled herself on the footstool in front of Madame Tanaka, hugging her knees and keeping her body still as her grandmother worked with the long shining mass of hair, deftly shaping it into an elegant French braid.

"So, little Kimiko," Madame Tanaka said, "the mayor will be there tonight?"

"Yes, he will. We invited the artist, but he refused. He says he avoids contact with the public because it inhibits his expression."

Madame Tanaka chuckled. "Picasso once told me the very same thing, but it wasn't true, you know. He loved contact with the public. He fed off the adulation."

Kim twisted to stare at her grandmother. The old lady frowned and gave her hair an impatient jerk, and Kim returned to her submissive pose.

"Grandmother," she murmured, "you never told me you met Picasso."

"I met all of them when I lived in Paris. They were always in the cafés, those artists. I don't know when they managed to work."

Kim sighed wistfully, thinking about her grandmother's extraordinary life.

Masako Kowashi grew up in a wealthy home in Japan, went to Paris to study in the 1930s and met her husband there. Yoshio Tanaka was a young Japanese-American who was teaching art history at the Sorbonne. He and Masako eventually had two children and developed a lively circle of friends, but everything changed with the advent of war.

"Tell me what happened when the war started, Grandmother," Kim said softly, relaxing as the skillful fingers worked in her hair.

"You've heard those old stories."

"I know, but we haven't talked about Paris for a long time, and I like to hear that story. You were so brave."

Madame Tanaka chuckled. "Not brave, my darling. A woman does what she must to survive. Especially when she has children to look after."

"Tell me," Kim insisted. "Tell me about my grandfather."

"He was so handsome, and so American," Masako began, her voice taking on a wistful tone as she spoke about the only man she'd ever loved. "I thought in those days that anything American was the last word in sophistication. I loved your grandfather's clothes, his funny accent, his talk of baseball, everything about him..."

"So you married him and had my father," Kim said.

"Yes. Laurence was born in 1938, and Genevieve in 1941. We gave them American names and made sure they were registered with French passports," Masako said, settling into the familiar story. "Your grandfather had the feeling something terrible was going to happen in Europe, even though we weren't at all political in those days. We were just having fun, and so much in love..."

Again the old lady's voice trailed off and Kim had to prompt her.

"But he changed when the war started, didn't he?"

"He certainly did. Suddenly, my carefree husband became obsessed with the war, and nothing I said would change his mind. He knew his beloved America would be drawn in eventually, and that Japan and the United States would be fighting on different sides, but nothing could stop him. He used his Japanese appearance and connections to get involved with an underground movement, and dropped off the face of the earth for a long, long time."

Kim frowned. "I've always wondered how he could do that. I mean, he was married and had responsibilities to you and the children."

"But there are different kinds of loyalty, dear heart. Maybe it was because he was living so far from America, and felt the need to help his country in some way. I never knew why he vanished."

"But how could he leave you in such a dangerous place with two little children? Aunt Genevieve must have been just a tiny baby."

"It was very difficult," Madame Tanaka said with a brief sigh. "Fortunately, I had their passports, and I'd received American citizenship when I married your grandfather. We always knew it wouldn't be safe in Paris, and he told me if Japan and the United States came into the war, I should take the children to America. I left in March 1942, a few months after the Pearl Harbor attack."

Kim frowned. Although she'd heard the story before, she was just beginning to acquire an adult understanding of the courage her grandmother had shown as a young woman, taking her little children to a country that was at war with her own nation and that was seething with anti-Japanese sentiment.

"Was it very hard for you, Grandmother? You were younger than I am now."

"Yes," Madame Tanaka said calmly. "It was very hard. Your grandfather had no family to speak of, just an old uncle who hadn't even heard of our marriage. I found shelter with some of my husband's friends from the academic community, and they concealed me until the worst of the anti-Japanese feeling died down. The children and I never went to an internment camp, although I expected every day that we would be summoned."

"Were you afraid?" Kim asked softly.

"All the time. Genevieve was a fragile child. She suffered terribly from asthma, and I was very much afraid she wouldn't survive if we went to a camp. Sometimes at night I cried from homesickness and fear."

"How did you support yourself and the children?"

"I took in sewing. I did so much fine sewing that my eyes ached and my fingers were always swollen. I think that's why they still hurt so much when the weather is damp."

"And you never heard from Grandfather?"

"Not until after the war. He was killed in the Philippines, smuggling messages behind enemy lines. The Americans said he was a hero, and gave me an award."

Kim nodded, thinking of the old military medal in a top drawer of her grandmother's dressing table. "Were you angry, Grandmother?" she asked finally.

"With whom? My countrymen, or the Americans, or fate, or your grandfather?" the old lady asked with a teasing smile.

Kim shrugged. "I don't know. With everybody, I guess. Your life was so happy and secure, and then it all got turned upside down, and you had to live through those hard lonely years, raising your children by yourself."

Even with her back turned, Kim could feel her grandmother's philosophic shrug. "War is inevitable," Masako said. "Ours is an ancient civilization, Kimiko. We understand that war is sometimes necessary before peace can exist, and that wartime horrors give way over the years to peacetime realities. One does not dwell on these things. One lives with courage and hopes to die with honor, and leaves the past to its own ghosts."

"So you have no regrets?"

"Why should I have regrets, my little one? I have you and your brother and sister, and their children to love. I live in this lovely home with you and your parents. My children are doing well. Your father is an investment banker, and Genevieve does interior design for rich people in Manhattan. My life is pleasant beyond compare. Of course I have no regrets."

"I love you, Grandmother," Kim said impulsively. She turned and knelt on the stool to embrace the old lady's tiny frail body.

"If you loved me," Masako said sternly, "you would sit still until I finish your hair. And of course you will be here on Friday night for dinner."

"Friday?" Kim asked blankly. "What's happening on Friday?"

Her grandmother sighed. "I've told you already, Kim. David Yamamoto is coming to dinner."

Kim felt a twinge of uneasiness. "Your friend's son, right? This wealthy and presentable young Japanese businessman of yours?"

"Your sarcasm is unbecoming. He's a very nice young man. He's a technical consultant at the computer firm where your brother works, and we've known his family for many years."

"Grandmother," Kim said gently, "you know that the days of arranged marriages are over, don't you?"

"Of course I do," Madame Tanaka said placidly. "It does no harm to introduce you to a nice young man, does it?"

"But I don't want to marry anybody. I'm happy with my life."

"You're thirty-three years old. I want to see you settled before I die."

"With a Japanese husband," Kim said.

"One should marry one's own kind, my child. A woman has enough conflicting loyalties, as it is. She has to be loyal to her parents and her husband's parents, her husband and her children, her home and her father's home. She shouldn't have to suffer a racial conflict within her marriage, as well."

Kim was silent, thinking about her grandmother's words. She'd seen all kinds of marriages among her friends, including a number of interracial and interfaith unions that seemed no more or no less successful than the traditional ones she'd observed.

"That's an old-fashioned attitude, Grandmother," she said at last. "Nobody thinks that way anymore."

"Is that so?" Madame Tanaka said, unimpressed. "Bend your head, dear. I just have to finish this last little bit."

"Grandmother, I don't think it's a good idea for me to meet this Japanese businessman of yours. I really think the whole idea is embarrassing."

"Voilà! C'est fini," Madame Tanaka said, lapsing into French as she always did when she wished to project an air of deliberate vagueness and avoid argument, while getting everything precisely her own way. *"Très, très jolie, ma petite."*

Kim got to her feet, gave her grandmother an exasperated kiss and left the room, pausing briefly to admire her image in the old lacquer-framed mirror, before starting down the hallway to her own suite of rooms.

As she neared the open door, she heard her telephone ringing, and broke into a run to get there in time to answer.

CHAPTER TWO

"COULD I SPEAK with Kim Tanaka, please?"

"This is Kim Tanaka."

Todd leaned back in the desk chair in his old room, trying to put a face to the voice he heard over the phone. It was a woman's voice, clear and low, with no trace of accent or inflection to give any hints about her background. But there was a note of brisk competence, a no-nonsense kind of manner. He imagined a tall woman with dark level eyebrows and an air of efficiency, dressed in mannish fashion, probably carrying a briefcase...

"Ms. Tanaka," Todd said hastily, realizing that the silence had grown uncomfortably long while he'd been trying to visualize the woman at the other end of the line. "My name is Todd McAllister. I'm calling about your ad in the newspaper."

"You're looking for studio space?"

"I sure am," Todd said cheerfully. "And the sooner the better. I really need to get to work."

"I see."

Todd sensed a slight hesitation in the woman's voice. He realized that the woman he pictured wasn't about to rent out half her studio over the phone. She would no doubt be sternly selective about a studio mate, probably even prepared to subject him to a battery of evaluative tests before awarding him the space. Todd felt a stirring of irritation. But he really needed studio space, so he made a conscious effort to summon his warmest inflection, and spoke with the easy cowboy charm that never failed him. "What kind of work do you do, Ms. Tanaka? Your artwork, I mean. I'm sure I've heard your name, but I just can't seem to—"

"I doubt it," the woman said briskly. "I've just moved back to Spokane this spring."

"Back?"

"I grew up here, but I attended high school and college in California, and I've been working there since I graduated."

"At an art-related job?"

"For a number of years, I taught art history and design at UCLA."

Todd gave a low whistle, considered that his initial perception had been correct. "That's impressive," he commented. "Did you have tenure?"

"Yes," she said briefly. "I did."

Todd sensed a stiffness in the woman's voice, a reluctance to give out personal details over the phone. Maybe this whole thing wasn't such a good idea, he thought. She didn't sound like the kind of person he was likely to get along with very well.

Todd McAllister was easygoing and didn't usually have much difficulty getting along with most people. But he was fairly certain that this Kim Tanaka wasn't going to appreciate his casual work habits. If she'd

achieved tenure at an art school in an institution like
UCLA, she was no doubt grimly competent and at
least middle-aged. He added a shock of iron-gray hair
to his mental image. "Why," he asked, unable to
control his curiosity, "would anybody leave a college
teaching job with tenure to come back to Spokane?"

"I was concerned about my family," Kim Tanaka
said, a little stiffly. This time there was no mistaking
her annoyance at his personal questioning, but she
continued to answer him with quiet courtesy. "My
grandmother is very old, and I wanted to be closer to
her."

"Your grandmother?" Todd rapidly subtracted the
gray hair, feeling increasingly puzzled.

How could anybody be old enough to have ac-
quired a professorship with tenure at a prestigious
college, and also young enough to have a grandmother?

"Yes. She's eighty-three, and getting quite frail. I
returned to Spokane and took a job at the public art
gallery. I work half days as a teaching curator, and
spend the rest of the time in my studio, but it's far too
much space for my needs and the rent is exorbitant. It
makes sense for me to share the place with another
artist."

"What kind of work do you do, Ms. Tanaka?"
Todd asked again.

"Mostly watercolors and silk screens," she said
briefly. "You don't need to worry. I'm very tidy," she
added dryly, surprising him with an unexpected touch
of humor. "I deal with small subjects."

"I don't," Todd said bluntly.

"I beg your pardon?"

"I deal with large subjects. Horses, buffalo herds, Cherokee raiding parties, that sort of thing."

"Oh," she said abruptly, after a moment's silence. "Todd *McAllister*. I'm sorry, I didn't recognize your name at first."

"I'm surprised you recognized it at all. I don't think I'm that well known in California."

"You're too modest. I believe you're well known all over America, Mr. McAllister."

Todd beamed at this praise, then frowned. The words were courteous but her voice was still carefully noncommittal, giving him no inkling of what she felt about his work.

"Thank you," he said at last. "Since you already know who I am, do you think you might consider renting me half your studio, Ms. Tanaka? I've got a major project to get started on, and I really need the space."

"Perhaps we could discuss it a little more before we make a decision," she said.

"Well, that seems fair." Todd forced himself to sound cheerful and relaxed. "When would be good for you?"

"How about Friday afternoon? I'm free at that time, and we'd have a chance to talk."

"All right. Should I meet you somewhere?"

"I think it would be best," Kim Tanaka said, "if you came to the studio. Then you can evaluate the space to see if it meets your needs, as well."

"I'm prepared to rent it sight unseen," Todd said, making a last desperate effort to wring a commitment from the woman. "I know which building it's in, and I'm sure the studio would be suitable."

"Are you? Well, I'm afraid I never do anything sight unseen. Two o'clock, Mr. McAllister? I believe you have the address."

"Two o'clock is fine," Todd said resignedly.

They said goodbye. He hung up, stared at the phone gloomily for a while, then wandered out into the hallway, wondering how he was going to fill in the long days until Friday.

Damn the woman, he thought with a restless frown.

Why couldn't she see him tomorrow? Now he had to hang around cooling his heels, waiting to unpack his art supplies and to order canvas. She sounded like a real martinet, this Kim Tanaka.

Probably built like a sumo wrestler, he decided uncharitably, with a black belt in karate....

He padded down the stairs in his stocking feet and ambled into the living room, where his grandmother sat by the fire working at her needlepoint.

Todd peered into Homer's basket. The old dog lifted his head and allowed his tail to thump slowly, before closing his eyes again. Todd bent to give him a few loving pats, then glanced into the other basket. "Where's the puppy?"

"Julia took him outside. He's paper-trained, but I want him properly trained to go outside, as soon as possible." The housemaid returned, carrying the wriggling Hugo, and tucked him into the smaller basket without looking at either of the people in the room.

"Did he go, Julia?" Barbara asked, lowering her glasses and peering over their gold frames at the thin woman who paused nervously by the door.

"I think so, ma'am," Julia said in a low tone. "But it's very cold out. He wanted to come inside quickly."

"I don't blame him," Todd said cheerfully. "Poor little guy."

The housemaid ducked her head and vanished with obvious relief. Todd knelt by the basket, stroking the shivering puppy, who rolled over in transports of joy at this attention and licked Todd's hand with a frantic pink tongue.

Todd lifted the puppy from the basket, crossed the room and lay on the couch, avoiding his grandmother's disapproving glance as he cradled the warm squirming body on his chest.

"Todd, I don't want that dog spoiled."

"He's not a dog, Nana. He's just a baby. He's scared and lonely."

"You're always so sentimental. Entirely too softhearted."

Todd considered this accusation, toying absently with the puppy's long silky ears. "Do you think it's possible to be too softhearted, Nana? Don't you think this poor old world can use every little bit of kindness and gentleness we can summon?"

"Of course not," Barbara said briskly. She knotted her thread and snipped it with a firm click of her scissors. "The world can look after itself, and so should you. If you keep being so softhearted, people will just take advantage of you."

"Spoken like a true humanitarian," Todd said with a grin.

His grandmother gave him a calm, level glance, then returned to her needlework.

Rain slashed and pounded against the windows, and the fire cast flickering shadows on the walls. Homer snored gently in his basket, while the puppy burrowed between Todd's shoulder and the couch, licking busily at his ear. Todd patted the small body, thinking about the woman he was scheduled to meet on Friday afternoon.

"MISS TANAKA, Jason made his house *blue!*"

Kim moved across the room in the direction of the complaint, picking her way around the sprawled bodies of small children who were working on the floor of the art gallery, painting with big brushes on rolls of newsprint.

It was her last class on Friday morning. The children were a third-grade group from a nearby school, part of the education component of Kim's curatorial job. She spent much of her time working with local schoolchildren, trying to teach them the rudiments of art.

She paused by an indignant small girl who crouched with brush in hand, glaring at the boy next to her. He worked in serene absorption, adding chimneys and windows to the house he was painting.

"He's making *everything* blue," the little girl shouted. "He can't do that!"

"Why not?" Kim asked, flicking back her ponytail and seating herself cross-legged on the floor next to the two children. She wore blue jeans, sneakers and a pale pink T-shirt, and when she sat down, it was difficult to distinguish the teacher from the students.

"The *sky* is blue. He can't make all the other stuff blue. It's not right."

Kim looked into the little girl's scowling freckled face and sighed. At what point, she wondered, were children robbed of their natural spontaneity and forced to conform? When did they really start to believe that sky was blue and grass was green and it was wrong to experiment?

"Angela," she said gently, glancing at the little girl's name tag, "do you see all those pictures on the walls?"

Still frowning, the child looked around at the stark array of photographs hanging on the gallery walls.

"Yeah?" she muttered suspiciously, then glanced sidelong at Jason, who had dipped his brush into the pot of blue paint and was now making a row of trees leading to his house.

"What color is the sky in those pictures?" Kim asked.

"It's gray," Angela said. "But that's different. Those are pictures that aren't colored."

"Haven't you ever seen a gray sky?" Kim asked gently. "Just before a storm, or when it's raining? Isn't the sky gray then?"

"Yeah, sort of, but..."

"And sometimes," Kim went on, "very early in the morning, the sky is all pale green like your sweater, and at nightfall, it's dusty mauve, and before a thunderstorm, it's often yellow, and deep in the night, it's pure black. So who says the sky is blue?"

"But he's making the houses and the trees and the flowers and everything, all the same dumb—"

"He's doing what artists call a monochrome," Kim said, ruffling the boy's hair as he labored over his painting.

"Why?" Angela asked.

"Because," Kim said with a smile, "he wants to see what it looks like. That's the only reason artists do anything, Angela. Just to see what it looks like. That's what makes it so much fun."

The little girl watched in puzzled silence as Kim got to her feet and moved off among the other children. Then she glared at Jason, who was now happily filling his sky with bluebirds.

AFTER THE CLASS, Kim went into the gallery workroom to get her lunch from a shelf, smiling at the head curator who was studying a wooden packing crate with a damaged corner.

"It'll have to be replaced, I'm afraid," he said, sighing. "I hope the shipping budget can stand another blow this month."

Kim's smile broadened. Jeffrey Holmes was always worrying about budgets.

"Did the children like the photographs?" he asked Kim, turning away from his gloomy scrutiny of the damaged crate.

"Not much, except for the candid shots and the portraits. Small children are generally more interested in human subjects than abstract ones."

"Children are true humanists," Jeffrey agreed. "They should enjoy our next exhibit. The collection of Inuit sculpture in soapstone."

Still smiling, Kim went into the office, unwrapped her lunch and seated herself at her desk, chewing absently on her sandwiches as she ordered new art supplies, then began to fill out a sheet of gallery statistics.

Jeffrey came in behind her and examined the sheet over her shoulder. "Those are excellent numbers, aren't they? Both public attendance and school involvement have gone up since your arrival, Kim. You're a great help to me."

Kim warmed at this praise and turned to look up at the elderly man. "Thanks, Jeffrey. You know, I'm surprised how much I enjoy this job. It's certainly different from teaching college."

"How's your own work coming?"

Kim brightened and set the sandwich down on its wrapping of waxed paper. "That's the best part of all. It's been years since I've had half days free for my painting. I'm getting so much done, and I'm really happy with my work."

Jeffrey beamed. "That's excellent news, my dear. Have you found a studio mate yet?"

"Not yet," Kim said, returning to her sandwich. "But I have somebody coming at two o'clock to look at the space. Actually," she added, after swallowing the last bite of her sandwich, "it's Todd McAllister. Have you ever met him?"

Jeffrey nodded. "He was a local boy, always a bit of a renegade. Never involved himself in conventional art programs. In fact, during his earlier years, I gather he was more involved in rodeo riding than painting. He's certainly made a name for himself in the art world now, though."

"I wonder what he'd be like to work with."

"I have no idea, my dear. Rumor has it that he's somewhat unconventional in his life-style, but then, that's the norm for artists, isn't it?"

"Are you unconventional, Jeffrey?"

"Well, let's see. I drive a Volkswagen, enjoy rock music, grow orchids in my attic and I'm trying to learn to knit. I've been happily married to the same woman for thirty-seven years. I've never run for political office, and I love eating at fast-food restaurants. Does that sound unconventional?"

"Is the sky blue?" Kim asked, giving her co-worker a fond pat on the shoulder as she passed him on her way out into the gallery foyer. "See you on Monday, Jeffrey. I'm off to meet Todd McAllister, the famous cowboy artist."

THE HARSH TONE of the buzzer caught Kim off guard. She'd been so absorbed in her work that she hadn't noticed the time passing. She jumped at the unexpected sound, almost spilling the jar of water on the shelf in front of her easel.

"Oh, no," she murmured, looking in dismay at her wristwatch. "He's here already, and everything's such a..."

Brushing her hair nervously back from her forehead, Kim hurried to answer the door, then stopped short.

A man stood in the dim light of the hallway, staring down at her, an expression of openmouthed amazement on his face.

He was quite a lot taller than Kim, but then, she thought dryly, so was everybody else. He had curly golden brown hair, broad shoulders, a square, tanned face and blue eyes that sparkled warmly as he gazed at her.

Slowly, his face broke into a grin.

"Are *you* Kim Tanaka?"

"Yes," Kim said, annoyed by the flutter in her breast and the shy awkwardness that suddenly came over her when she became aware of his frank admiration.

I feel more like a schoolgirl than a professional woman in her thirties, she thought furiously. *This is so silly....*

"I'm Todd McAllister. It's a pleasure to meet you, Kim. A *real* pleasure."

"Hello," Kim said briskly, shaking his hand in a businesslike manner and then moving back into the studio. "Please come in."

The man followed her, still looking at her intently. "You're so... different from what I expected," he commented, with the warm professional appraisal of an artist admiring a model. "I thought you'd be... older, I guess. More formidable."

"Well, I hardly think that's relevant to the business at hand, is it?" Kim said firmly. "Now, the studio is almost eleven hundred square feet, as you can see, with strong northern light. There are storage cabinets on both end walls, and another small cupboard behind that door. The utilities are—"

"I'll take it," Todd said, hardly glancing around at the room. "It's perfect. Can I move in this afternoon, do you think?"

Kim felt a brief stirring of panic. There was something about the man that she found deeply unnerving. In particular, he had an easy confidence of speech and behavior that made her feel awkward and unsure of herself.

Although, she admitted privately, there certainly was no denying his physical appeal. She stole another glance at his muscular shoulders and his cheerful tanned face, which was even more handsome in the bright daylight of the studio. But this man had another kind of charm, as well, a boyish appeal and a warm, crooked grin that made her heart beat faster whenever he smiled at her.

He wore leather cowboy boots and jeans, and a blue denim shirt that brought out the vivid color of his eyes. While Kim watched, he strolled across the room and stood looking at her painting on the big easel.

She tensed, feeling the same sensitivity she always felt when somebody was about to pass judgment on her work. In fact, waiting for Todd McAllister's comment, she was even more nervous than usual, and a little annoyed as she looked at his curly head and the powerful grace of his body.

"Very nice," he said, stepping back a few paces from the easel and inclining his head as he squinted at the delicate watercolor. "What's going to be down here in the corner?"

He indicated a patch of untouched paper at the edge of the painting where a bridge vanished over a shining river into a patch of mist.

"Nothing," Kim said briefly.

"Nothing?" the man echoed, arching an eyebrow at her. "Just blank?"

Kim fought a rising irritation. "It's the Japanese style to leave a portion of the painting blank, Mr. McAllister. It's considered presumptuous to declare that a work is finished."

He looked at her thoughtfully for a moment, obviously considering what she'd told him.

For some reason, Kim found herself dreading his next words. "We haven't discussed terms," she said hastily, to draw his attention away from her painting. "Would you be prepared to assume half the rent? I mean, would you be working here a fair amount of time and requiring that much of the space?"

"I'll probably be working around the clock for a few months," Todd said. "Once I get started, my hours can get pretty erratic. In fact, if you don't mind,

I'd like to move a cot and hot plate into my half, so I can eat and sleep here if things are going well and I don't feel like leaving. And I'm more than willing to pay any price you name."

Kim stared at the man, feeling her panic increase. When she'd considered renting out the unused portion of the big studio, she'd pictured someone faceless and silent, someone working quietly, almost invisibly, over on the other side of the room. She certainly hadn't imagined a vigorous personality like Todd McAllister's, a man whose work habits and tastes were vastly different from her own.

The vivid glow of his blue eyes, the charming grin and tousled curly hair suddenly made the room seem much smaller, almost dangerous. Kim felt uncomfortably close to him, even though they were standing a considerable distance apart. In fact, she had a sudden, irrational fear that if she took a step toward him, she'd be in his arms, touching him . . .

She shivered and hugged herself briefly, rubbing her bare arms with nervous hands. "Mr. McAllister," she ventured, "look, I'm not sure if this . . ."

But he wasn't listening. He paced eagerly around the studio, looking with enthusiasm at the tall windows, the ample storage cabinets, the long shelves and double porcelain sinks and numerous electrical outlets.

"Perfect," he was saying happily. "Just perfect. Kim, I probably ought to warn you . . ."

"Yes?"

He turned to glance at her. "My studio can get pretty lively at times. I mean, I like to have company drop by. I enjoy visiting with people while I work, and I know a lot of old cowboys around here who'll likely be stopping in. They criticize the technical details of my work and give me inspiration."

Kim absorbed this, momentarily shocked into silence.

"And," he went on, pacing off the dimensions of the empty half of the room, "I tend to use a lot of props, too."

"Props?" Kim echoed weakly.

"Saddles, taxidermists' wildlife models, things that I need to look at while I paint. Once I brought a live horse into the studio, but I don't think I could do that here, unless there's a freight elevator. Is there, do you know?"

He looked at her with sudden interest. While Kim was searching for an answer, footsteps sounded in the hall and two women appeared in the doorway.

Kim turned to look at the newcomers. One was an older lady, tall and regal with snow-white hair and a long coat of fine tan wool. The other was small and shy, probably Filipino, Kim decided. The smaller woman looked so nervous that Kim smiled at her, then tensed with rising excitement when the woman smiled back.

For a moment, Kim forgot all about Todd McAllister. She was caught in a rapt study of the young woman's face.

This was the face that Kim had been seeking for over a year. She'd been commissioned to undertake an ambitious project, a mural depicting the plight of women through the ages. She wanted a woman's face to appear prominently in the foreground, a symbol of Every Woman, shadowed by smaller intersecting images in a rich collage. And the woman standing in the doorway, huddled shyly in an overlarge jacket and clutching something in her arms, had just the face Kim had envisioned.

The way the woman was holding the bundle, she might be cradling a baby. That would be a good touch—sorrowing-woman-with-child. Maybe she should incorporate the image of the baby, too....

"Ms. Tanaka, this is my grandmother, Barbara McAllister," Todd said. "And her housekeeper, Julia Adolpho. Ladies, this is Kim Tanaka. Is there some kind of problem, Nana? Why are you here?"

"We were driving past and saw your truck. I wanted to let you know that the Stevensons are coming for dinner tonight, Todd, and I'd like you to be there."

Kim found herself privately enjoying the peremptory note in the woman's voice. It was exactly the same tone her own grandmother used when she wanted Kim to do something and intended to brook no resistance.

In fact, Madame Tanaka had used that precise inflection when she'd informed Kim that her attendance was expected at tonight's family dinner with the young Japanese businessman, David Yamamoto.

But Kim's smile faded when Barbara McAllister's gaze shifted in her direction. The woman's eyes were as blue as her grandson's, but they held none of the warmth of his. Kim sensed a cold disapproval that chilled and puzzled her. Todd obviously felt the sudden tension in the room and moved forward to lift the object from the housekeeper's arms, holding it out to Kim. "Meet Hugo," he said. "I believe he's on his way to the vet for his shots, poor little guy."

Hugo lifted his blunt head and gazed soulfully at Kim. He looked so woebegone that Kim smiled in spite of herself and reached out to lift one of his silky ears. "Isn't he darling," she murmured. "Hello, Hugo."

The entire situation was becoming awkward and disorganized. This was a feeling that Kim hated above all, the uncomfortable sensation that she was losing command of herself and her surroundings.

She looked quietly at the tall, white-haired woman, the shy little housekeeper and the smiling handsome face of Todd McAllister.

"So," Barbara was saying as she surveyed the room, "this is where you're going to be working, is it?"

"I'm afraid not," Kim said.

She felt Todd glance at her sharply, but forced herself to remain calm and expressionless.

"I've decided not to rent out my studio, after all," she said. "I'm sorry to have bothered you, Mr. McAllister. I hope you're successful in finding a work space somewhere else."

Kim smiled courteously at the others, then moved toward her easel, conscious of their eyes resting on her in startled silence.

CHAPTER THREE

TODD STARED at Kim in dismay, hardly noticing when his grandmother and her housekeeper left the studio and vanished down the hallway. He moved back into the room and looked at the woman's slim straight back and dark ponytail as she studied the painting on her easel.

What had happened to upset her? Was it something he'd said, or...

Todd frowned as he thought about his grandmother, and her ancient bitterness against the Japanese. She hadn't said anything that Todd could recall, but maybe Kim had read something in the old woman's face or voice—caught an expression or an inflection that had troubled her.

He was angry at the thought that his grandmother's prejudice could possibly have robbed him of a career opportunity. But on a deeper level, Todd was also saddened to think that the exquisite woman before him might have been hurt by someone associated with him.

She was so delicate and beautiful, this Kim Tanaka. At first, Todd had been powerfully struck by her fragile, flowerlike beauty, but now he was even more impressed by the contrast between the woman's appearance and her personality. She might look like a dainty orchid, but she had a soul of steel. He could see it in the clear intelligence of her dark eyes, the determined set of her mouth, the erect look of her back as she turned away from him.

"Was it something I said?" he asked abruptly, moving to stand near her. "Have I upset you somehow?"

If she'd been disconcerted by something that had happened, she was fully composed now. She looked up at him calmly.

"Of course not," she said. "Renting out a studio is a business proposition, Mr. McAllister, not a personal one. And I think that our trying to work together would probably be quite uncomfortable for both of us. I believe our work would suffer from the tension."

"Why?"

"Because our styles are so different. I'm sorry if I've caused you any bother or delay," she repeated. "But you're sufficiently well known that I don't think you'll have any problem finding a place to work. In fact," she added, clearly anxious to get rid of him so she could return to her painting, "I'll ask around for you, if you like. I meet a lot of local artists in the course of my work."

"That's at the city gallery?"

"Yes. Now, if you'll excuse me . . ."

Todd McAllister was not accustomed to being dismissed. Nor was he used to sparring with a personality as strong and obstinate as his own. Throughout his

life, a combination of charm, energy and sheer determination had almost always managed to get him
whatever he wanted. But now, looking into the face of
this woman, he felt defeated and he could hardly bear
the disappointment. He didn't want to look anywhere
else for space. He loved this room and the light, and
he wanted to unpack his equipment and start working
this afternoon.

Most of all, he wanted to work with Kim Tanaka.
He liked the idea of her quiet presence being on the
other side of the room. There was something about her
that was calming to him. Watching her evoked the
same sense of peace as did gazing at a calm lake or a
silvery autumn moon.

She turned to him, her face withdrawn and cool.
Todd was reminded again that this woman had
achieved teaching tenure at one of the country's most
distinguished art schools.

"Mr. McAllister..."

"Yes?"

"Your grandmother's housekeeper...did you say
her name was Julia?"

"Julia Adolpho," Todd said, a little confused by
the change of subject. "Why?"

Kim looked at him directly. "Her face is perfect for
a painting I've been commissioned to do by a na-
tional women's political group. I think they want to
use it as a poster. I've been holding off a long time
because I just haven't been able to find the right
model."

Todd nodded, knowing how difficult and often frustrating it was for an artist to find the perfect model.

He looked at Kim when she paused. "And?" he prompted.

She turned aside uncomfortably, inclining her head and toying with one of the brushes in her paint jar. "And I wondered if you thought she might be willing to sit for me."

Todd studied her bent head, the long silky pony-tail, the sweet line of her cheek and mouth. He was strongly tempted to offer some kind of deal; he'd deliver his grandmother's housekeeper as a model if Kim would change her mind about the studio. But as soon as the thought occurred to him, he dismissed it as petty and childish.

At the same moment, Kim looked up at him with her unsettling clear gaze. "Never mind," she said. "It was probably a bad idea, anyhow. I hope you find a studio, Mr. McAllister."

"Thanks," he said, turning away. "I'll see if I can talk to Julia about sitting for you, but I wouldn't count on it. She's awfully shy."

"Please don't bother. As I said, it was just a thought, really. Goodbye, Mr. McAllister. Thanks for coming."

Todd paused in the doorway with a last regretful look at the big airy room and the beautiful woman who stood at her easel. He watched her as, frowning, she dipped a paintbrush into a jar of water, then rubbed it in a block of dark pigment before adding some exquisite Japanese calligraphy to the side of the painting.

Finally, reluctantly, he turned and walked down the empty hallway.

JULIA STOOD by the window of her attic bedroom, gazing out at the crescent spring moon hanging above the treetops. She shivered despite the warmth of her flannel nightgown and rubbed her arms, thinking wistfully about the young Japanese woman she'd seen earlier that day. What must it be like to be that woman, Julia thought in wonder.

She could hardly imagine a woman her own age working to make such beautiful pictures, paying her way in the world with her talent and renting a whole huge room just for herself.

In Julia's home in the Philippines, five or six families would live together in a place that big, and consider themselves lucky to have it. Yet, here in America, the room was occupied by one small woman who didn't even live there.

A series of squeaks and small yelps rising from a cardboard box next to Julia's bed, caused her to shake her head and turn back into the room.

"Hugo!" she whispered, hurrying across the room to kneel by the box. "You be quiet, or Mrs. McAllister will hear you and we'll both be in trouble."

As if he could understand her words, the puppy fell silent and gazed up at her with bright eyes, then began scrambling out of the box. In his eagerness, he

forgot himself and whimpered noisily. Julia gave him
a rueful smile.

"All *right*," she whispered. "But just for a little
while, you bad puppy." She lifted the squirming animal from the box and carried him with her to the bed,
patting his fat silky body to keep him quiet.

Julia had been unable to bear the puppy's doleful
crying when he was left alone at night in his basket.
She knew that she could put him in with Homer for
comfort, but she was afraid that the bigger dog might
inadvertently smother the puppy against the side of the
basket.

Still, she was also afraid that Mrs. McAllister would
find out she was taking the puppy into her room and
be angry with her. Julia was terrified of displeasing her
mistress. She couldn't imagine losing this job and
having to search for another position. Possibly she'd
even come to the attention of the immigration officials and have her work visa suspended.

Julia moaned and huddled under her blankets,
pressing her face against the puppy's fat body.

Hugo snuggled with her gratefully, burrowing into
the softness of the pillow. Julia patted his back, smiling at him in the glow of the bedside lamp. Finally, the
puppy rolled over, exposing his pink stomach, and fell
asleep in a tumble of ears and paws, his eyes squeezed
tight like a baby's.

When the little dog was sleeping soundly, Julia
reached across his head and took a letter from the
bedside table, moving carefully so as not to disturb her
bedmate.

She shook the letter and it fell open at the fold lines. The paper was already worn from many readings. The letter was written in English, in a child's large block letters, and decorated with bright crayon-colored pictures of trees and flowers. It read:

Dear Mother,
    I am very well. I have a new ball. It is red. I miss you and pray for you every day.
                                    Your loving son,
                                        Roberto

Julia smiled through her tears, thinking proudly that Roberto's printing was very good for a little boy who was barely six years old. Of course, his uncle Cesar had probably helped him with the wording and punctuation, but she knew that Roberto had done the printing by himself.

Again she studied the colorful letter, hungry for details about the child. Was he happy? Was he well? Her mother always said in her letters that everything was fine in the village, but then, Julia knew her mother would be reluctant to worry her daughter who was so far away.

Roberto had a new ball. That was good.... It showed that the family could afford a few small luxuries, and that somebody was thinking about Roberto. And they were making sure that he said his prayers....

Again the tears burned in Julia's eyes. She dashed at them with her free hand, still holding the letter tenderly.

She had known it would be hard, leaving her son behind and coming to America alone. But the immigration officials had warned Julia that despite her high-school education and secretarial training, domestic work was all she could hope for in the beginning, and American families weren't interested in hiring women with small children.

"Your records indicate that you are divorced, Mrs. Adolpho. Is that right?"

"Yes," Julia had whispered, intimidated by the cool efficiency of the American lady at the immigration office.

"Could your husband possibly help with some of your son's expenses?"

"No. He never sends any money. He's remarried and has two other children."

"I see. Well, the best plan would be to go to the United States by yourself and get a good job, and save some money," the woman had advised her briskly. "Then send for your son. Prospective employers and the government will be more likely to look on you favorably if you do it that way."

Terrified at the possibility of missing this opportunity, Julia had agreed to everything. She'd left Roberto in the village with her brother Cesar and his family, where her mother lived, as well. There were lots of people to look after her son, and they appreciated the money that Julia sent to them. It was all working out well, except that Julia missed her little boy with a visceral ache that never went away.

Sometimes she entertained wild thoughts of telling Mrs. McAllister about Roberto, casting herself on the old lady's mercy and begging permission to bring her son to America. But something always prevented her at the last minute. Mrs. McAllister was unpredictable in her reactions, and very stern when displeased. She might be angry if she learned that Julia had a child she'd never mentioned. Besides, Julia thought, swallowing hard and toying absently with the puppy's silky ears, it shouldn't be more than another year or two. Despite sending a large portion of her pay every month to Cesar, she was managing to save a little. Her bank account was growing, slowly but steadily. Maybe next year, or certainly the year after that, she'd be able to go to the government officials, show them her bank statements and ask permission to go to the Philippines and bring Roberto back with her. But the time seemed to go so slowly....

Julia folded the letter and tucked it back in the nightstand. Then she settled under the covers, switched off the light and drew the puppy's warm body close to her. She lay still, gazing out the window at the moon caught in the branches of the elm tree.

BARBARA MCALLISTER, too, was looking at the silvery scrap of moon among the branches.

This was obviously going to be one of the nights when sleep was especially elusive. Barbara hated those nights that seemed to happen more often recently, dark hours when she lay awake till dawn, staring out the window and thinking about the past.

The house seemed bigger and emptier since Todd had moved into an apartment. He'd only been home a few days, but his noisy, cheerful presence had seemed to fill the whole world with sunshine. When he left, the place felt huge and lonely.

Nobody would ever know how much Barbara McAllister adored her grandson. She was careful not to display any emotion, keeping her reactions sternly controlled and her conversation crisp and detached. Even Todd himself, though he understood her better that anyone else, would probably have been surprised to know how deeply Barbara loved him, and how painfully she missed him when he was gone.

Barbara stirred restlessly in the wide bed, wondering if she should get up and make herself some cocoa. It was past midnight, and she still didn't feel at all sleepy. Maybe a cup of hot milk and a slice of toast…

She heaved herself out of bed, put on her slippers and dressing gown and padded softly through the silent house, pausing on her way to the kitchen to sit by the fireplace and look down at Homer in his basket.

The puppy's basket was empty, and Homer was alone, Barbara noted. Julia must have taken the little creature into her bed again.

Barbara smiled briefly in the darkness.

She'd known from the beginning that Julia was breaking house rules by comforting the puppy at night, but she had no intention of saying anything. The new housekeeper was so shy and timid, so obviously frightened of her mistress, that Barbara maintained a tactful silence on the subject of Hugo's nighttime adventures.

"Between Todd and Julia, that animal's going to be spoiled rotten," Barbara told Homer, who had awakened and was gazing at her with bleary surprise. Homer nodded agreement and fell asleep again, one of his long ears dangling comically over the edge of the basket.

Barbara leaned back in the chair, reaching up to toy absently with her braid and wishing she hadn't stopped here in the living room. If she'd gone straight to the kitchen, her cocoa would be made by now, resting warm and comforting in a mug on the lamp table beside her.

But she made no move to get up, just settled deeper in the chair and looked around with a sigh at the darkened room.

Barbara had no need of artificial light to see the contents of the big room. Many of them hadn't changed in the seventy-odd years of her life, and she'd hardly been away from the house at all in those years.

More than fifty years had passed since she and her sister and brothers had all lived here together, but their childhood ghosts seemed to fill the room. Barbara could see her brothers hurrying off to tennis matches and ball games, her sister whirling down the staircase in a party dress, herself going out to meet young Alex McAllister, who looked so handsome in his uniform...

But her marriage to Alex had been so brief that sometimes it seemed never to have happened. Barbara hadn't even moved out of the house, except for a month in rental accommodations in Texas where Alex was waiting to be shipped overseas. She never saw him after that one precious month, but he left her something to fill her lonely days.

Lillian was born nine months later, when Alex was on a destroyer in the Pacific. Barbara still had his letter, the one he'd sent to her after they telegraphed him news of his daughter's birth.

"Love you both," he'd said. "I'm coming home soon to see my girls!"

But he never made it home. The destroyer took a direct hit just before his leave was due. Alex was pulled from the water by a Japanese patrol boat and taken prisoner. Barbara heard from him only sporadically after that, and not at all for the final two years of the war. She could only imagine how he'd suffered before his death.

Barbara sighed, thinking of the beautiful Japanese woman she'd met that afternoon in the art studio, her small erect body and sweet face.

Todd kept telling his grandmother that war was a historical imperative, that everybody had suffered equally and that people, as well as nations, were required to put the past behind them and establish cordial relations with one another again.

Barbara understood what her grandson was telling her, and there had been times in the past when she'd honestly tried to leave the old bitterness behind and get on with her life. But she'd lost so much, and she needed to blame someone for that loss. Otherwise, her years on earth seemed like a senseless and tragic waste.

She stared at the empty grate, brooding over her memories, thinking how badly she'd been cheated. How she'd spent her whole life in this house, a lonely aging woman without a husband, caring for her elderly parents until they died, and then looking after the little boy her daughter had abandoned.

Her daughter...

Again Barbara's face twisted with bitterness and sorrow. That was another thing she needed to blame somebody for. After the death of her young husband, Barbara had pinned all her hopes on their baby, devoted so much love and energy to the raising of Alex's child. But Lillian had been a problem right from the beginning. She'd been headstrong, selfish and rebellious.

Barbara truly believed things would have been different for her daughter if Alex had lived. He could have handled Lillian. Their daughter was always better behaved and anxious to please if a male was involved. Barbara just seemed to irritate the girl, bringing out the worst in her.

Barbara shuddered, thinking about the stormy years of Lillian's adolescence in this house. Barbara had been caught between the demands of two sick parents and her equally demanding daughter. There were times during Lillian's teenage years when Barbara had thought she would die of weariness. And just when it had started to get a little better, when the girl was eighteen years old, showing a few fleeting signs of growing up and getting ready to take charge of her life, she'd become pregnant with Todd.

Poor Todd . . .

Barbara remembered the thoughtful little boy he'd been, so sunny and cheerful on most days, but so deeply hurt by his mother's casual cruelty. Lillian never even tried to make a pretense of wanting him or caring about him. She left the baby with her mother and went on with her life as if he'd never been born, flitting from man to man and city to city, dropping by once or twice a year to see her mother and her son.

When he was little, Todd would anticipate these visits eagerly. Barbara could tell that he was anxious because he would become unnaturally quiet, and spend hours up in his room working on careful drawings with which to impress his mother. But often, Lillian came and stayed for just an hour or so, then went on her way with obvious relief, leaving the little boy crushed and pale with disappointment. And sometimes she didn't bother to come at all, even when she'd promised.

Lillian hadn't been back to Spokane for several years. She telephoned sometimes from California, where she lived with her husband, a much older man who had enough money to keep her interested, at least for a time. Todd never mentioned his mother's name, and refused to speak to her on the telephone if he happened to be in the house when she called.

Barbara knew that Todd didn't trust women, even now, and that his happy-go-lucky manner concealed painful scars that others would never be allowed to see. Somebody had to be blamed for so much suffering. These things didn't happen out of the blue, and they weren't accidental. People did wrong things, and others had to pay. Lives were ruined. Worst of all, the damage extended all the way into succeeding generations, harming the innocent.

Again Barbara thought about the Japanese artist with her serene demeanor and lovely pale face. She remembered the way Todd had looked at the woman as she stood by her easel, his expression of warm interest, the sudden flare of intensity in his eyes.

Barbara's mouth tightened with resolve.

"Never," she whispered aloud to Homer, who slept on undisturbed. "Never in a million years. I'd die first."

CHAPTER FOUR

"THIS ONE is called *Childhood.* I wanted the work to represent the joy and freedom a small child feels before social pressure dulls his experience of the world."

The people in the gallery nodded solemnly at the sculpture, consulted their catalogs and moved across the carpeted floor, following the burly young artist as he introduced his new collection. The artwork was being displayed in a private commercial gallery, well known for its cutting-edge collections.

Kim lingered to examine the sculpture, which was a broad piece of angle-iron welded to an old metal pump and riddled with rusty bolts.

A young woman beside her gazed at the twisted metal shapes with rapt approval. "It's so *strong,* isn't it?" she murmured. "Quite visceral, I think." Kim turned aside hastily, coughing to hide the fit of giggles that threatened to disgrace her. She glanced up, her eyes bright, to see if her companion shared the joke.

But David Yamamoto was looking politely at the sculpture, his handsome face impassive. He frowned at his catalog and prepared to move across the gallery behind the artist. When he became aware of Kim's glance, he arched his eyebrows in courteous inquiry.

Suddenly, Kim was desperate to know what David was thinking. Maybe if she could find a glimmer of understanding somewhere in this man, she wouldn't feel so alone when she was with him. She took his sleeve and held him back as the crowd trooped across the gallery.

"David," she whispered, "tell me the truth. Don't you think this is all just really silly?"

"What do you mean?" he asked, looking concerned. "Kim, you wanted to come to this exhibition tonight. You said it was important to your job."

"I know. I'm supposed to be here so I can write a critique for our own gallery. But it's just so ridiculous." She pointed at the ugly metal structure. "Calling this *Childhood!* He should call it *Old Pump Filled With Rusty Bolts.* At least it would be more sincere, wouldn't it?"

David's eyes widened in surprise. "I'm surprised you'd feel that way. After all, you're an artist yourself."

"That doesn't mean I can be taken in by a charade like this! David, an object isn't art just because someone says it is."

"Art, like beauty, is in the eye of the beholder," he read aloud from his catalog.

Kim made an impatient gesture. "But do you really believe that, David? Doesn't all this—" she waved her arm to take in the roomful of welded metal and scrap iron "—doesn't it all make you feel just a little bit like giggling? Tell me the truth."

David looked at her soberly. "I never laugh at other people's work," he said. "Would you like some champagne, Kim?"

"That would be nice, thank you," Kim said in defeat, then watched as he made his way calmly through the throng. David was slim, graceful and impeccably dressed in a gray suit and tie, his dark hair gleaming in the muted light.

Her grandmother was probably right, Kim thought sadly, still watching as he approached the wine and cheese bar.

David Yamamoto was an extremely nice young man. Even Kim's irreverent spirit couldn't stir him to unkindness. He was tactful, intelligent, considerate and hardworking, and she should probably marry him and fill Masako's heart with joy. Kim stood still visualizing what her life would be like as the wife of David Yamamoto.

It wasn't hard to picture. In fact, she'd have an existence much the same as her mother's. Kim would be prosperous, secure and well respected in her home and community, free to pursue her artistic goals and indulge her charitable instincts while raising a family. Their home would be largely Western in orientation, with a few Japanese touches for the sake of atmosphere.

Still, their shared heritage would form the background of her life with David, just as it did for Kim's parents, and would give their children a strong sense of continuity and the security of a proud, ancient lineage. It would be, Kim realized, a most pleasant and fulfilling life.

But would she always suffer these moments of intense loneliness, when something struck her as funny but there was nobody with whom to share the joke?

Kim and David had gone out together several times in the weeks since the dinner at her father's house. Their dates came about because whenever he phoned or visited, David showed his respect by speaking for a few moments to Madame Tanaka before talking to Kim. Masako always knew when David called, and Kim understood with weary certainty that her grandmother would start looking weak and frail and develop alarming palpitations if Kim refused to go out when he asked. So she usually accepted.

But, Kim thought, despite the fact that David was such an ideal partner for her, so well suited in every way, there was no chemistry between them. Kim had no intention of marrying a man who couldn't laugh with her, no matter how perfect he was.

Kim shook her head restlessly and moved across the floor of the gallery. She leafed through the glossy catalog, which claimed that the work of this "exciting young sculptor" was "a joyous celebration of the essence of art and life."

Maybe David was right, and it wasn't proper to laugh at another artist's work, regardless of how silly she thought it was. Still, Kim felt those distressing giggles threatening to bubble up again when she paused by another sculpture.

It was a shiny metal hoop about eighteen inches in diameter, apparently the rim of a small tire, with a couple of metal plates welded to its surface by coarse gobs of soldering iron. Chains of various thickness hung in untidy loops from the flat surface of the hoop.

The title plate was affixed to the other side of the display column. Kim couldn't find the piece in her catalog, though most of the others were listed, their prices in the thousands of dollars. And several works already displayed the small red dots that indicated they'd been sold.

"*Springtime,*" a voice said unexpectedly, somewhere near her left shoulder.

Kim jumped a little and turned around, finding herself looking up into a square, tanned face, and eyes that were an amazing shade of blue. Though a whole month had passed since she'd last seen those eyes, Kim realized she hadn't forgotten them. Not at all.

Todd McAllister waved his hand toward the sculpture in front of them. "It's called *Springtime*. It's a late entry in the show. The artist says it's a depiction of the eternal sweetness and fertility of the vernal equinox."

Kim stared at him, trying desperately to keep from laughing. But when she saw the wicked gleam that danced in his eyes, and a dimple that kept appearing in one cheek, she was undone. She covered her face with the catalog, gasping and shaking with laughter while Todd pounded her back and smiled apologetically at the people who glanced in their direction. "Choked on a bit of cheese," he explained to the onlookers, fanning her with his catalog. "Hey, Kim," he whispered urgently, bending his curly head close to hers, "are you going to be all right? Should I call an ambulance, or something?"

Kim shook her head, waving her free hand helplessly. After a few moments, she was able to get her breath, but she was afraid to meet his eyes in case that dangerous twinkle set her off again. Instead, she concentrated on the rest of him, which was casually dressed in jeans, boots and a tweed sport jacket over an open-necked white shirt.

"Vernal equinox?" she murmured when she was able to speak again.

Todd took her elbow and steered her into a corner of the room near the windows, where the May evening was deepening to purple twilight and a gentle fragrance of lilacs wafted into the crowded gallery.

"C'mon, girl," he whispered, "don't you believe in eternal sweetness and fertility?"

"Sure I do." Kim glared at the offending sculpture. "But to me, that thing looks just the opposite. You know what it looks like? One of those medieval chastity belts that knights fitted onto their ladies before they rode off to the Crusades."

"Ow!" Todd winced and looked thoughtfully at the metal hoop with its dangling links of coarse chain. "That's not a real pleasant thought, is it?"

He still had a hand on her elbow, and he gently pulled her against him as the crowd swelled and pressed closer to their corner. Kim had a sensation of masculine warmth and strength, of steel-hard muscle as her body pressed into his.

She drew herself away hastily and turned to give him a polite smile. "Thank you," she murmured. "I think all I really needed was to laugh a bit over this . . . collection. I feel much better now."

The dimple was very pronounced in his cheek. "You sure had a fit of the giggles, all right. Even if you do look a whole lot more grown-up and serious without the ponytail."

Kim reached up to touch her hair, surprised that he'd even remembered her ponytail. "My grandmother likes to do my hair in a French braid for important occasions like this."

"It's very glamorous," Todd said with approval, looking at her glossy dark hair and her slim-fitting white woolen dress. "But I kind of miss the ponytail," he added, his eyes dancing again.

Kim looked down in confusion, clutching her catalog.

Still, she no longer had any desire to be away from this elegant carpeted gallery. In fact, the room suddenly seemed warmer and brighter, the light more sparkling, the crowd more animated. Even the sculptures, she thought in surprise, didn't look quite so awful.

"Are you here with somebody?" Todd asked.

Kim nodded. "He's trying to get me some champagne. There he is," she added, catching sight of David across the room, still waiting patiently at the bar.

Todd studied her escort with interest. "Looks like a nice guy," he commented. "Are you two serious?"

"We're friends," Kim said quietly. "My grandmother introduced us," she added, surprised that she was telling so much to this virtual stranger. "She's very anxious for me to be . . . settled."

"I see. How about you?"

Kim dropped her head, looking away from his disconcerting blue gaze. "I don't think so. In fact, the idea of settling down doesn't appeal to me very much at all."

He seemed on the verge of saying something else, then must have thought better of it and smiled at her casually. "Tell me, Kim, have you rented out the other half of your studio yet?"

She made a face, thinking about all the bizarre types who'd been disturbing her work as they came to look at the space. "No, I haven't. I've had quite a few offers, but none of them seemed right to me."

"Anybody I'd know?"

"As a matter of fact, our sculptor was one of them."

"This guy?" Todd asked in surprise, looking around.

Kim nodded. "He was all set to move in, with his acetylene torches and fuel tanks and everything. Apparently, he couldn't believe that I wasn't flattered by the prospect."

Todd squinted at the display of sculptures, looking thoughtful for once. "Funny thing about artwork, isn't it?" he said. "You know, I went to a showing of welded metal sculpture at the Metropolitan in New York three years ago, and it was wonderful. It left me practically breathless."

"I know that exhibition," Kim said eagerly. "That was Paquette's work, wasn't it? I saw the show in San Diego."

"That's the one. And it's abstract work, too, but it's sure a whole lot different from this stuff."

"That's always been my complaint about abstract art," Kim said. "I know it's terrible for me to have laughed the way I did, but it's so easy for someone to produce something and call it art. And no matter what it's like, there's always somebody ready to jump on the bandwagon and say it's beautiful, and that just annoys the public and makes artists look ridiculous."

"Naked emperors, many of us," Todd agreed. "But not you," he added. "Those watercolors of yours are exquisite, Kim. I've been looking through all the local galleries for one to buy, but I can't find any that people are willing to part with."

His praise was sincere. Kim flushed with pleasure and looked down again, suddenly tongue-tied.

"Anybody else?" he asked.

"I beg your pardon?"

"Anybody else look at your studio?"

"Well," Kim said, "there were two teenage boys in baggy pants and cotton bandannas. They paint eagles and coyotes on the sides of vans."

Todd chuckled. "No kidding. How were they planning to get the vans up to the second floor?"

"No sweat, they said. I think they said they would bring up the doors and side panels, and paint them in the studio with airbrushes. It was hard for me to tell because they had their portable tape deck playing rap music the whole time we were talking."

"Maybe not quite your cup of tea," Todd said, giving her a sympathetic smile.

"Not quite. And then there was a really strange woman who paints nudes of men. She seemed to think I'd be so intrigued by her models, I'd be willing to give her a reduced rent just for the privilege of looking at them."

He threw back his head and laughed aloud, then sobered. "I wish you'd change your mind and rent the space to me," he said. "I'm so anxious to find a studio, I'll pay the whole rent, not half. And I'll *work* in the nude, if that's what you like."

Kim was assailed by a sudden mental image of Todd McAllister without clothing. His shoulders would be broad and flat, his body lean, graceful and muscled.

Kim savored the picture, wondering if his chest was hairy or smooth, if his legs were as good as the rest of him, if his body was tanned like his face...

She blushed again, horrified by her thoughts, and looked up in confusion as David returned, bearing a tray that held champagne glasses and cheese.

"David Yamamoto, this is Todd McAllister," she said, composing herself with an effort. David handed her the tray and shook Todd's hand. "I've seen your work, Mr. McAllister. I think you're one of the country's great artists."

"Thank you. Call me Todd, please."

"David, I think I'm going to rent out the other half of my studio to Todd," Kim said suddenly, and felt Todd looking at her with startled delight. She kept her face turned away, almost as surprised by her own rash statement as Todd obviously was.

But she was getting tired of trying to sublet the space, and this man seemed so pleasant and comfortable tonight. And he really needed a studio. This way, she could solve both their problems. And working with him might not be so bad. At least they shared a sense of humor....

David seemed unaware of her confusion. He beamed with pleasure, turning back to Todd. "Well, that's wonderful news. I know Kim's been anxious to find a studio partner. Perhaps I'll be fortunate enough to watch you work sometime."

"Anytime," Todd said, still looking at Kim. "I like having company while I work."

KIM HADN'T EXPECTED Todd McAllister to waste a lot of time following up on her offer. Still, she was a little surprised the next day when she walked over to the studio after lunch and found a dusty pickup truck parked by the curb. The man himself was stretched lazily behind the wheel with an old baseball cap tipped over his eyes to block the sun's glare.

Kim paused by the truck and peered uncertainly through the open window, wondering if he was asleep. But Todd sat up at her approach, tipped back his cap and studied her. Kim shifted awkwardly on her san-

daled feet, suddenly conscious of her bare shoulders
and legs in the white cotton sundress.

"It's...quite hot today, isn't it?" she said, feeling
unaccountably nervous. "Really humid."

"It sure is," Todd agreed, swinging himself out of
the truck and reaching for a leather portfolio. He wore
faded jeans and a yellow T-shirt with a beer logo on
the front. "I like that dress," he said abruptly. "It
looks nice with your coloring."

"Is that a compliment, or an artist's observation?"

"Is that a serious question, or are you fishing?" he
asked, giving her a quick, penetrating look. Kim
tensed with irritation and turned aside. She went into
the building and started to climb the stairs, not looking to see if he was following.

"Sorry," Todd said behind her. "I didn't mean to
offend you. I just can never understand why a woman
can't accept a compliment without making an issue of
it."

"Maybe because we hear so many tired lines, we
can't help questioning the sincerity," Kim said, trying
not to let her annoyance show in her voice. She paused
by the studio door and inserted her key in the lock.

But Todd caught her arm and turned her around,
forcing her to look at him. "Look, I may have a lot of
faults, Kim," he said quietly, "but I don't tell lies.
When I pay you a compliment, you can be damned
sure it's sincere."

She shrugged, very aware of his hand on her bare
skin. "I'm not sure it even matters," she said with
forced casualness as she turned from him, opened the

door and walked inside. "After all, we're just going to be working partners, right? And I think it's a good idea to keep it that way."

"Sure," he said, crossing the room to examine the worktable. "That's fine with me. Have you decided how to allocate the space?"

"Not yet. First we have to set up some kind of formal agreement and get it down on paper."

"I did all that last night," he said. "I drafted some forms on my computer. Here, have a look."

Kim glanced at the papers he took from his portfolio, surprised by his businesslike manner. In effect, the forms spelled out a joint lease agreement binding on both parties, but able to be broken by either signee with two weeks' notice for "just cause."

"'Just cause'?" Kim asked with raised eyebrows. "Like what?"

"Well, say you chew tobacco and spit on the floor, and I can't stand it. Or if you and your boyfriend insist on having sex in the studio while I'm trying to work. That would probably constitute just cause."

Kim bit her lip, reminding herself that she was being deliberately teased and she shouldn't keep rising to the bait. But there was something so maddening about this man...

"Actually," she said calmly, "those would be good rules to write into the agreement, don't you think? No spitting in the studio. And absolutely no sex."

"Except between leaseholders," he said, giving her a look of cherubic innocence.

"*Especially* not between leaseholders," Kim said firmly, but when his dimples flashed again, she found herself smiling along with him.

"Okay, now about money," he said, looking at his papers again. "I ordered canvas this morning and it'll be delivered later in the week, so I should be able to get started right away. I'm proposing to pay rent for the whole month of May, even though I'm starting well into the month, because it's not fair to you otherwise. So we'll—"

"Why?" she asked, leaning against the worktable and folding her arms.

"Beg pardon?"

"Why isn't it fair to me? What's fair about making you pay rent for days you haven't even worked here?"

Todd sighed and turned away from his careful examination of one of the sinks. "Look, are you going to fight about every single detail?"

"I'm not the one trying to be the boss and run everything. I have no intention of charging rent for weeks you haven't been here. I'd just as soon have the rent start in June, but if you insist, it shouldn't be all that hard to prorate it and figure out the balance owing. Especially since you're such a whiz with computers."

He came across the room and stood in front of her, almost too close for comfort. "What a woman," he said quietly, only half teasing. "You look like an orchid blossom, but you sound like one of my college professors."

"Then you'd better trust your ears more than your eyes," Kim told him briefly. "That's a lot closer to my true personality."

"Is it really? Do you just work and think all the time?" He watched while she got her paints out and slipped into a discolored smock.

"All the time."

"No fun or romance? No fooling around?"

Kim turned to look at him. "What do you define as 'fooling around'?"

"You know," Todd said, shrugging.

Kim kept her back turned so he wouldn't see her smile. "I'm afraid I don't. By the way, those forms of yours..."

"Yeah?"

"I'd like to take them to a lawyer and have them checked over before we sign them. Just to make sure we haven't...missed anything."

"Okay." Todd moved toward the door and then lingered, looking back at her. "Should I come by and sign them tomorrow, then? Will you be here in the afternoon?"

She nodded, already absorbed in her work.

"And if I can move in by Friday, will that be okay with you?"

Kim looked up. "I guess it'll have to be, won't it?"

"I guess so. I'm an inevitable part of your life, Kim. From now on, you're stuck with me."

She sighed. "Todd..."

"Yeah?" He paused by the doorway, looking around quickly.

"No horses in the studio. Okay?"

He laughed and vanished down the stairs, leaving Kim smiling at the empty doorway.

TODD PARKED his truck outside the city art gallery and entered the foyer, moving quietly so his boots wouldn't clatter on the polished marble floor. He hesitated, then approached a glassed-in office at one side of the gallery doors.

"Mr. Holmes?" he asked, looking in at the elderly man perched behind the desk. "I'm Todd McAllister. Is Kim Tanaka anywhere around?"

"Ah!" The man's eyes sparkled beneath his bush of eyebrows. He got up and extended his hand. "A pleasure to meet you, Todd. Kim's in the gallery, teaching a class."

Todd shook the proffered hand, then glanced hesitantly at the closed gallery doors. "Will she be finished soon? I'm moving into her studio this afternoon and I've got a truckload of my supplies outside. I'll need the keys."

Jeffrey Holmes consulted his watch. "I think her class ends in fifteen minutes or so. Why don't you go in? It's a fifth-grade class. I believe they're working on composition this morning."

"Will she mind if I sit in?"

"Oh, I don't think so. She's a very experienced teacher."

Todd nodded, smiled gratefully and moved out into the foyer again, heading for the big double doors. He opened them and slipped inside the main gallery, where a group of ten-year-olds were sprawled on the floor among a display of soapstone sculptures.

The children had big pads of drawing paper propped up on the floor and on their knees. They were drawing the sculptures, struggling to reproduce the images of animals, birds and hunters standing on the marble display columns.

Todd looked around for Kim, unable to see her at first. Finally, he spotted her, sitting cross-legged on the floor next to a couple of girls. She wore jeans and a yellow cotton shirt and looked almost like one of the children, Todd thought. He smiled, enjoying the opportunity to watch her work. Unaware of her audience, Kim bent close to one of the girls, her face animated and her ponytail swaying as she pointed to the child's drawing.

A few of the children glanced up at Todd and Kim followed their eyes, then got hastily to her feet and crossed the floor toward him, brushing back a few strands of long black hair.

Todd watched her hungrily, surprised by his own reaction. He'd found Kim Tanaka attractive the first time he'd looked at her, but with each new encounter he was more fascinated. There was something so extraordinary about her, a winsome grace and a kind of shimmering, exotic loveliness that he'd never seen in another woman.

At first he'd only wanted to gaze at her, feasting his eyes on her as if she were a delicate spray of blossoms, or a peaceful moonlit garden. But lately, especially since he'd watched her dissolve in helpless laughter at the art showing, and seen her working at the studio, Todd found himself thinking of Kim Tanaka not simply as beautiful but as a warm and sexually desirable woman.

And he wanted her, in a way that he'd seldom wanted anyone else. He wanted to hold her, undress her and look at her slim body. He wanted to learn all the secrets that were hidden behind her shining dark eyes.

But, Todd warned himself sternly, he had to be careful. Those feelings, if he dared to express them, were likely to cost him the use of some prime studio space, so he'd better just keep a firm rein on his emotions.

He forced himself to smile casually, and kept his voice low so he wouldn't disturb her. "Hi, Kim. I just came by for the keys to the studio, if that's all right with you."

"No need to whisper," she said in a normal tone. "We're pretty easygoing here. Want to see what they're doing?" she added.

"I sure do." Todd moved among the students and looked down at their efforts, intrigued by the varying degrees of artistic skill represented on the sheets of drawing paper.

"This is Todd McAllister, class," Kim told the children. "He grew up here in Spokane, and painted the large mural down at city hall that we went to look at a few weeks ago. Remember?"

One of the boys looked up at Todd with wide eyes. "The really neat one with all the horses and cannons and everything?"

"It shows the Battle of Bull Run," Todd said. "That painting took me almost a year to finish. There are more than four hundred figures in it."

The children gazed at him in awe. Todd made himself comfortable on the floor and commented on the children's drawings, borrowing a pencil to demonstrate some tricks of perspective, delighting them with a rapid sketch of a horse so realistic that it almost leapt from the page. When Kim dismissed the class, he watched their noisy departure with a smile, then turned to her.

"That's a nice group," he said. "They seem really keen."

"Most kids are, if they're given half a chance and not bored to death by all kinds of technical stuff."

He looked with pleasure at her shapely body and sparkling face. "It's pretty hard to imagine anyone being bored in a class that you were teaching, Kim."

She shifted nervously under his frank, admiring gaze, and Todd reminded himself again that this sort of flirtation was strictly out-of-bounds. For one thing, she had a boyfriend, and the guy seemed like a decent person. Besides, Todd admonished himself, their working relationship would suffer immediate strains if he didn't learn to control himself.

But she was so adorable. Todd couldn't seem to quit thinking about her, couldn't help wondering how it would feel to hold her, how her lips would taste, what she'd be like in bed ...

She moved briskly from the gallery, and headed into the office to collect her things while Todd followed, trying very hard not to think about going to bed with this woman.

"Well, Jeffrey, I'm off," she said to the curator. "Have you met Todd?"

"Just now, my dear. I take it today is moving day?"

"Yes, it is. We're heading over to the studio right now. Wish us luck, okay?"

The little man beamed at them, and Todd saw a look of private amusement in his eyes. Jeffrey Holmes clearly was no fool; he seemed to have his own opinions about the wisdom of this working arrangement.

Todd liked the man. Under normal circumstances, he would have stayed to discuss Jeffrey's tastes in art, his curatorial duties and his own work. But he had no time for socializing right now. He wanted only to get into the studio, unload his supplies and get a canvas set up and ready to go.

Outside, he paused beside his truck and looked down at Kim. "Do you have a car here?"

She shook her head. "I usually come down on the bus in the morning. It's a lot easier than fighting for a parking space, and the studio's just a few blocks away from the gallery."

"Hop in, then. I'll take you over."

She climbed into his cluttered vehicle, looking quite incongruous on the high leather seat as she sat amid a tumble of paint pots and brush cases.

"You know, I'm being pretty inconsiderate," Todd said as they rounded a corner and headed for the studio. "I guess it would be polite to take you to lunch first, wouldn't it? I've been so damned anxious to get moved in, I keep forgetting things."

She held up a brown paper sack for his inspection. "I bring my lunch," she said. "It's quicker and cheaper. Besides, I tend to feel just like you," she added, giving him an understanding smile. "When I finish work in the morning, I'm so anxious to start painting that I don't really want to take a lot of time over lunch."

Todd nodded, swallowing hard. He wondered if she had any idea how bewitching her smile was, and what a devastating effect she was having on him.

Probably not, he decided. There was a lot of strength and complexity to this woman's personality, but she was certainly no flirt.

"Have you been able to do any work at all on your commissioned paintings since you got home?" she asked, looking down at a pack of sable brushes on the seat next to her.

He shook his head. "Not much. The canvases need so much space. I've just blocked out the composition and spent a few weeks at the library doing research on historical details, but that's about it."

He parked in front of the studio and got out, handing her some smaller canvases from the back of the truck and hefting out a weighty box of paints and turpentine.

"How many paintings are you going to do?" she asked, leading the way up the stairs.

"Four," Todd answered, trying not to watch the way her rounded hips swayed. "Each of them will be four feet by six feet. It's a series depicting the influence of the horse on American history."

She unlocked the door and stepped inside. Todd followed, sighing with pleasure when he entered the airy room with its bank of windows.

"God, this is so perfect," he murmured, crossing the room to deposit his burden on the workbench. "We agreed that I'll take this side, all right?"

Kim nodded, watching as he paced around the studio. "I've already marked it off with chalk," she said. "You get this floor space, and the cupboards from here to the wall. The others are mine. We'll share the bench and the sinks. Does that sound reasonable to you?"

"It sure does," Todd said. "You know, this is sort of like a marriage, isn't it?" he added, teasing her again, despite his firm resolve to keep things on a businesslike footing.

It was so much fun to tease Kim. Her cheeks turned a delicate pink, and her huge dark eyes looked alarmed. But her voice was casual when she turned away and reached for her lunch bag. "I wouldn't know," she said. "I've never been married. Have you?"

Todd grinned. "Marriage isn't my cup of tea, I'm afraid. I can't imagine any woman putting up with me for more than a week or so."

She looked at him in disbelief. "But you expect me to share a studio with you?"

"That's different. This is my job, and I'm really serious about work. I'm just not all that serious about my personal life."

"Well," she said calmly, "as long as you're able to keep your personal life out of the studio, we should be fine."

"Yeah," Todd said, watching her intently. "We should be just fine. In fact, Kim, I think we'll be great together."

But she didn't hear him. She was munching on a sandwich as she fiddled with a gray stone jar containing a spray of flowers. She moved the jar back and forth on the bench, looking at it through narrowed eyes.

A partly finished watercolor stood on her easel, and Kim was obviously trying to arrange the flowers so they'd catch the same light she'd been working with the previous day. She was so absorbed in what she was doing that she seemed to have forgotten his existence.

"I know just how you feel," Todd murmured, watching as she set her sandwich on the easel tray and reached for a brush. "I really think we're going to be great together, Kim," he added softly.

She nodded absently, and dipped the brush into a jar of water, then frowned at her painting.

Todd felt lighthearted and full of optimism. He paused a moment longer, then hurried down the stairs to his truck to bring up the rest of his supplies.

CHAPTER FIVE

JULIA STOOD on the street outside the studio, looking up at the bank of windows that glimmered warmly in the afternoon sunlight. She hesitated, almost sick with tension, and opened the lid of the picnic basket she carried.

Hugo gazed anxiously out at her from the shadowed interior, whimpering pitifully when he caught her eye. The puppy had been to the vet for another shot, and Julia was taking him home. She wished that she could get on the bus and go straight back to the house, but Mrs. McAllister had given her another errand to do on the way home.

"Stop in at the studio, Julia," she'd said, "and take this shirt to Todd, would you? He left it behind when he moved to the apartment."

Julia had looked dubiously at the folded shirt, wondering in silence why Todd couldn't just pick it up when he came for dinner on Sunday.

"And while you're there," Barbara went on with forced casualness, "see how things look down there, all right?"

"What things, ma'am?"

Barbara waved her hand and turned away. "Oh, just how they seem to be getting along, and so forth.

He's been working there almost two weeks now. I'd like to know if everything's all right."

Why couldn't Mrs. McAllister come down herself, if she wanted so badly to know how things were at the studio, Julia thought rebelliously, still lingering on the sidewalk with the picnic basket over her arm.

But she knew the answer to that question.

Mrs. McAllister didn't want to visit the studio because she didn't like the pretty young woman with whom Todd worked. In fact, Mrs. McAllister seemed to dislike all Japanese people, which was strange because she had no apparent prejudice against Julia, and she was quite fond of the young Korean couple who operated the neighborhood grocery store.

For some reason, her dislike was reserved for Japanese. Julia found her mistress's attitude mildly puzzling, but it was none of her business.

Until now, Julia thought gloomily, when she was expected to spy on Todd and his studio partner and report back to Mrs. McAllister.

She sighed, knowing that Mrs. McAllister held complete power over her. Julia would do exactly what her mistress requested because she had no choice. She had to keep her job so she could save enough money to send for Roberto.

Julia's face tightened with resolve when she thought about her son. She peeked into the basket again, thinking how much Roberto would have loved the puppy. By the time Roberto got to America, Hugo would probably be a lazy old dog like Homer. It was such a shame . . .

Finally, she could put it off no longer and trudged up the stairs to the second floor, holding the picnic basket and another heavy canvas bag containing Todd's shirt, some puppy food, three balls of knitting yarn and a pile of books.

Julia hesitated outside the closed door of the studio, knocked timidly and then pushed the door open when she heard Todd's voice call a greeting. Inside, she looked around with astonishment.

The studio had changed drastically since Julia's last visit. Then the big room had been almost empty, stark and orderly and silent. Now it overflowed with color and noise, at least on one side. The wild disorder was all concentrated in the area nearest the door, where Todd worked at a huge canvas propped up on a wooden frame.

His half of the workbench was littered with art supplies, books, saddles and pieces of sculpture depicting horses, buffalo and other animals. Various bits of riding equipment hung from the walls. Country music throbbed from a stereo on one of the shelves, and Todd sang along, dancing an impromptu two-step, brush in hand, as he squinted at the canvas.

On the far side of the room, Kim Tanaka stood painting quietly at her easel, surrounded by tidiness and sparse order. Her brushes were lined up neatly on the bench, flanked by pots of tempera colors and pigment blocks arranged in symmetrical rows. Two white irises stood in a crystal vase near the window, the only adornment in her half of the studio.

The contrast was so striking that Julia almost giggled aloud, but caught herself in time.

All at once, she tensed nervously, thinking there was a third person in the room. But it was only a dressmaker's dummy near Todd's easel, wearing the metal breastplate and helmet of a Spanish conquistador, looking haughty, while Todd's eyes moved from it to the image he was creating on the canvas.

"Hi, Julia," Todd said with an easy smile. "Did Nana send you up here to check on me?"

This was so close to the truth that Julia was momentarily tongue-tied.

"Never mind," Todd said at once, evidently recognizing her discomfort. "It's real nice to see you. Would that by any chance be Hugo in the basket?"

"Yes," Julia whispered, conscious of the two artists looking at her curiously. "He's just been to the vet for his shot."

"Well, then, let him out for a while. He's not likely to do anything unacceptable on Kim's nice clean floor, is he?"

Julia shook her head, her cheeks warm with embarrassment. "He...he did it outside, in the park, just a few minutes ago."

"Good. Let's see him."

Todd grinned when Hugo tumbled out of the basket, all clumsy paws and flapping ears. The puppy cowered for a moment on his haunches, blinking in the bright sunlight that flooded the room. He nosed at Julia's foot for reassurance, then began to trot around, investigating happily while Kim stopped her work to smile at him.

"Julia, this is Hernando," Todd said, indicating the handsome figure in the armor. "He's one of Kim's boyfriends. Hernando dropped by to visit and I talked him into modeling this stuff for me. He's a pretty sexy-looking guy, don't you think, considering that he's almost four hundred years old?"

"Very handsome," Julia agreed, smiling.

"It's nice to see you, again, Julia," Kim said, moving out from behind her canvas. "Todd, look, that puppy's getting into your cupboard. He might eat something and make himself sick."

Todd hurried over to extract Hugo and close the cupboard door, while Julia placed the laundered shirt on a clean portion of the table. "Mrs. McAllister sent this," she murmured. "You left it in your room."

He nodded absently and picked up his brush again. "Thanks, Julia. A half turn to the right, please, Hernando," he added, adjusting his model slightly. "Just so the light reflects on your breastplate. Good . . ."

Julia looked at the huge canvas, where a group of mounted Spaniards had been blocked out in charcoal against a rough background of canyons and plains. One of the figures was beginning to emerge from the canvas, a noble dark face wearing the breastplate and helmet that the dummy modeled. Julia thought how majestic the finished painting was going to be, and looked with new respect at the handsome young artist.

She crossed the room to stand shyly near Kim, and watched Hugo with close attention as he sniffed at Todd's feet.

"This isn't as massive as Todd's work," Kim said, smiling and moving aside to let Julia see the painting on her easel. She was putting the final touches on a delicate study of flowers in a gray stone jar.

"Oh, I think it's beautiful," Julia said softly. She gazed at the painting, deeply moved by its grace and simplicity. "It makes me feel peaceful and happy."

Kim looked at her with surprise and sudden interest. "Why, thank you, Julia. That's probably the nicest compliment you could give me."

Julia shifted awkwardly, touched by the woman's kindness but unable to think of anything to say.

Kim dipped her brush in the water, swirled it thoughtfully, then turned to look at Julia again. "You know, Julia..."

"Yes, ma'am?"

"Call me Kim, please. I was wondering if you might be interested in modeling for me."

"Modeling?" Julia gaped at her. *"Me?"*

Kim nodded, looking intently at Julia's face. "I'm doing a special project, and I need a face just like yours. It might take a while," she warned. "Probably at least twenty hours. I'd most likely want you an hour or two a day for several weeks."

Julia was flabbergasted, wondering what to say. It seemed wonderful to her, the thought of coming to this warm and exciting place every day, being allowed to stay for hours and listen to the music and the conversation, watching beautiful pictures grow under the hands of these talented people.

"I usually have some free time in the afternoons," she said shyly. "Mrs. McAllister doesn't care what I do then. And it's easy to get here on the bus."

"Good. Afternoons are best for me, too. Now, I'll pay you my standard model rate, which is twenty-two dollars an hour. Is that all right?"

Julia's head spun. She hadn't even considered the idea that Kim might be intending to *pay* her for modeling. "Twenty-two dollars an hour?" she whispered. "For... for twenty hours?"

"If it's not enough—"

"Oh, no, it's fine," Julia said hastily. "It's... wonderful," she added, smiling at Kim with sudden radiance. "I can hardly believe it."

She hurried to collect Hugo who had dragged an old leather cowboy boot into the center of the floor and was shaking it furiously.

"Could you start on Monday?" Kim asked.

"Yes," Julia said, still feeling dazed.

She was so excited, she couldn't even do the arithmetic. How much was twenty times twenty-two? Possibly enough for a one-way plane fare for a small boy. And she'd have it in a couple of weeks. Now, if she could just save enough to buy her own ticket, and convince the authorities that she would be able to care for Roberto when he arrived...

Her thoughts were so far away that Julia was hardly aware any longer of the people in the room. She tucked Hugo into the basket, murmured hasty goodbyes and hurried toward the door, her heart singing with excitement.

Todd glanced around at Kim after Julia left, giving her a thoughtful look, which she ignored. At last he turned to his model, leaning forward and speaking in a theatrical whisper.

"Hernando," he murmured, "I've been used. I feel so...so dirty."

Still Kim ignored him.

"Why do I feel that way, you ask?" Todd looked at the haughty conquistador and frowned, reaching out to rearrange one of the plumes. "Well, isn't it obvious? She doesn't love me at all, Hernando. All this time, I thought she wanted me working by her side, and instead she was just using me to get the model she wanted for her painting. I feel so..."

He paused, and melodramatically lay a paint-stained hand against his chest.

"I feel so *cheap*," he concluded mournfully.

"Oh, shut up!" Kim muttered. "You know perfectly well that my offering you this studio space had nothing to do with Julia. As a matter of fact, I'd forgotten all about her until she stopped by here today."

"So it's true?" Todd asked, waving his brush in the air and doing a few line-dance steps to "Achy-Breaky Heart," which was now blaring from the radio. "You really love me, after all?"

"No, I don't. I hate you," Kim said, "with a deep, bitter passion. Almost as much as I hate that bloody song."

"Come on," Todd said. He set the brush on his easel, hooked his thumbs through his belt loops and sidled close to her. "Dance with me, Kim. I've showed you a hundred times. It's step, side, step, side, kick, *hitch*..."

Kim shook her head and went on painting. He watched her for a moment, sighing. "You'd be so cute if you'd learn to line dance. You should see the girls down at the saloon on Saturday night in their tight jeans and red cowboy boots. They're truly a joy to watch."

"So go and watch them. I can't imagine anything I'd enjoy less."

"Yeah?" He straddled a chair and leaned his chin on the back of it as he gazed at her canvas. "Do you mind if I look?"

"Not at all," she said dryly. "Feel free. I never mind as much," she added, "once I'm finished."

"The light's wrong," he said after a moment. "There, behind the vase."

"What do you mean?"

He got up and moved over beside her, picking up one of her brushes and gesturing with it. "See? The light strikes the vase and the petals on this side, right? So the table here should be in partial shadow. You've got too much highlight there."

"Oh, *damn*," Kim muttered. "You're right."

"I'm always right," Todd agreed, giving her a placid smile and returning to his own painting. "Otherwise, it's probably the nicest thing you've done this spring," he added. "Hey, Kim..."

"What?" she asked, frowning as she stood back and contemplated the watercolor.

"What do you make of Julia?"

"Make of her?" Kim looked at him blankly. "I don't know what you mean. She seems like a sweet woman. Why?"

"I think she's a woman with a secret. I think she's hiding something about her past."

Kim stared at him. "What makes you think that?"

Todd opened the storage cabinet and sorted through his tubes of green paint. "Damn! I'll have to mix some, I guess," he muttered. "I've seen more of her than you have," he said over his shoulder. "She seems so timid and buttoned-up, but there's banked fires in her soul. You can tell by the way her eyes look sometimes."

"Banked fires in her soul," Kim repeated dryly. "I see. And what causes these fires, in your professional opinion?"

"I don't know. Maybe she's an illegal alien. Maybe she's got some dark secret in her past that she's hoping won't be discovered in America. But I think that's what gives her face that arresting quality you noticed. It's the secrets in her eyes."

Kim looked at him. "You know, you could be right," she said slowly. "But maybe it's nothing so dramatic. Todd, does Julia ever talk about her family?"

"Not much. Why?"

"Maybe she's got children back in the Philippines, and that's why she looks so sad. A lot of Filipino women are forced to leave their husbands and children behind so they can get domestic work over here. I saw a documentary about it on television a couple of weeks ago.''

"So, do they ever see them again?"

"Of course. They work and save like mad until they can afford to sponsor the rest of the family. Poor Julia," she added thoughtfully. "I wonder how I can find out more about her."

Todd chuckled and punched his dummy on the shoulder. "You hear that, Hernando? That's women for you. Let them hear that maybe somebody's got a secret, and what's their immediate reaction? They want to find out what it is."

Kim glared at him. "Don't you think it's sad? Don't you feel sorry for Julia, if it's true?"

"Why? For leaving a bunch of kids behind? You'd think she'd be overjoyed." Todd frowned, stirring a bit of cobalt blue into a swirl of green on his palette and studying the result.

Kim was watching him, shocked. "You can't be serious," she said slowly.

"About what? Kim, do you think this is anywhere close to the color of blue spruce?"

She ignored the glob of paint on his palette. "About Julia's being overjoyed to leave her children behind. Todd, that's such an awful thing to say."

He shrugged. "My mother left me behind, and it never bothered her in the least. I'm sure my reaction would probably be the same if I were foolish enough to have kids, which I wouldn't be."

"You mean you'd never want to have children?"

"God, *no,*" he said fervently. "I can't imagine being tied down with kids."

"But—"

"Look at Julia. If you're right that she was forced to leave her kids behind, imagine how she's suffering. Why have kids and make yourself vulnerable like that?"

"But children bring so much joy, too. My little nieces and nephews..."

Todd shook his head. "I never learned much from my parents, Kim. After all, I never even knew who my father was, and my mother was never around. The only thing they taught me, by their complete absence, is that this whole thing about family love and warmth, it's mostly a myth. I don't ever want any part of it."

"But don't you—"

"Let's go get something to eat," Todd said, tossing his palette aside and moving restlessly toward the sink. "I'm starved."

"You go," Kim said automatically. "I want to finish this."

But long after he'd cleaned up and left the studio, she stood looking absently out the window at the warm summer sky.

"THIS IS GOING so well, Julia. I'm almost done. Just another few days, I think."

Kim tilted her head to one side and looked at the woman sitting on a stool near the window, then back to her painting.

She'd decided to place Julia in partial sunlight, so that half of her face was illuminated and the other half in shadow. The uneven light gave the picture a troubling, two-edged aspect that was very effective. And the planes of Julia's face, with its fine bone structure and huge dark eyes full of strength and sorrow, were perfect for the mood Kim wanted to project.

Julia had been coming to the studio several afternoons a week for the past month. It was now late June, and Kim had almost finished the foreground of the portrait to her satisfaction. All it needed was a bit of refining and highlighting of the flesh tones, as well as some more detail on the face of the baby in Julia's arms. They'd used a life-size doll for the sittings, but Kim hoped to borrow one of her small nieces to get the actual shading of the child's face perfect.

"Almost finished, did you say?" Todd asked from across the room. "Can I look, Kim?"

"Only if you let me look at yours, and allow me to dish out an equal amount of criticism."

Todd grimaced. "I hate criticism."

"I know you do. So you'd just better be gentle with me."

"Oh, honey," he assured her fervently, "you can count on it. I'll be gentle with you."

Kim blushed and turned away.

It was hot in the studio despite the big fan they'd installed in one of the windows. Kim didn't like air-conditioning and Todd hadn't pressed her, although both of them knew she might have to reconsider as the summer heat intensified. For now, he seemed content to work in the moving gusts of air from the fan, wearing ragged denim cutoffs, canvas deck shoes and a white tank top that left most of his upper body bare. Kim remembered the night at the sculpture gallery when he'd teased her about his working in the nude and she'd found herself wondering what his body was like. By now, she'd seen as much of the man as could be decently exposed while working, and there was nothing that didn't please her.

His shoulders were broad, flat and well-muscled, as were his legs. Both his chest and legs were dusted with curly golden hair, more visible because of the dark tan that still remained from his months in a tropical climate. Todd McAllister was such a superb physical specimen that he could easily have found work as a male model.

However, it was difficult to visualize this man doing anything but painting. Todd loved his work so passionately that watching him was a pleasure, and the huge painting that grew under his hands seemed more beautiful every day, sweeping and breathtaking in its intensity.

She hesitated while he came toward her, then turned to her model. "Julia, shall we take a break? Let's have some tea and cookies."

Julia gave her a shy smile and climbed down from the stool, moving across the room toward the hot plate that Todd had bought for the studio. Kim felt a pang of guilt when she noticed how stiffly Julia walked. Absorbed in her work, Kim had kept the woman sitting too long again. But Julia was such a wonderful model, always silent and uncomplaining, no matter how long the session lasted.

Todd stood behind Kim, brush in hand, resting one hand on her shoulder and studying the portrait on her easel. Only Julia's face and body were visible, and the outline of the child in her arms. The background was still misty, with a blurred suggestion of figures and shapes that would be filled in later.

"I'm afraid I don't work nearly as fast as you do," Kim told him as he studied the painting. "It's been a month and I've only done one figure. You've finished about eight of them."

"It's breathtaking," he muttered, staring at the portrait. "Just amazing. God, Kim, you've absolutely captured the feeling you wanted. It's almost magic, the mood it evokes."

She flushed, delighted by his words. They seldom commented on each other's work, but Kim knew that praise from this man was always sincere. She glanced over at him, feeling a sudden disturbing awareness of his physical presence.

His face was rapt with pleasure as he looked at the painting, his body taut and powerful. The muscles bulged in his upper arms, even when he stood casually next to her, and his whole being gave off an almost palpable aura of strength and masculinity. Kim had to fight an urge to lean against him, touch his skin and feel his warm body pressing into hers.

"Do you think the flesh tones are right?" she asked hastily. "I've been tinkering with them for days. I want the effect to be both warm and cool, if you know what I mean, and I can't seem to get it quite right."

"I know what you mean." He squinted at the painting, rubbing a finger thoughtfully over his jaw where a bit of golden stubble was beginning to glisten in the late-afternoon sunlight. "What about a touch of raw sienna here, Kim?" he said at last, indicating a highlighted cheekbone on the portrait. "Don't you think? Maybe about two shades darker than you've used, and then rubbed down a bit."

She considered a moment, nodded in sudden excitement and reached for a brush.

"Not yet," Todd said, gently prying the brush from her fingers. "Time for a break, honey. Julia's making tea."

Kim stared at him blankly, then gave him a sheepish grin, surrendered the brush and followed him across the room to the little alcove where he'd installed the hot plate. They settled themselves on the mismatched chairs and sipped their tea happily, feasting on cucumber sandwiches and cookies that Julia had brought in her basket.

Kim wondered how they'd look to a casual visitor dropping into the studio. There was Todd in his cutoffs and tank top, Kim was barefoot in a brief pink cotton sunsuit covered with paint stains and Julia in the outfit Kim had chosen for her sittings, a shapeless brown caftan woven from linen so coarse that it resembled burlap.

But their appearance didn't matter, not up here in their private place.

They'd had some company, mostly eccentric cowboy friends of Todd's who had dropped in briefly and dispensed some tall tales or entertained them with guitar music. Various members of Kim's family, too, had visited them from time to time.

And once, Todd had made good his threat and brought up a plump gray-haired woman in cowboy boots who'd spent an entertaining hour or so trying to teach Kim to line dance.

Mostly, though, they'd been too busy the past month to invite their friends to the studio.

"You know," Todd said casually, helping himself to another sandwich and picking up on Kim's thoughts, as he often did, "we're not all that sociable up here, are we? Not exactly flooded by visits from family and friends."

Both women looked at him in silence. Todd grinned and leaned his chair back at a dangerous angle, tilted against a wall containing a display of antique bridles and bits.

"Tell us about your family, Julia," he said, waving the sandwich and propping up his long bare legs on the workbench, "My studio mate, the lovely Kimiko, has a large and interesting family, several of whom we've met this past month. I myself have a much smaller family, consisting of my grandmother and a mother conspicuous by her absence. How about you?"

"Todd," Kim began.

"I don't really like to talk about...my family," Julia said in her soft, halting voice. "They are...so far away." Her shining dark hair fell forward, partially covering her face, but Kim could see the dusky glow of her cheeks and the tension in her shoulders.

She took pity on the shy woman and gave Todd a warning glance.

"I have to go," Julia whispered as she looked at her watch. "Mrs. McAllister wants pepper steak for dinner, and I've left the beef marinating since lunch."

"Then it should be nice and tender," Todd said casually, levering himself from the chair and moving back to squint at his painting.

He turned to look closely at Julia who'd peeled the caftan over her head to reveal a plain yellow T-shirt, a pair of brown walking shorts and heavy leather sandals.

"Is she nice to you, Julia? My grandmother, I mean," Todd asked. "She's not...harsh, or mean, or anything?"

Julia shook her head, looking surprised. "Oh, no. She's stern, but very fair. Actually," she added in her softly accented voice, "she's very nice to me. The other day Mrs. McAllister even showed me the old photo album, with all the pictures of your grandfather in his uniform, and your mother when she was a little girl, and your baby pictures."

Kim noticed how Todd's face tightened at the mention of his mother. He frequently made casual comments about his early abandonment and lonely childhood, but he seemed uncomfortable if anybody else brought up the subject. Still, she was more interested in his casual questioning of Julia about the old woman's attitude toward her housemaid.

Kim had been fully aware of the emotion smoldering in Barbara McAllister's eyes on the one occasion when they'd met.

A lifetime of belonging to a visible minority had made it easy for Kim to recognize prejudice when she encountered it. There was no doubt that Todd's grandmother, for some reason, had deep-seated feelings of anger and resentment.

Apparently, Barbara's prejudice didn't extend to all Orientals, though, not if she was willing to be kind to her housemaid, even entertain Julia with family pictures. Kim suspected that Todd was thinking the same thing, and she wondered if his interest was partly on her behalf.

She put the thoughts aside and smiled at Julia, who was packing her basket and getting ready to leave. "Did you want to look at the painting before you go, Julia? I got a lot more done today."

Julia smiled shyly and came over to look at the face on the canvas. "I can't ever believe it's me," she murmured, gazing at the painted image. "She looks so... beautiful."

"Well, of course she does. *You're* beautiful, Julia," Kim said warmly. "From the inside out," she added, giving the other woman an impulsive hug.

Julia blushed and fled, leaving both artists smiling at the door after she'd gone.

"So, what do you think?" Todd said at last, frowning as he squeezed a glob of deep turquoise onto his palette. "Is there something going on there?"

"With Julia's family? I don't know. But she's so sweet, I find it hard to believe there isn't a man in her life somewhere.... Todd, there's one sandwich left. Would you like it?"

"Sure, if you're not going to eat it."

"No, thanks. I'm stuffed." Kim carried the sandwich over to him, paused briefly to admire his work, then returned to her own canvas.

"Speaking of men in one's life, are you still going out with David?" Todd asked suddenly.

"Not really. He calls occasionally and we go out for coffee or a walk, just to keep my grandmother from getting really annoyed with me. But when we're together, we seem to spend all our time talking about your work. He seems completely fascinated by it, particularly as an investment. He thinks your paintings are going to sharply appreciate in value over the next ten years, and he wants to get in on the ground floor."

"I see. And does that bother you?"

Kim looked at the back of Todd's curly head, watching as he leaned forward to apply some deep azure shading to the wall of a canyon. "Why should it bother me that he admires your work?"

"That's not what I mean," Todd said without turning around. "The two of you had something going back in the spring, didn't you? It wouldn't be unreasonable for you to resent the fact that nothing seems to be coming of it except David's newfound interest in painting."

"Are you kidding?" Kim smiled and began to mix the raw sienna he'd recommended for her flesh tones. "David and I really didn't have much of anything to talk about before. Now at least we have something in common."

"Funny, I would have thought the two of you had all kinds of things in common. Your grandmother obviously thinks so."

Kim put down her palette knife and stared at him. "What exactly do you think David and I have in common, Todd?" she asked quietly. "The fact that we're both Japanese?"

Todd turned and gave her a thoughtful look. "Don't be so sensitive. What you have in common is a good education, a shared background, family friendship, all kinds of things."

Kim relaxed and smiled at him. "I know. Sorry to be so touchy. I just hate the assumption that two people should be instantly compatible because they share a racial heritage."

"So, is that what your grandmother thinks?"

Kim stirred the paint thoughtfully, frowning at the dark brownish red pigment. "I suppose that's part of it. My grandmother certainly doesn't believe in interracial marriages. Mostly, though, I think she just considers David to be good husband material."

Todd's dimple sparkled briefly. "I see. And how about you?"

"*I* don't know," Kim said abstractedly. "I guess he probably is. He just doesn't..."

"Turn you on," Todd suggested when her voice trailed off into silence.

Kim grinned. "That's right. David doesn't turn me on."

Todd crossed the room to get a drink of water. He leaned against the counter, glass in hand, his long legs casually extended. He looked at Kim with interest, then came over to stand near her easel, watching as she touched paint to the sharply defined line of the cheekbone.

"So, who turns you on?"

Kim moved back and studied the image with narrowed eyes, took a cloth and rubbed the paint down a little, then looked at it critically.

"That's better," she said.

"Who turns you on, Kim?"

"You really want to know? Well, I like men who are quiet, reserved, thoughtful, family-oriented, sort of scholarly..."

Todd laughed. "In other words, you prefer guys just like me," he suggested. "Right?"

She turned away to hide her smile. "Go back to work, Todd."

"Add a little more paint," he advised, "and rub it down once again."

"Do you think? Maybe it's too—"

"Try it, woman. Don't be so stubborn."

Kim obeyed, and realized with delight that the flesh tones were now exactly what she'd hoped for.

Todd studied the painting and nodded, then leaned back against her workbench once again, staring absently at his own canvas. "Kim, when you were going out with David..."

Kim's cheeks warmed and she concentrated on her painting.

"Tell me the truth. Did he ever kiss you?" Todd asked.

"I really don't think that's any of your business," Kim said calmly.

"You don't? Well, I think it's definitely my business."

She looked at him in surprise. "Why on earth would it be any business of yours?"

He moved closer to her and smiled. "Because I plan to kiss you pretty soon, my Kimiko, and I want to know what kind of competition I'm facing."

Kim turned away and stirred her paint furiously. "Don't be ridiculous," she said, her voice sharp.

"Ridiculous?" he echoed. "You think kissing you would be ridiculous?"

She stared at him, conscious of a heightened sensual awareness. Everything seemed more real and vivid, like a moment caught in time and magnified. Kim was powerfully aware of the light streaming in the window, the caressing warmth of the summer air, her own body in the brief cotton sunsuit, Todd's shoulders and tanned face, the dusting of golden hairs on his forearms and the stubble on his cheek, even the sound of their breathing in the quiet room.

"I think this whole conversation is ridiculous," she said at last. "Go away and let me work."

"You've already done lots of work today. Come here." Todd reached out a lazy hand and stroked her ponytail, then gripped the silky mass and tugged gently.

Kim allowed herself to be drawn toward him. But when their bodies were very close together, almost touching, she looked up at him with quiet pleading.

"Todd, this really isn't a good idea," she murmured. "We have to work together all the time. Let's not complicate things, all right?"

He met her gaze soberly, his eyes such a vivid blue that they seemed to burn her flesh. "Things are already complicated," he whispered, reaching up to stroke her cheek with a gentle hand. "I'm so conscious of you all the time that it's starting to interfere with my work. I really need to do this."

Kim shivered at his touch and closed her eyes as he drew her into his arms, enfolded her in a powerful embrace and bent to kiss her. His mouth was warm and firm, moving hungrily against her lips, then roaming over her face and throat as he pulled her even closer in his arms.

"Oh, Kim," he whispered at last, his mouth on hers again. "Kim, you feel so good. You're just the sweetest thing, you know that?"

She nestled in his arms, lost in the pleasure of the moment. Only now did she realize that she'd been wanting this embrace as much as he did, even though she hadn't allowed herself to think about it.

But he was right. It felt so good. Todd's body was big and muscular, hers small and dainty, but they fit together so sweetly, they seemed to have been made for this embrace. And the man's kiss satisfied something deep inside Kim, an aching need that had been part of her ever since she could remember.

"Yes," she murmured, pressing her face against his chest. "Yes, it feels good. But we mustn't do it again, Todd. Please, can't we just be friends and working partners?"

"Why?" he asked, reaching up to gather handfuls of her hair and pull it across his mouth.

Because my grandmother would be horrified if she ever saw this, Kim thought. *Because she would probably die of shock, and I love her too much to cause her that kind of pain.*

"Why?" he repeated, tipping his head back to look down at her.

"I just...don't think it's a good idea." Kim drew herself from his arms and turned aside, staring out the window at the summer sky.

"It seemed like a pretty good idea a minute ago. In fact, I could have sworn that you were enjoying it as much as I was."

Kim looked back at him steadily. "Sure I was. I'm a woman, and you're a reasonably attractive man. That doesn't mean we automatically have to fall into each other's arms. It *is* possible for us to exercise some self-control, you know."

"Exercise some self-control," he echoed softly, giving her a bright teasing glance. "That's my Kim, all right. What a woman."

His grin was so infectious, she found herself laughing with him, relieved that the intensity of the moment seemed to have passed. She started cleaning her palette while he watched with calm interest.

"What are you doing tonight?" he asked finally.

"I'm taking my grandmother to the symphony. Are you working late?"

"I think so. I'd like to finish that canyon before the weekend. Want to come with me and grab some spaghetti down at Luigi's? Then you can go home to your grandmother and I'll come back to work."

"Sure. That sounds great." Kim smiled gratefully at him, happy to leave the dangerous emotions behind them.

Still, she knew that many hours from now, when it was dark and starry and the night wind sighed around the eaves of the house, she'd lie alone in the stillness of her room and think about his kiss, and yearn to feel that sweetness once again.

CHAPTER SIX

JULIA STOOD in the big sunny kitchen, chopping green peppers to add to the simmering meat that filled the room with a spicy aroma of ginger and soy sauce. At the back of the stove, a heavy saucepan of wild rice was heating slowly, and the dancing lid was like music in the afternoon stillness.

Hugo lay under the heavy oak table, gnawing with his sharp puppy teeth at a bone from the steak. Julia bent to look at him briefly, then straightened and returned to her task.

A shadow fell across the floor and the mistress of the house appeared in the doorway. Barbara nodded, coming a few steps into the room, then looked sharply at Hugo.

"Julia, are you quite sure he won't choke on bone splinters?"

"It's all right, ma'am," Julia said in her soft musical voice. "It's a very, very hard bone. I checked it before I gave it to him."

Barbara seated herself at the table, watching as Julia finished chopping the peppers and started on a big white onion.

"When Homer was a puppy," she said with a faraway look, "Todd gave him a turkey drumstick and part of it got caught in his throat. We almost lost him, poor baby. He had to be rushed to the vet at nine o'clock on New Year's Eve."

"Poultry bones are very dangerous for dogs," Julia agreed, brushing at her tears as she chopped the onion. "People don't seem to realize that."

Barbara reached down to fondle the puppy's ears while Julia scooped the onion slices into the meat sauce along with the green peppers. Then, Julia began to work on a plateful of snow peas, snipping off the ends with quick motions of her hands.

"Would you like a cup of tea, ma'am?" she asked, glancing up at Barbara. "I made a fresh pot when I got home."

"Thank you. That would be very nice." Barbara leaned back in her chair and watched as Julia crossed the room to get a fine porcelain cup from one of the cabinets. "Did you have a nice afternoon?"

Julia nodded. "The painting is almost finished. Soon I won't need to go there anymore."

The prospect of ending her visits to the studio made her feel sad, but she didn't tell her mistress that.

"I've never sat for a portrait," Barbara said. "It must be very tiring."

"It was quite hard at first, but I've gotten used to it."

"Does it really look like you?" Barbara asked curiously.

Julia considered, setting the teapot and a jar of milk on the table. "Sort of, but better," she said at last. "I think it's the way I would look if I were pretty."

Barbara smiled. "You're very pretty, Julia. You just aren't aware of it, which adds to your appeal."

Julia shook her head, and poured her mistress a cup of tea. Then she sat down and went on snipping peas.

"So you think she's a fairly good artist?" Barbara said casually.

"She's wonderful. You should go to the studio and see some of her work, Mrs. McAllister. The flowers she does, and the portraits, they're just beautiful. You'd love them."

The older woman's face turned scornful, making Julia regret her impulsive words.

"Oh, I doubt that very much," Barbara said curtly. "And I haven't the slightest desire to visit her studio, thank you."

Then why do you always ask so many questions about it? Julia wondered silently, her face impassive as she finished stripping the peas and got up to wash them under the faucet.

"So, are they still getting along well?" Barbara asked, sipping her tea.

"They seem to be," Julia said in a noncommittal voice. "Sometimes they argue, but it's not in anger, it seems. It's more like..."

She was going to say Todd and Kim's amiable wrangling was rather like that of a cheerful married couple, but changed her mind and let the words trail off into silence. She switched the water off and stared out the window, looking at her well-tended flower beds and small vegetable plot beyond the flagstone terrace.

Just as well, Julia thought, that the painting was almost done. Her visits to the studio, all that teasing and laughter and easy conversation, were making her lonely and discontented with her life, impatient for the day when she and Roberto could be a family again.

She turned aside with a weary gesture and crossed the room to stir the meat sauce. Barbara bent and gathered the puppy into her arms, then came over to sniff the delectable mixture, smiling at Julia.

"Perfect, as usual," she said. "Julia, you are really a treasure, my dear. Did you know that? An absolute treasure."

She swept out, carrying the puppy, leaving Julia staring after her in surprise.

"THIS IS DELICIOUS, Nana," Todd said with affectionate enthusiasm, looking across the table at his grandmother. "Where did Julia learn to make Yorkshire pudding?"

"I taught her. She never forgets anything once she's learned it. The girl's a marvel."

It was their regular Sunday dinner, and Todd was savoring the roast beef and crusty browned potatoes, the rich gravy and feather-light Yorkshire pudding.

"Maybe," he said casually, reaching for his napkin, "Julia's too capable to be a housemaid, Nana. We should help her to get some training and find a more profitable job."

Barbara looked worried. "I know," she said. "I hate to admit it because she's such a wonderful cook and housekeeper. Isn't that selfish?"

"Completely selfish," Todd agreed amiably. "Nana, you know you have to make sure Julia has the opportunity to achieve her full potential. After all, you can always find another cook."

"But she's happy here," Barbara said wistfully. "She appreciates the comfort and security she has. We're even becoming quite good friends. Besides, whenever I suggest that she make any kind of move, even in the most roundabout way, she just looks alarmed and gets really quiet."

"Nana..."

"Please, don't press me, Todd. I know you're right, and I intend to do something about it. You don't have to pound me over the head."

He nodded, satisfied. He moved his foot gently beneath the table, dislodging Hugo who had crawled under the chair and fallen asleep with most of his body resting heavily on Todd's shoe.

"Is that puppy under the table again?" Barbara asked sharply, bending to peer beneath the heavy damask cloth. "Todd, you *know* he's supposed to be sleeping in his basket."

"He's just being friendly," Todd protested. "He's like a little kid, Nana. He gets excited when there's company in the house."

"A well-trained dog knows enough to leave the guests alone," Barbara said. "I simply cannot abide a dog that leaps and climbs all over people. Julia," she added when the woman came in to remove the dinner plates, "that puppy is under the table again. Please remove him."

Julia exchanged a glance with Todd, then bent and scooped up the fat puppy, carrying him over to his basket and depositing him there with a warning murmur. Hugo whimpered a little but didn't move.

"Wonderful meal, Julia," Todd said, smiling up at her.

The woman's shy face lighted with pleasure. "Thank you," she said as she moved around the table.

"Are you coming to the studio tomorrow afternoon?" Todd asked as she stacked the plates on the sideboard with deft efficiency.

Julia glanced cautiously at his grandmother, then back at Todd. "Yes," she murmured. "I think the painting will take a few more hours to finish."

Todd nodded and watched Julia leave the room.

He felt his grandmother's gaze resting on him and looked at her with mild inquiry, then tensed a little. Todd knew this woman very well, and he recognized that particular gleam in her eyes. Barbara McAllister had something important to discuss.

Todd sipped his wine, annoyed with himself for the sudden tightening in his stomach.

He was over thirty years old, with an impressive international reputation. He'd graduated from college and traveled the world, and he was able to produce paintings that sold for astonishing sums of money, enabling him to live in luxury.

So why did he still feel like a resentful little boy every time his grandmother looked at him with disapproval?

"Nice wine," he commented, frowning into the crystal goblet. "What is it, Nana?"

She shrugged. "It's just a domestic Cabernet. Do you really like it?"

"It's very rich. Nice with beef."

"Yes," she said. "I thought it would be." But Todd could tell from the set of her mouth that she wasn't really interested in discussing the merits of their dinner wine.

"How's your work coming?" she asked, nodding as Julia came in and poured coffee from a tall silver pot.

"Fine. Great, in fact. It's a terrific studio, Nana. The light is so good all day long, and I'm getting more done than I figured I would. At this rate, I could possibly finish all four paintings in a little more than a year."

Barbara raised her eyebrows. "Really? I thought you'd planned to spend two years on them."

"I did, but it's going so well, I'm already giving some thought to what I want to do next.... Julia, this looks too good to be true."

Todd smiled at the young woman, then at the heaping plate of strawberry shortcake she was placing in front of him.

"Our own strawberries," Barbara said proudly. "They've been quite good this year, haven't they, Julia?"

"Yes, ma'am," Julia said, spooning more whipped cream onto the shortcake. "The strawberries are delicious."

Todd dug happily into his dessert, savoring the rich flavors. But part of him was still wary, knowing that his grandmother hadn't yet broached whatever was on her mind.

"What will you do next, then?" she asked, sipping her coffee and toying with her dessert fork.

"I'm not sure. I thought I might go to the Southwest and live on the road for a while in Arizona and New Mexico, do a series on working cowboys. The dying breed, that sort of thing."

"Do you have a commission?"

Todd shook his head. "I don't want one. I'd rather work independently and mount my own exhibition, maybe in one of the New York galleries, and sell the paintings to private collectors. That's always a lot of fun, but I haven't done it for years."

Barbara nodded thoughtfully. "Your mother called last week," she said at last. "She thinks she'll drop by for a visit later this summer."

Todd kept his voice light. "That's nice," he said. "Let me know in advance, would you, Nana? Then I can arrange to be out of town when she's here."

"That's very unkind of you, Todd. I'm sure she wants to see you."

"Well, I don't want to see her."

"Todd..."

"The woman's an embarrassment, Nana! She makes a mockery of any kind of decency and moral values, and I want nothing to do with her."

"You're so harsh, dear."

"I'm not harsh at all. I'm just speaking the truth and you know it."

"She's coming with that man," Barbara said, frowning. "The one she mentioned on the phone last month."

"You mean her boyfriend, not her husband?"

"We don't *know* that he's a boyfriend, Todd. Lillian says he's an old friend of the family."

"Sure he is. And I'm the tooth fairy," Todd muttered. He took a scalding gulp of coffee and reached hastily for his water glass. "I don't know why her stupid husband puts up with her behavior. I guess the poor old guy's just too feeble to find anybody else. But I hate to see her squandering his money and cheating on him openly at the same time. It's so...corrupt."

Barbara stared at the candles with a faraway look. "It's hard to believe that Lillian's over fifty," she said at last. "She turned fifty-one her last birthday. I always thought maybe she'd settle down when she was older, and start living differently."

Todd thought about his mother with her garish clothes, her brightly dyed hair and heavy makeup and shrill girlish laughter. "She's never going to grow up, Nana," he said coldly. "She's stuck in adolescence forever, and everybody associated with her suffers because of her behavior. It's best just to avoid her."

"She's my daughter," Barbara said calmly. "It's difficult for me to avoid her."

"Well, it's not difficult for me." Todd took another cautious sip of hot coffee. He gazed into the cup for a moment, then set it down with an air of finality.

"Julia says her portrait is going quite well," Barbara said after a few moments of silence. Her tone was casual, but Todd sensed that they were finally getting to the real issue.

"It's almost finished. You should see it, Nana. It's such a strong painting."

"So I've been told," Barbara said dryly. "This Japanese woman...you feel that she's really talented?"

"Nana, she has a name, you know," Todd said, struggling to control his sudden anger. "Her name is Kim. I hate it when you call her 'the Japanese woman.' Especially in that tone of voice."

"I see," Barbara said coldly, sipping her wine. "Now I'm supposed to be concerned about my tone of voice as well as what I say?"

"I wish you'd try to be a little more fair and charitable, that's all," Todd said wearily.

"You're not particularly fair or charitable about your mother," Barbara said pointedly.

"My mother doesn't deserve my charity. You know that she's treated me miserably for most of my life. But Kim Tanaka has never done a single thing to hurt you or anyone else. She's a sweet, kind, intelligent and talented woman, and I really resent the way you talk about her."

As he spoke Kim's name, Todd remembered how she'd felt in his arms, her curvy body and glossy hair, the silken ivory of her skin and the sweetness of her mouth.

The woman was as delectable as the rich dessert in front of him...like strawberries and cream with a dash of pure sexual excitement that made her irresistible. Todd's body stirred and began to ache, and he shifted uncomfortably on the hard wooden chair.

He looked up to find Barbara watching him with cold appraisal and slightly raised eyebrows. Todd gave her a level glance. "I mean it, Nana," he said quietly. "In fact, I intend to bring Kim here as soon as I can talk her into coming for a visit, and I want you to be cordial to her."

"Have you ever seen me treat a guest with anything less than cordiality?" Barbara asked, carefully setting her wine goblet on the table.

"No," Todd admitted. "But I've certainly seen you treat people with something less than warmth."

"Of course," his grandmother said calmly. "False warmth is nothing but hypocrisy. You know how I despise hypocrisy."

Todd sighed in defeat, then grinned at a sudden thought. "Well, if it's any comfort to you," he said, taking another mouthful of dessert, "you're not alone, Nana. Kim has a grandmother, too. Did you know that? And the woman absolutely detests the thought of me."

"What on earth are you talking about?"

"Kim's grandmother. An old lady named Masako Tanaka, with the most extraordinary life story."

"Have you met this woman?"

Todd shook his head. "I'd love to, but Kim is reluctant to invite me to her house. But while we're working, she spends hours telling me stories about Madame Tanaka and her student days in Paris before the war when she hobnobbed with Picasso and Somerset Maugham."

"Before the war? She must be older than I am."

"I guess she's in her eighties. But she's apparently still as sharp as ever. Kim really adores her."

"So why doesn't this Kim want you to meet her grandmother?"

"I guess she's dealing with the same problems I am," Todd said, looking down at his plate. "Apparently, her grandmother doesn't approve of me."

Barbara stared at him in disbelief. "*She* doesn't approve? Why?"

Todd shrugged. "She wants Kim to marry a person of Japanese descent. It's very important to Madame Tanaka. In fact, she's already lined up a prospective husband. I think Julia's probably told you about David, hasn't she? He's a..."

But Barbara had become so pale and agitated that Todd stopped talking and looked at her in concern. "Nana, what's the matter? What is it?"

"I had no idea," Barbara murmured in a shaky voice, "that there was any danger of a...a serious relationship between you and this woman."

"Who said there's a serious relationship?"

Barbara looked up at him, her eyes dark with emotion. "You just said that her grandmother was upset because she wants this...this girl to marry a Japanese person. Why would she be upset unless there was some possibility that the two of you might be getting seriously involved?''

"Come on, Nana..."

"Marriage!" Barbara whispered with a shudder. "My God, boy, what on earth are you thinking? How could you possibly be so *stupid?*"

"You don't know a damned thing about Kim," Todd said with rising anger. "Except that she's Japanese, but that's enough for you, isn't it, Nana? That's enough to condemn her, no matter how sweet she is, because of some ridiculous fifty-year-old resentment that you can't seem to rid yourself of."

"You can call me ridiculous if you want, but I honestly can't imagine anything more unsuitable than the kind of marriage we're talking about."

Todd's anger faded. "We're not talking about marriage, Nana," he said in a weary voice. "I have no intention of marrying Kim Tanaka or anybody else. She may be sweet, bright and delightful, but a lifetime of contact—or should I say, no contact—with my mother has fully convinced me that a man's better off alone than tied to a woman. *Any* woman. There, does that satisfy you?"

Barbara picked up her wineglass and looked at him across the gold rim with a long appraising glance. "Eat your dessert," she said at last. "It's far too good to be wasted."

Todd nodded and attacked the strawberry shortcake again, and nothing more was said about Kim Tanaka or her grandmother.

THE MEMORY of his conversation with his grand-mother troubled Todd greatly. By tacit agreement, his relationship with Kim returned to its old casual foot-ing, and both of them acted as if the passionate kiss they'd shared had never happened. But he hadn't quite managed to shake his unhappiness even a week later, when he picked up Julia at the house and the two of them drove downtown to meet Kim in Riverfront Park for the Fourth of July celebrations. Julia had the puppy with her, as she often did. Todd had wanted to bring Homer, as well, but the dog was too old and lazy to stir from his hearth, even on a warm summer eve-ning like this.

Hugo, though, was in a frenzy of delight at the outing. He was learning to walk on a leash, and looked proud and sprightly as he trotted up the path ahead of them, dragging Julia along while he nuzzled ecstati-cally at the damp grass, the tantalizing scent of ham-burgers and frying onions and the feet of passersby.

Julia scanned the throng on the grassy riverbank, shading her eyes with her hand.

"There!" she said, pointing into the crowd. "There she is, over by that big tree."

Todd waved, catching sight of Kim, who had spread out a blanket and was unpacking a huge picnic bas-ket. She was dressed in an outfit Todd had never seen before, a matching top and shorts of white silk pat-terned with tiny red apples. Her hair was pulled into the casual ponytail that he loved, and she wore no makeup except for a touch of lipstick. She looked childlike, radiant and absolutely delicious.

Todd remembered the taste of her lips when they'd kissed, a memory that was somehow jumbled up in his mind with the remembered richness of the strawberry shortcake at his grandmother's house. He felt a stab of hunger, deep and urgent, and struggled to keep his voice calm as he greeted her.

"Hi, Kim. Nice outfit."

"It's brand-new. Do you really like it?" She smiled at him, then laughed as Hugo leapt on her and began licking her face.

"Mrs. McAllister would be so upset if she saw him doing that. Hugo, don't jump. Be a good dog." Julia hauled the puppy away, seating herself on the blanket next to Kim, who leaned over and hugged her.

"Hi, Julia," Kim said. "I'll bet you've never been to a Fourth of July celebration before, have you?"

Julia shook her head. "I came here in the wintertime," she said, shivering as she recalled her arrival in America. "It was so *cold!* I was afraid that it was always going to be windy and snowy like that, and I wouldn't be able to stand it."

The others laughed. Todd lay back on the blanket, folding an arm under his head and grinning as Hugo climbed onto his stomach. He fondled the puppy's ears, then reached up to tug idly on Kim's ponytail.

"What does your hair look like when it's down?" he asked. "How long is it?"

She glanced at him in surprise. "It's almost to my waist. Why?"

Todd gazed up at her in the fading sunlight, his mouth suddenly dry as he imagined that glorious hair falling all around her body in a rippling black cascade.

"Let's undo it for a minute, all right?" he said, his voice husky. "I want to see what it looks like."

Kim laughed and turned away, rummaging busily in the picnic basket. "Don't be silly, Todd," she said, in the same reproving tone that Julia used with the puppy. "Does anybody want some potato salad?"

"Is there potato salad?" Todd asked with interest.

"Julia made the salads, and I brought sandwiches."

"Then I guess for my own safety, I'll have to eat lots of both, won't I?"

"Absolutely. Won't he, Julia?"

But Julia wasn't listening. Instead, the young woman was staring at a family group below them on the grassy riverbank. Puzzled by her expression, Todd followed her gaze and saw a little boy playing with a red ball.

He was a plump, dark-haired child about four years old, with a bright laughing face. He threw the ball into the air and ran around clumsily trying to catch it, then wandered over and leaned against his mother, who gathered him into her arms and gave him a loving kiss before turning to say something to her husband.

Tears glittered in Julia's eyes. She clambered hastily to her feet and attached Hugo's leash, muttering something under her breath as she hurried away with the dog, heading for the pathway down near the river.

Todd leaned up on his elbow and watched her in surprise, then turned to exchange a troubled glance with Kim.

She shook her head, frowning, and stretched out next to him on the blanket, watching Julia's slight figure in her yellow sundress as she walked with the puppy along the edge of the water.

HOURS LATER, the night was warm and murmuring, as softly enclosing as a mantle of black silk. People whispered quietly all around them, lying and sitting on blankets and waiting for the fireworks display.

Todd watched as Kim pulled a red sweater over her head and flipped her ponytail out of the neckline. "Are you getting cold, honey?" he murmured.

"A little. It feels good to put my sweater on." She smiled at him, her face indistinct in the glow of the starlight. "I wish Julia could have stayed for the fireworks, don't you?"

Not really, Todd thought. *I love being alone with you, sweetheart....*

"Well, she was probably right to go home," he said aloud. "Hugo would have hated the noise. I remember how it used to make poor old Homer howl with agony. We only brought him once, I think."

"Did you and your grandmother always come here for the Fourth of July picnic?" Kim settled next to him on the blanket, fitting her jacket under her head as a makeshift pillow.

Todd was deeply moved by the strange intimacy of the moment. Despite the hushed crowd on the riverbank, he felt as if he and Kim were all alone, lying close together but not touching, waiting for something momentous to happen. . . .

"Yes," he murmured. "My grandmother is very patriotic. She stopped coming to the picnic when I grew up and moved away, because she found the day too long when she was here by herself."

"You know, my grandmother's just the same," Kim said unexpectedly. "She loves the Fourth of July."

"That's a little surprising, isn't it?"

"Why? Because she's Japanese? You think it's not possible for a Japanese-born woman to be a patriotic American?"

"Come on, Kim. You're always so touchy about this. How come?"

Kim gazed at the black sky above her while Todd looked at her profile, etched with silver in the summer moonlight.

"I hate prejudice," she said finally. "I can't think of anything more unfair than judging and dismissing people because of the way they look, or their racial or ethnic background. It just infuriates me."

"Have you experienced much of it yourself?" Todd asked gently, grateful for the sheltering darkness that made this conversation easier, more detached and impartial.

"Not really," Kim said. "Of course, there are always people who treat you a little differently. But I almost never encounter any real hostility over my being Japanese. It only happens very occasionally, with people like—"

She stopped abruptly, and the darkness was suddenly charged with tension.

"People like my grandmother," Todd finished quietly. "Isn't that what you were going to say, Kim?"

She nodded reluctantly. "It's not hard to tell," she said at last. "That first day when she came to the studio, I could see by the look in her eyes that she hated me for being . . . what I am."

"Oh, honey, I'm so sorry." Todd reached out to touch her cheek, longing to take her in his arms and hold her.

Kim smiled. "Don't worry, Todd. It's not your fault. And I'm well able to look after myself, you know."

"I know. You don't look it, but you're made of tempered steel, aren't you, kid?"

"You'd better believe it," Kim told him with a fleeting grin. "Actually," she went on, sobering again, "I feel sorry for people like your grandmother. I can't help wondering what makes them the way they are."

"With Nana, it's no big mystery. My grandfather died in a Japanese prisoner-of-war camp almost fifty years ago, and she's never gotten over her bitterness."

"I thought it might be something like that. How long were they together?"

"About a month. They got married while he was on leave and had a little time together before he was shipped out. Just long enough for my grandmother to get pregnant with my mother."

"Did she ever see him again?"

Todd shook his head. "His ship was blown up and he was taken prisoner right after my mother was born. He died a couple of years later. Meanwhile, Nana moved back with her parents and spent the rest of her life looking after them and raising her kid all alone."

"The poor woman," Kim said softly. "No wonder she's bitter."

"Is your grandmother bitter? She lost her husband in the war, too."

"I know, but my grandmother is very philosophical. She believes in fate and destiny."

"You know what the strange thing is about all this?" Todd asked, reaching to take Kim's hand and idly caressing her fingers.

He could feel her sudden tension, and realized that even the most casual touch had a powerful effect on her, just as it did on him. But she kept her voice light and cheerful. "What?" she asked, smiling at him. "What's strange about all this, Todd?"

"Our grandfathers fought on the same side in the war. In fact, your grandfather was just as American as mine, wasn't he? You know, if I tried to tell Nana that," he added gloomily, "she'd never ever believe it. She just wouldn't be able to accept the truth."

"I guess she needs someone to blame. Some people are like that, Todd. It's all so simple and clear-cut to them. There are good guys and bad guys, and a visible enemy is easier to recognize."

"Doesn't your grandmother feel that way? I know she doesn't like me much."

Kim was silent a moment, thinking. "With my grandmother, it's a lot more complex. She's really not prejudiced, but she still doesn't believe in mixed relationships. Not because she feels there's anything basically wrong with other races, but because she honestly believes that intermarriage causes too many problems."

"So are there any mixed marriages in your family?"

Kim shook her head. "No, but it's a very small family. My aunt Genevieve never married. Both my parents are third-generation Japanese-Americans. And my brother and sister both married Japanese people, too. Although," Kim added with a reminiscent smile, "my brother, Yosh, gave my grandmother a few bad scares during his college years."

"He did? How?"

"Well, Yosh was brilliant and handsome, really popular, and he dated a steady stream of blue-eyed blond cheerleader types. I always thought he did it just to tease my grandmother, and it certainly worked. She almost died with worry over him."

Todd chuckled. "You know, our grandmothers actually have a lot more in common than they'd ever suspect. We should get them together for tea."

Kim lay staring up at the starry sky above the treetops. "What a picture," she said at last. "I wonder what they'd talk about. Maybe they'd— Oh, Todd!" she whispered in hushed awe. "Look at that! Isn't it beautiful?"

He gripped her hand, watching as a soft golden flower exploded in the darkness and rained down on them in a shower of fire. The sky filled with bursts of flame and blossoms of color. Pink and green, red and blue, violet and amber and silver glowed in the darkness and fell softly to the grass amid murmurs of delight from the crowd on the riverbank.

Kim laughed, her face sparkling in the rainbow-tinted darkness with a childlike pleasure that brought a lump to Todd's throat. Suddenly, he wanted her with an urgency that he could neither control nor understand. "Kim," he whispered huskily, rolling toward her and gathering her in his arms. "Sweetheart, you just don't know what you do to me. You don't know how much..."

He buried his face against her neck, breathing in the silken fragrance of her skin, holding her tightly in his arms.

"I want you," he muttered in agony. "God, I want you so much."

She moved against him, gripping his head in gentle hands. "Todd, please..."

He kissed her, and realized when their lips met how much he'd hungered for this moment, how the memory of their last embrace had haunted him. No woman had ever made him feel like this, so weak with tenderness and afire with lust at the same time.

"Kim," he whispered, his mouth roaming over her face and throat. He reached under her sweater with shaking hands to undo the buttons on her shirt, his body rigid with desire. "Kim, let me..."

"No," she murmured, moving away from him. "Todd, we can't."

"Why can't we?"

"For one thing," she said, her eyes bright with laughter in the darkness, "we're in a fairly public place, in case you'd forgotten. There are about a thousand people jammed onto this riverbank, Todd."

"They won't notice," he breathed, gripping her in his arms as showers of gold fell all around them and his hunger raged. "They're watching the fireworks."

"Yes, they are. And we're not providing them with any other fireworks to watch." Kim pushed him away gently and sat up, brushing at her tangled ponytail. "I mean it, Todd."

"Oh, Lord," he groaned, still lying full-length on the blanket. He reached for her in agony. "Kim, I'm dying here, sweetheart. Don't you have any pity for a dying man?"

She looked down at him, her face softly illuminated by a fiery pink blossom that filled the sky. "What do you want, Todd?"

"Dammit, you know what I want!"

"You want to go to bed with me."

He paused, a little chilled by the calm, practical tone of her voice. "Yeah," he said at last. "That's what I want."

"And then what?"

Todd sat up and moved to put his arm around her, but her matter-of-fact approach was beginning to make him uneasy. "What do you mean?" he asked.

"What if we go to bed together? What happens then?"

"You know what happens! We both have a whole lot of fun and enjoy it thoroughly. What's wrong with that?"

"And when it's over, do we keep working together like old friends, or what? If there are bad feelings, who leaves the studio after the romance ends?"

Todd shook his head in despair. "Why are women always like this? Why do they have to worry about the end of the romance before it's even started?"

"Because women are much more practical than men, that's why. Men let themselves get carried away by passion and don't give a thought to what's going to happen tomorrow. But women," Kim said in that same quiet tone, "are always thinking about tomorrow."

Todd was silent, realizing that she spoke the truth.

The simple fact was that Todd McAllister couldn't bear to think about tomorrow, or the possibility of a long-term relationship. He couldn't endure the prospect of commitment to one woman. All his life, he'd avoided any kind of serious entanglement, deftly extricating himself before the situation got out of hand.

Until now, he thought. For the first time in his life, Todd McAllister wanted a woman badly enough to think about the future, and the idea utterly terrified him.

CHAPTER SEVEN

HOMER LAY on the grass, drowsing in the warm August sunlight. Hugo capered nearby, sniffing at insects and plants and occasionally giving little yelps of happiness. He galloped across the lawn, still clumsy and puppylike though his body had grown considerably since early spring, and fell against Homer, then rolled over playfully, tugging and gnawing at one of the old dog's ears.

Homer opened his eyes and bared his teeth, causing the overgrown puppy to draw back cautiously, still gripping Homer's ear. After a brief confrontation, Hugo let the trailing ear drop and turned away in a dispirited fashion to explore one of the flower beds. His eyes brightened as he began to dig furtively in the soft dirt, glancing over his shoulder at Julia who was weeding the vegetable garden.

She saw him almost at once and called to him sharply. "Hugo! Stop that!"

Hugo stiffened and sat back on his haunches, giving her a look of soulful innocence before gathering himself together and hurtling across the lawn in pursuit of a big yellow butterfly.

Julia rested on her heels and watched him with a smile. She wore old shorts and a T-shirt, and a wide-brimmed straw hat that shaded her face from the afternoon sun. After a moment, her smile faded and she reached into a pocket to take out Roberto's letter, which had arrived that morning and still carried a precious feeling of closeness to her little boy.

She read the letter hungrily, trying to see beyond the brief labored sentences. "I am very well. Uncle Cesar has a new saw. It is very sharp. Grandmother has a sore knee..."

This was all interesting, but not the kind of detail that Julia yearned to know. She frowned as she held the neatly lettered paper up to the sunlight, trying to make out a couple of lines at the bottom of the page that had been firmly crossed out with ballpoint pen.

Beneath the blue lines, she could see the smeared black of Roberto's pencil, faintly discernible in the glaring light. "Please come home," Julia read with difficulty. "I cry at night."

She caught her breath and stared at the paper.

Until now, Julia had generally managed to convince herself that all was well with Roberto, and that her family had told her the truth when they said the child was happy and well adjusted. But here was absolute proof that he was lonely and sad, and that they were keeping things from her.

Julia looked around. Normally she loved working outside, welcoming the change from cooking and housecleaning. But now, with evidence of Roberto's sorrow in her hands, the place enclosed her and she longed to escape. She wanted to run inside and pack her shabby bags, take her careful hoard of savings and buy a ticket on the first flight back to the Philippines. "Roberto," she whispered. "It's all right, my little darling. Please, be brave. Mother will come back right away..."

But, of course, that was impossible. Leaving now would mean giving up everything she'd gained by her hard work and sacrifice. Worse, it would mean the end of any chance for a better life for Roberto. The only way to ensure a decent future for him was to stay here, save money and send for him. Otherwise, he could expect nothing but a life of grinding poverty and hopelessness, suffering all the things that Julia had hoped to save him from.

But how could she bear the thought of Roberto's being lonely and frightened, and crying for his mother in the darkness of the night? She tried to comfort herself by remembering the sound of his voice on the phone the last time she'd telephoned.

Long-distance calls were terribly expensive, a luxury that Julia only allowed herself on rare occasions. When she'd spoken to Roberto two weeks after the Fourth of July celebration, he had been subdued but cheerful enough, telling her about his schoolwork and the baseball team he and his friends had formed in a vacant lot.

Of course, Cesar was always close at hand when Julia talked to Roberto on the phone, and she was sure he wouldn't allow the little boy to say anything that might be upsetting to his mother, so far away in America....

"Hello, Julia," a voice said nearby. "We've been looking for you."

Julia looked up in surprise. Todd and Kim stood at the edge of the garden, smiling at her, both of them looking relaxed and casual in jeans and cotton shirts.

Hugo approached them and sniffed happily at their feet, then loped off toward the fence where he was digging up a cache of bones. Julia clutched the hoe and smiled awkwardly at her visitors, conscious of her baggy shorts, the ragged coolie hat she wore, the smears of dirt on her hands and legs.

"There was no answer at the door, so we came around the back. That looks like a pleasant job," Kim said. "Do you take care of this whole yard and garden?"

"Most of it." Julia leaned the hoe against the fence and crossed the garden toward them, nervously wiping her hands on her shorts. "There's a gardener who does the heavy work and mows the lawn once a week, but I do . . . everything else."

"And she cooks and cleans and does the grocery shopping," Todd said, smiling. "And looks after the dogs and takes classes besides. What a woman."

Julia flushed at his praise and stood shyly on the path, wondering why they'd come.

"It's too hot in the studio to work there this afternoon. We're going horseback riding," Kim said. "Todd has a friend who owns a ranch just north of the city, and he's offered us the use of a couple of his horses this afternoon. We thought you might like to come along."

"Horseback riding?" Julia said in astonishment. "Oh, my goodness, I can't remember the last time I..."

"Come on, Julia," Todd urged. "All you ever do is work. This friend of mine, he's got some really gentle, quiet old saddle horses we can use. The only way I could get Kim to go," he added with a look of boyish appeal, "was to promise that you'd come, too. Don't make a liar out of me."

Julia felt a flutter of excitement. She looked over at the dogs, then back at the two people by the garden. "But... horseback riding! What would I wear?"

Todd threw up his hands in a gesture of despair. "Women! You're all the same. Offer to take a woman on a trip to a distant galaxy, and right away she'd start worrying about what to wear."

Kim glared and punched his arm, then turned to Julia. "Just wear some jeans or cotton slacks, and a long-sleeved shirt for protection from the sun," she said. "And a hat, if you've got one. But...maybe not that one," she added, looking at Julia's tattered coolie hat.

Julia laughed again. "No, not this one. Don't I need... cowboy boots, or something?"

"I'm wearing running shoes," Kim said. "I don't have any cowboy boots. Although," she added, with a pointed glance at Todd, "there *are* people who seem to feel that it's a serious deficiency in my wardrobe."

"I refuse to take her line dancing until she buys cowboy boots," Todd said placidly. "And she feels terrible about it, poor girl."

Suddenly, Julia realized how much she'd missed Todd and Kim. She hadn't seen much of them lately, not since the portrait was finished, and the outing would take her mind off her own problems for a while.

"If you don't mind waiting a minute," she began, "I'll just run inside and..."

"Hello, Julia. I got back early," a voice said, startling all of them. Julia whirled and saw Barbara McAllister marching down the flagstone walk from the garage, carrying a pair of shopping bags.

The three younger people stood silently near the garden, waiting for her to approach. Barbara's eyes widened when she saw Todd and Kim, but she said nothing, just stopped and gave her grandson an inquiring glance.

"Hi, Nana," Todd said nonchalantly. "You've met Kim, haven't you?"

Barbara inclined her head with cool politeness. "Yes, I was in her studio one day last spring. Hello, Kim," she added.

"Hello, Mrs. McAllister. We're going horseback riding," Kim said. "We stopped by to see if Julia might want to come with us."

Julia waited with growing tension, afraid to look at her employer. Barbara handed the heavy grocery bags to Todd and sighed with relief.

"Horseback riding," she said, looking amused. "Is that a favorite pastime of yours, Julia?"

"I haven't done it in years," Julia said. "But I'd really like to go," she added tentatively, "if it's all

right with you, ma'am. There are some cold cuts and
salad in the fridge, and I can—''

"Don't worry. I'll be fine," Barbara said, waving
her hand casually. "I don't have much of an appetite
on these hot days. Hurry up, my dear," she added
when she saw Julia hesitating. "You mustn't keep
them waiting. Run inside and change your clothes.''

Julia hurried toward the back door while the other
two women followed more slowly. Todd brought up
the rear, carrying Barbara's grocery bags, with Homer
and Hugo trotting at his heels.

A COUPLE OF HOURS later, Kim rode her placid mount,
smiling with pleasure at the gentle rocking motion of
the horse and the spectacular scenery around them.
Todd's rancher friend had been as good as his word,
supplying the two women with saddle horses so quiet
that the animals seemed like nursery toys on springs.
And Todd had been right, as well, Kim thought, when
he'd assured her that the back of a horse was the best
vantage point for enjoying the beauty of this summer
afternoon.

Out in the open, the landscape rolled off on all sides
to a limitless horizon, misty in the far distance and
swirling with wisps of low cloud. Besides the rhyth-
mic thump of their horses' hooves and the creak of
saddle leather, the only sounds were the occasional trill
of bird song from the brush, the lowing of distant
herds of cattle and the gentle whispering rustle of the
summer breeze.

The tranquillity and stillness were almost mesmerizing. Kim couldn't remember when she'd felt so utterly at peace with herself and the world. She sighed with contentment and looked over at Julia, who rode beside her and sat very erect on a plodding gray mare, gripping the reins firmly in both hands.

Julia wore jeans, a plaid shirt and one of Barbara's wide-brimmed straw hats. She looked like a child, bright-eyed and delighted with this unexpected adventure.

Kim smiled fondly, then glanced at Todd, who rode at her other side on a big, high-stepping sorrel gelding. His long body seemed relaxed and comfortable in the saddle, his hand low on the reins. He looked like part of the horse he rode, as he swayed and shifted effortlessly with the movements of the animal.

"Todd, you're such a good rider," Kim commented enviously. "You make it look easy."

His teeth flashed in a smile beneath the brim of his Stetson. "During a portion of my misspent youth, I was actually a working cowboy, you know. I had a job on a ranch in Idaho, lived in a bunkhouse and herded cattle for a living."

"With a college degree?"

"Why not? Just because a man has graduated from college doesn't mean he automatically has a burning desire to sit at a desk and be an executive. I've always loved the wide-open spaces, Kim. This landscape is so beautiful in all kinds of weather. Even in the dead of winter, when the trees are covered with hoarfrost and your saddle's like a cake of ice, and your breath practically freezes in the air."

"So that's why you liked cowboy life? Because of the *scenery?*"

"I'm a visual person, Kim. I'm turned on by beauty. I always have been."

He looked at her face and body deliberately. She gripped the reins, hastening to distract him. "When you were a cowboy, what did you do? I mean, what were your days like?"

"Mostly not that glamorous. We got up early and went to bed late. We spent a lot of time breaking and gentling horses, hunting strays in the brush, stringing fence line and vaccinating calves, getting dirty and tired and soaked in the rain."

"It doesn't sound all that great. Especially not for a sensitive artist like you."

"That's what my grandmother used to say. But I was young and full of energy in those days. Besides," he added with a reminiscent smile, "the weekends were always the best part."

"Oh, really? And what did you do on weekends?"

Still smiling, Todd reined his horse in closer to hers. "We went to town, or to rodeos. We were just a bunch of wild, reckless kids, dancing and partying all night long, riding bulls and chasing girls."

Kim felt an irrational stab of jealousy, thinking about all the women over the years who'd held that big muscular body, kissed that sexy mouth...

Todd grinned as if he could read her thoughts. "Don't worry, sweetheart," he murmured. "Not one of them was ever as beautiful as you."

"Oh, yeah," Kim said with mild scorn. "I'm sure that's true. I'm *much* more attractive than all those rodeo princesses in their tight pants and tooled leather boots, right?"

He pretended to consider this, frowning solemnly. "Well," he said finally, "I have to admit that they were cute, but I'm pretty sure that none of those girls was ever a college professor."

Kim chuckled and turned to Julia who seemed to be in a world of her own.

"Having fun, Julia?" she asked.

"Oh, yes," Julia breathed, patting her horse's neck. "I can't remember when I've enjoyed anything so much."

"You should get out more," Todd said, leaning across Kim to look at the other woman. "You really should, Julia. My grandmother should let you off the leash occasionally."

"Mrs. McAllister has been very kind to me since I came to America," Julia said loyally. "I appreciate everything she's done for me."

Kim thought of the elderly woman they'd met earlier in the day. Even laden with grocery bags in the garden, Barbara McAllister was a regal, imposing presence. And when they went inside the house to wait for Julia, the older woman had made it quite clear that she hated seeing Kim standing next to her grandson. The woman's frosty manner still rankled.

"You know, you've got a pretty good seat on that horse, Julia," Todd was saying. "You must have done some riding back home in the Philippines."

"Yes, I did," Julia said. "When I was a girl, we had an old horse in the village that we all took turns riding. And then a couple of times before Roberto was born, I—"

She fell abruptly silent, while Todd and Kim exchanged a glance.

"Julia?" Kim said gently. "Who's Roberto?"

Julia gripped the reins and bit her lip, avoiding their eyes.

"Julia?" Kim asked again.

Tears gathered in Julia's eyes and began to spill down her cheeks. She looked up with a pleading expression that tore at Kim's heart.

"He's . . . Roberto is my son," she whispered. "My little boy."

EARLY THE FOLLOWING evening, Kim sat on the stool near her grandmother's chair, holding a skein of green embroidery silk as Madame Tanaka wound it onto a plastic spool.

"It's so pretty," Kim murmured, watching the rippling emerald lengths of silk fall away from her hands. "What's this one going to be, Grandmother?"

"It will be a scroll depicting the four seasons. I want you to look at the pattern and give me your opinion, *chérie*. Some of the colors are quite pale. I thought I might do some substitutions."

"All right," Kim said absently. "I like it when you use vivid colors like this one. It makes the scrolls so beautiful. The last one was—"

"So this Julia, the woman who sat for the portrait you were painting, she's left her son behind in the Philippines so she could find a job as a domestic?" her grandmother asked, with one of the rapid conversational shifts that Kim always found disconcerting. Her grandmother's body might be ancient, but her mind was still rapier sharp.

Kim nodded. "I feel so sorry for her, Grandmother. She's suffering so much. You can't imagine how terribly she misses him."

"Oh, yes. I can imagine," Masako said quietly.

"It's such a dreadful system, making a woman leave her child behind when she's trying so hard to make a better life for him," Kim said with passion. "I can't believe Julia's kept him secret all this time. If it were me, I'd be wanting to talk about him every minute, just for the comfort of saying his name."

"Perhaps Julia has been afraid of her employer's reaction," Masako suggested, studying her embroidery pattern.

Kim cast a quick glance at her grandmother, but the old woman's face was impassive.

"If she is, she has no reason to be," Kim said. "Todd and I talked about this for a long time last night after we took Julia home. He's going to tell his grandmother all about it today, and suggest that the family sponsor Roberto. He's certain that Mrs. McAllister will be willing to give both Julia and her son a home, so there's no reason the little boy couldn't come here and live with his mother right away."

"There's a great deal of legal complication involved in sponsoring a nonfamily member."

"I know, but surely they can get around all that. After all, originally, Julia was planning to deal with the bureaucracy all on her own. You should hear how much money she's saved, Grandmother."

"It's very generous of Todd to be so interested in Julia's problem," Masako said. "He must be extremely fond of children."

Kim shifted awkwardly on the upholstered stool. "He's concerned about Julia," she said at last. "He's anxious to do whatever he can to make sure she's happy."

"So, it's the housemaid he's concerned about? Not her child?"

"He doesn't know the child," Kim said with a touch of annoyance.

"Neither do you, Kimiko. But still, your eyes fill with tears when you speak of him. He is a little boy, just six years old and many thousands of miles from his mother, and his plight tears at your soul. I was merely wondering if Todd McAllister feels the same way."

"Were you? Well, I don't think he does. As a matter of fact, I don't believe that Todd is all that fond of children."

Masako frowned. "How can one not be fond of children?"

Kim's tension increased. "He's never been around children, Grandmother. Besides, Todd had quite a traumatic childhood himself, you know. He was abandoned by his mother... that's Mrs. McAllister's daughter... soon after he was born. His grandmother raised him, and his mother hardly ever came to see him when he was growing up. And he never even knew who his father was. Isn't it understandable that he'd have some reservations about children and family life?"

"An unhappy childhood can be a source of great bitterness," Masako agreed.

Kim looked at her suspiciously. "So, do you feel sympathy toward him? I don't get the impression that you do."

"Whether or not I feel sympathy for Todd McAllister is of little importance. It's your happiness I'm considering, nothing else."

"I don't understand what connection you could possibly see between my happiness and Todd's attitude toward children."

But as soon as she'd spoken the words aloud, Kim could see the connection all too clearly. She turned on the stool and looked out the window at the gathering twilight, uncomfortably conscious of her grandmother's eyes resting on her.

"So," Masako asked after a long silence, "you see no connection?"

"Grandmother, it's not like that," Kim said. "We're just friends. Todd and I work together every

day. We enjoy each other's company. It's not...
anything else," she concluded lamely.

Masako shook her head. "When attractive young
people of opposite sexes spend a great deal of time together," she observed, "it's always something else. I
was young once, too, you know. I remember what it's
like."

"I doubt it," Kim said rebelliously. "If you really
remembered what it's like to find somebody attractive, you wouldn't be so harsh in your judgments."

Masako dropped the green silk into her lap and
stared at her granddaughter. "I had the impression
that you and David Yamamoto were getting along very
well together," Masako observed, her voice quaver-
ing a little. "Obviously, I was wrong."

"Grandmother," Kim said in despair, "we *do* get
along very well together. I like David. He's a fine person, and a good friend. But," she added gently, "he
could never, ever be more than that to me, Grandmother. He just couldn't."

"Why not? He's handsome, intelligent, considerate, a good provider... What on earth is wrong with
David Yamamoto?"

"Nothing," Kim said. "Nothing's *wrong* with him,
Grandmother. There's just... there's no spark, that's
all."

"Spark!" Masako echoed with profound con-
tempt. "What nonsense. You silly children, you over-
look all the fine qualities in a person and look for
sparks! Those fires can burn out very quickly, my love,
and you're left with nothing but cold ashes."

Kim lowered the skein of silk and looked at the lined face above her. "Grandmother," she murmured, "look me in the eyes and tell me there were no sparks between you and my grandfather."

Masako's mouth twitched, and her eyes softened with memory. She turned away, and stared out the window. "That was different," she said at last, with a fond faraway look. "Completely different."

"Why? You had the chance to live with a man who thrilled you, Grandmother. I know how you felt about him. Why is it so wrong for me to want the same thing? I'm not prepared to settle for reliability and comfort. I want some sparks when I pick a man to spend my life with. I want the same thing you and my grandfather had."

"And this man... this cowboy of yours... does he thrill you, Kimiko? Does he light up your world, as they say in the song?"

Kim tensed, a little taken aback by the suddenness of this attack. "I don't... I'm not sure what you're talking about," she faltered.

"Oh, I think you know very well what I'm talking about," Masako said calmly. "I think you're falling in love with this wild young man. And you're making a terrible mistake. Absolutely terrible."

All of Kim's indignant protests died away as she looked up at the quiet face by the window. "Even if what you say is true, Grandmother," she murmured after a few moments, "how can you be so sure it's a terrible mistake? You've never even met Todd Mc-

Allister. How do you know that he's a wild young man, as you say?"

"I know enough about him. I don't think you're even aware, my child, of how much you talk about him. I know that he's been an unstable wandering man for most of his adult life. He's footloose and irresponsible, and his background and heritage are so different from yours that you could never hope to find happiness with him. You're being completely foolish, Kimiko. A woman your age should know better."

"A woman my age should be free to do as she pleases without a lot of interference and unwelcome advice! In fact, Grandmother—"

Kim stopped herself partway through her heated remarks, alarmed by Masako's expression and the droop of her frail body.

"Grandmother, I'm sorry," she whispered, getting up to hug the old lady. "I'm sorry, darling. I didn't mean to talk to you like that. And there's nothing for you to worry about. Nothing's happening between me and Todd. Nothing at all."

Masako peered up at her anxiously. "Nothing? You promise?"

"Honestly, Grandmother. We just work together, that's all."

It was the truth, Kim told herself firmly. Except for a couple of slips—a few stolen passionate kisses that thrilled her to the core and haunted her in the night— she'd managed to keep Todd at arm's length during these past few months. And she intended to keep on doing that, because Kim knew in her heart that her grandmother was right.

She and Todd were utterly unsuited to each other.

Even if she could never forget the feeling of his mouth and hands, the dimple in his cheek and the warmth of his laughter. Even if his light footsteps on the stairs were enough to set her heart beating madly, and her hands shaking. Even if...

A knock sounded at the door. Kim gave the old woman in the chair another fierce hug. She crossed the room to open the door, then stood frozen in dismay.

"Todd!" she whispered, looking in confusion at the tall man in the hallway. "I...didn't expect... Why are you here?"

"Hi, Kim. I stopped by to see if I could coax you out for a walk. It's such a beautiful evening," Todd said. "Your father told me you were down here, so I thought I'd drop by to pay my respects to your grandmother."

"Who is it, dear?" Masako called from within the room.

Kim took a deep breath, staring at Todd. She groped for words, still openmouthed and speechless with the shock of seeing this man on her grandmother's threshold.

"Kimiko?" the old lady asked from behind her, with a touch of impatience.

Kim trembled and clenched her hands nervously, then stood aside to let Todd enter the room, trying to keep her voice casual. "It's Todd," she said. "Todd McAllister."

Todd crossed the room with a few long strides and paused by Masako's chair, giving the woman his most charming smile.

"It's an honor to meet you, Madame Tanaka," he said with sincerity. "Kim's told me so much about you and your fascinating life."

"Ah, but life is only fascinating in retrospect," Masako replied, looking up at him soberly. "While one is living it, the most fascinating life can seem merely confusing and frightening. Especially," she added with quiet emphasis, "if one insists on making the wrong decisions."

Kim paused uncertainly by the door, watching this unlikely scene in the gracious Japanese bedroom. More than anything, she was conscious of Todd's handsome golden presence, and the way he and Madame Tanaka looked at each other with calm appraisal.

They were like two fighters, Kim thought, each taking the measure of the opponent before joining in battle.

A cloud slipped in front of the dying sun, casting the room into deep shadow. Kim shivered and hugged herself, suddenly chilled with a nameless sadness.

CHAPTER EIGHT

IN SEPTEMBER, a couple of weeks after Julia's startling revelation, Todd left to conduct a four-day art workshop at an eastern college. Kim, who'd been looking forward to having the studio to herself for a whole week, was surprised how much she missed him.

She'd expected to use the peace and quiet to get all kinds of work done, but instead she felt lost and lonely. She spent a lot of the time wandering around the studio or staring restlessly out the window, missing Todd's irreverent conversation and easy laughter, even his annoying teasing and the constant thump of his country music.

On Friday, she left the gallery at noon and walked the few blocks to their studio, thinking about the last evening they'd spent together.

After the awkward moments in Madame Tanaka's room, she and Todd had escaped with relief into the gentle summer evening.

For hours, they'd walked along the streets together, talking quietly about Julia and her little boy. Todd told her that he'd spoken with his grandmother, and that Barbara was going to talk to the immigration officials as soon as possible but didn't want to say anything to Julia until she'd gotten a clearer idea of the legal position.

Kim frowned when she thought about Masako's insinuation that Todd had no concern for the child. He was simply trying to help Julia.

It wasn't fair for her grandmother to judge Todd when she didn't know him. But in spite of herself, Kim couldn't help remembering Todd's cynicism whenever he spoke about family life.

Some people really did feel that way, Kim realized. Anyone with a few basic courses in psychology knew that fractured childhoods and early betrayals made some people reluctant to form attachments in their adult life. They tended to be rootless and uncommitted, wandering from place to place, never settling down and giving their love to any one person.

They were people like Todd, she thought reluctantly.

Another image flashed into her mind as she hurried toward the studio. She thought of Barbara McAllister. Kim hadn't seen Todd's grandmother since that encounter the day they'd taken Julia horseback riding, though Todd reported frequently on Barbara's determination to find a way to bring Roberto to America.

Still, Kim remembered the feeling of Barbara's cold blue eyes upon her, and shivered at the memory of the woman's obvious dislike.

Both grandmothers, it seemed, were solidly opposed to the idea of a serious relationship between

Kim Tanaka and Todd McAllister. But their concern was ridiculous.

There was no relationship of the sort they feared, none at all. And there never would be.

Kim frowned again, wondering if there was any truth to her grandmother's accusation that she was falling in love with the man.

It was hard for Kim to analyze the depth of her feelings, because she was with Todd so much. But during an enforced absence like the week just passed, she was able to examine herself and her own reactions with somewhat more clarity.

The conclusion she reached, after a lot of thought, was that she and Todd McAllister were friends. Their friendship was based on their mutual love of painting. Unfortunately, this friendship was becoming more and more complicated by a powerful sexual attraction that affected both of them.

Kim shook her head impatiently, thinking about the way Todd made her feel, especially when he touched her or kissed her. It was a distressingly adolescent reaction, all tingly thrills and hot breathless yearnings, the kind of thing she should have outgrown a dozen years ago. A woman Kim's age should have more control of herself.

Still, she missed Todd every day. And despite their friendship, when she thought about him, her memories were sharply physical.

Kim sighed and trudged around the corner toward the studio, then paused, her heart pounding.

Todd's truck stood at the curb. The windowed canopy was jammed full of saddles, western gear, art supplies and a stuffed bobcat that snarled at Kim through the dusty glass.

She stood on the sidewalk, staring back at the bobcat for a moment, feeling absurdly happy. Then she turned and ran up the stairs, as breathless and excited as a child on Christmas morning. Long before she reached the studio she could hear the steady, elemental beat of Todd's favorite country music, and smell the paint and turpentine wafting into the hallway.

"Well, he's certainly back," she muttered aloud, with a sigh of mock resignation. But there was nothing resigned about the singing in her heart as she opened the door and slipped into the studio.

Kim paused in confusion, looking around. Todd was nowhere in sight, although there was a lot of fresh paint on his canvas. In fact, she thought, examining the big painting, he must have come home sometime during the night and worked for hours. He'd finished detailing the last of the background and had begun blocking in some major figures at the edge of the canvas.

But where was he?

The studio was empty, throbbing with the plaintive beat of a country love song, while the flowers on Kim's workbench dipped silently in the gusts of air from the fan.

Perhaps he'd just stepped out to his favorite Italian restaurant for lunch. Maybe she'd run down to Luigi's and surprise him. Kim certainly didn't feel able to settle in and start working, not when Todd was nearby. She wanted to see his face and body, hear his voice and absorb the warmth of his physical presence. Despite her resolve to get these dangerous feelings under control, the nearness of the man was enough to...

Suddenly, Kim caught sight of a shoe behind the big canvas, and a hairy bare leg.

She let the door close behind her and moved into the room on tiptoe, peeked behind the canvas and smiled. Todd was fast asleep on the cot he'd brought into the studio. He wore ragged cutoffs, a T-shirt and deck shoes, and he lay on his back, sprawled like a child on the tumbled sheets.

His face, too, looked childlike in sleep. Kim edged forward and stood by the cot, gazing down at him. She was overcome by a flood of tenderness so powerful that she was weak and dizzy for a moment, almost swaying on her feet. She felt a deep, maternal yearning to take off his shoes, pull the covers over him and smooth the tangled lock of hair on his forehead. But a darker, more urgent part of her wanted to lie beside him, nestle close to him and kiss his smiling mouth, touch her tongue to the pulse that throbbed at the base of his throat...

While she hesitated next to the cot, appalled by her thoughts, a hand reached out with lightning swiftness and grasped the bare flesh of her leg.

"Gotcha!" Todd whispered without opening his eyes.

Kim gasped and tried to pull away but he held her tightly, his hand sliding up her leg as he pulled her closer to the bed.

"C'mere," he muttered. "I'm having an erotic dream, and you're in it."

"Oh, no. Not unless I choose to be," she told him, mustering her last shred of dignity.

"Oh, sweetheart, you really want to be in it. You should have seen all the naughty things you did in my dream."

"Look, Todd, I don't think this is..."

But even as she spoke, Kim felt herself being drawn relentlessly toward the rumpled bed, pulled down into his arms.

"Did you miss me?" he whispered, his breath warm against her cheek. "Did you miss me while I was gone, little Kimiko? Are you glad to see me?"

"Not at all. It was so nice and quiet while you were away... Let me *go!*" she added furiously, struggling to pull away as his hands began to roam over her body, cupping and caressing her breasts through the light fabric of the dress she wore.

"Shh. Don't yell like that, sweetheart. You'll wake me up, and I'm having such a nice dream."

"Todd..."

"Such a nice dream," he said, sighing. He reached to unfasten the clip on her ponytail. Her hair spilled over his face and shoulders. "Oh, God, Kim..."

Kim tried vainly to resist, then subsided into helplessness as she felt his arms tighten around her. She buried her face against his chest, giving herself up at last to the warmth and strength of him, the clean scent of his skin and his powerful thrusting maleness.

Again she had a confused sense of beauty and rightness, of opposites fitting together into a perfect unity. Soft and strong, small and large, dainty and blunt, silk and sand... They were meant to be together, to blend their bodies and souls into a soaring harmony that wouldn't be denied.

She was tired of resisting all the urges that drew her to this man. She wanted to yield, to give way, to lose herself in him and let the tide carry her wherever. Kim was sharply aware of the moment, the instant when all her defenses crumbled and she made a conscious decision to give herself to Todd McAllister.

She felt a wave of sheer terror, followed by delight and a kind of abandon she'd never known.

"If it's going to happen," she whispered against his throat, "it might as well be good."

He leaned up on his elbow and drew away to look at her in surprise, then grinned and lifted a handful of her hair, burying his face in its silky blackness.

"My sentiments exactly," he said softly. "Tell me, how do I get this dress off? The damned thing's getting in my way."

"There's a zipper at the back," Kim told him. "Much like this one," she added solemnly, reaching toward his bulging denim shorts.

"I see." He looked at her soberly, his eyes sparkling. "And what do we do with zippers, Kimiko?"

"We grasp them like this..." She gripped the tab on his zipper, avoiding his teasing grin. "And we pull gently, like this."

The zipper slid down and his denim shorts fell open, leaving no doubt about his level of interest. Todd stood up with a lithe motion, stripped off shoes, shorts and T-shirt and stood in front of her wearing nothing but his cotton undershorts.

Despite the fact that she was accustomed to seeing almost this much of his body on a regular basis, Kim found herself awed by his naked male beauty. She reached out to touch his hard belly and run her hand over the powerful curve of his thigh, then gasped when he sat on the bed and swept her onto his lap, cuddling her fiercely in his arms.

"Okay, now it's my turn," he whispered, reaching for the zipper at the back of her dress. He eased it down and pulled the straps gently over her shoulders until she was naked to the waist.

Todd leaned forward to kiss each of her bare shoulders, running his lips across the base of her throat with a sigh of pleasure. Then he sat back to look at her, his eyes wide with appreciation.

"Little Kim," he murmured, reaching to cup her breasts in his hands. "You're so exquisite. You're like a lovely porcelain sculpture."

"You're not...not so bad yourself," Kim whispered, smiling at him.

She couldn't believe how much at ease she felt, sitting half-naked in his arms while he studied her body with frank admiration. They were in full sunlight, bathed in golden warmth, but there was nothing awkward about the moment, no shyness or embarrassment. Kim felt that she'd been created for this moment, shaped and designed to fit within the circle of his arms and fill his eyes with pleasure.

He lifted her easily and pulled the dress down over her hips, then tossed it aside and stroked her legs with a wondering smile.

"Perfect," he murmured. "Perfect in every way. What a woman you are, Kim."

She nestled close to him, hungry for his kiss, and sighed when his mouth closed over hers and he pulled her down onto the bed to lie beside him. The kiss went on forever, drawing both of them deeper and deeper into a fire that glowed and shimmered like the sunshine all around them. Their hands moved over each other's bodies, stroking and caressing, exploring and discovering and savoring.

Kim loved his body, the hard planes of bone and muscle and the surprising silky texture of his skin. Most of all, she loved the feeling of being in his arms, lost in his caress. She felt utterly safe and cherished, as if she'd found a place where pain could never intrude, and happiness was complete. They moved as one, drawn instinctively as if they'd done this together a thousand times before. There was no awkwardness or unfamiliarity, no sense of strangeness. Their bodies shaped and fitted to each other like two halves of a whole, melding smoothly and sweetly. When he entered her, she felt a mounting tide of excitement, an urgent need that made her cry out with longing. The wave of feeling intensified, pounded and thrust at her, grew to an elation that was almost unendurable, and finally crashed and broke around her in shivering waves of ecstasy.

Kim lay in his arms, drowsy and rich with contentment. She felt at one with the rays of sunlight that streamed over the bed, all golden and warm and lustrous, utterly spent and satisfied.

Gradually, her awareness returned and she rolled her head to look at Todd, who lay beside her with his eyes closed. Kim smiled, loving the fine strength of his aquiline profile. She reached out with a lazy finger to trace the line of his nose and mouth, then grinned as he opened his eyes to look at her.

"Wow," he muttered, his voice hushed with awe. "So, what did you think, Kim? Did that feel all right for you?"

She frowned judiciously. "I guess it was okay," she said. "You're not bad, for a wild cowboy."

He chuckled and rolled over to take her in his arms, burying his face in her hair. "Cowboys are great lovers," he murmured. "Didn't you know that, woman?"

"Actually, no, I didn't. It's the first time I've made love to a cowboy."

"Yeah, maybe. But not your last."

"Is that so?" Kim asked, pulling away to look at him. "How do you know?"

"I'm psychic," Todd told her with a grin. "My instincts tell me that you're going to make love to a cowboy many, many more times. Possibly starting within the next fifteen minutes or so."

She leaned over to kiss him. "No kidding. Tell me, do your instincts say anything about how the cowboy plans to get any work done in the midst of all this activity?"

"God knows," he muttered sadly. "I love this," he added, gripping a handful of her hair. "It's like black silk. Like getting lost in midnight. I could drown in your hair and eyes, Kim."

She felt a need to keep the moment light, to tease him about his sudden flight of poetry and hide her own emotion. But she knew exactly how he felt. His eyes were as deep and beautiful as a mountain lake, and she, too, wanted to plunge into those calm depths and lose herself forever.

She gazed at him, wide-eyed and silent, until his hands began to roam over her body again. Then she forced herself to pull away and laugh. "That's enough!" she said with mock sternness. "I'll bet you haven't even had lunch yet."

He bared his teeth and nibbled at her shoulder. "No, but I'm about to."

"You are not," Kim said. She swung her legs over the side of the bed and sat up, looking around for her clothes.

"I'm not? What am I going to do?"

"First, you're going to get dressed and come with me for a real meal. Then you're going to have a nap while I get some work done, because I'll also bet you haven't slept all night. And *then*," Kim went on, ignoring his bright teasing glance, "we'll decide what's going to happen next."

He laughed and reached for her but she evaded his grasp, walking toward the bathroom with her clothes while he lay and watched her.

MASAKO TANAKA dropped her embroidery into her lap and gazed out the window, feeling every one of her over eighty years. It was unusual for her, this sense of weary futility. Usually Masako felt vigorous and full of confidence. She was sometimes startled to catch a glimpse of herself in a mirror and realize how ancient she'd become.

Masako grimaced as she watched the scene beyond the window, bathed in rich October twilight. Kim and her parents were strolling in the courtyard, with two of the smallest grandchildren tumbling at their feet. Todd McAllister walked beside them, a tall incongruous figure among the small trim bodies and shining black heads around him.

His muscular breadth and golden coloring were like an affront, an unpleasant note in the harmony beyond the window. Masako was troubled by everything about him. She couldn't get accustomed to his easy laughter, the blue fire of his eyes, his charming dimple and bright curly hair and the catlike grace of his big arrogant body.

She watched nervously as he lifted little Alice and held her aloft. Masako's youngest great-grandchild, just three years old, laughed and kicked her small running shoes in the air, her round face pink with delight. Todd grinned fondly at the dark-haired toddler, then hugged her and set her carefully on the path again, where she gripped his hand and trotted beside him, looking up at him with an adoring gaze.

Laurence and Midori, Kim's parents, smiled at him with affection, too. They liked the man, and could see no reason for Masako's firm opposition.

"He's a fine artist," Laurence had said mildly when they'd discussed the man last night at dinner while Kim was away. "He has an international reputation, Mama. His work is in collections all over the world."

"And he's *so* charming," Midori had added with a smile. "The grandchildren worship him."

Masako frowned again, recalling the conversation. Midori Tanaka was an intelligent woman and a good mother, but she didn't understand the importance of heritage and traditional values. Nor, apparently, did Laurence.

He'd even accused his mother of being racist, saying that she objected to this man simply because he wasn't Japanese.

Masako picked up her embroidery again and began to stitch mechanically, wondering if there was any truth in what her son had said. Could her reaction be nothing more than bigotry?

Masako Tanaka despised any trace of prejudice. She'd done her best to teach all the children that people deserved to be evaluated on their own merits, not on their appearance and background.

Obviously, she thought with a wry smile, her teaching had been very effective, at least where Kim was concerned. But this was different, Masako thought, her smile fading. All those views of equality and tolerance were supposed to be applied in a general sense. They surely didn't mean that the most precious person in one's life should be allowed to run out into the world and make a terrible mistake.

And Masako knew that this relationship was a mistake.

The old lady was so attuned to Kim's emotions that she'd been aware of the dangerous feelings long before her granddaughter. She'd known when Kim began to find the man intriguing, then sexually attractive. She'd watched the growing tenderness in Kim, and the hunger when she spoke his name.

Finally, Masako had looked at her granddaughter one hot day in late September and seen the sleepy languor in Kim's eyes, the bloom of fulfillment on her cheeks. Masako had known at once that her worst nightmare had come true. Kim had bedded the charming, footloose young man, and been drawn under his sexual spell.

In the weeks since then, Kim had brought Todd to the house several times, and he'd been met with general approval by all the family except Masako. Kim's father, who loved fine art, respected Todd's talent, and her brother Yosh spoke to him with easy friendship. Both Midori and Kim's sister, Reiko, flirted with him happily, obviously smitten by his laughing cowboy charm. And, as Midori said, the little children adored him.

Only Masako kept her distance. She watched Todd McAllister with suspicion, knowing that he was going to hurt Kim terribly. Masako also knew she had to prevent this disaster. She had to stop Kim from getting more deeply involved with the man. And Madame Tanaka knew exactly what she was going to do. She folded her embroidery with sudden decision, then sat quietly in the twilight stillness of her bedroom, making plans.

JULIA WAS POLISHING furniture, part of the massive fall housecleaning that she'd undertaken. Much of the motivation for this effort was Barbara's desire to have the old house sparkling before her daughter, Lillian, paid her long-promised visit. But Julia was also eager to immerse herself in the task of cleaning out closets, turning mattresses and vacuuming carpets.

The hard work kept her from thinking about her problems.

At first it had been such a relief to tell Kim and Todd about her son, and have them, in turn, let Mrs. McAllister know about Roberto. There were no longer secrets, and she could talk about him whenever she wanted. But soon the relief changed to a yearning more fierce than any that Julia had ever known.

Now that she could speak freely about Roberto, he seemed closer every day. His face filled her mind while she worked, and she heard his voice in her dreams at night. If she couldn't see him soon, she was afraid she would go mad....

Julia moaned softly and tried to distract herself by thinking about Kim and Todd.

Anybody who spent any time with the two artists on these mellow autumn days could see clearly where their interests lay. They could hardly keep their hands off each other, even in public, and the blazing intensity of their passion shone from their eyes whenever they met.

Julia smiled briefly, thinking about her two friends, then sobered again. Their love made her realize how alone she was, even though Julia had no wish to involve a man in her life. She had room in her heart for only one love just now, and it was her son.

"Julia!" Barbara called from the kitchen, interrupting Julia's thoughts. "Where are you?"

"In here, ma'am. I'm polishing the dining-room furniture."

Barbara appeared in the doorway. She wore her best silk trouser suit, Julia noticed in surprise, a pair of fawn-colored slacks and a high-necked tunic with a vivid russet scarf.

"You look very nice, ma'am," Julia said softly. "That's such a lovely outfit."

"What? Oh, this. Thanks, Julia," Barbara said, looking abstracted. "My daughter called again last night, did I tell you? She and her friend are coming out later in the fall, probably for Thanksgiving. It's certain, this time."

Julia nodded and returned to her work, hiding her skeptical expression from Barbara.

Lillian McAllister had already called at least three times to cancel or postpone her visit. And on one memorable occasion, she hadn't even bothered to notify them, just failed to turn up at the expected time. They were left with the house fully prepared and a refrigerator so stuffed with food, they'd had to give much of it away.

Julia was beginning to develop a fairly clear picture of Barbara's daughter, and to understand why Todd spoke about his mother with such resentment. The woman was absolutely unreliable, he'd told them angrily after the last cancellation. Lillian had never kept a promise in her life, unless it suited her for some personal reason.

Julia shook her head and leaned forward to polish the pedestal of the big oak table. She wondered how a strong woman like Barbara tolerated this behavior from her daughter. Julia could never act that way, but Lillian, it seemed, had no fear of her mother.

"Julia? Could we talk for a moment, please? Sit down here in one of the chairs, my dear."

Julia looked up in surprise, then nodded and got to her feet. She dusted a cobweb from her hair and sat nervously on the edge of a dining-room chair, gripping the polishing cloth in her hands.

"Julia," Barbara said gently, "I've spent some time these past weeks speaking with immigration officials. I didn't want to tell you about it until I had some definite information."

"Immigration officials?" Julia repeated. Her mouth went dry, and her heart began to pound with alarm.

Barbara smiled and reached over to pat the woman's hand. "There's nothing to be concerned about. The fact is, I'd like to sponsor your little boy."

Julia licked her lips and stared, trying to understand. "Roberto?" she whispered at last. "You'd like to... to bring him over here? Mrs. McAllister... you'd do that for me?"

"Well, partly for myself, too," Barbara said calmly. "I'm very pleased with your work, Julia. I was hoping we might make a deal, you and I."

"A deal," Julia echoed numbly.

"Perhaps I should call it a business arrangement. I thought that if I were to sponsor your little boy, and agree to have both of you live here while the two of you get more settled, perhaps you'd be willing to work for me a little longer. Of course," Barbara added hastily, "I'd give you a raise in pay, as well. I know that you deserve more than you've been getting, Julia, but I had no idea at first how capable you'd prove to be, and how much responsibility you'd be assuming in my household."

Julia's mind groped through all of this, unable to grasp the wonder of it. "You'll *sponsor* Roberto?" she asked. "And we can both live here in this house?"

"I hope you will. Todd's old room is perfect for a little boy, and I rather doubt that Todd will ever need it again," Barbara said with a distant smile. "Now, it all takes a great deal of time, Julia," she added. "I've already begun the process, but there are masses of papers to be filled out, and they have to be processed in both countries. Still, one official did tell me that if I got started right away, possibly we could have your son here by Christmas.''

"Christmas!" Julia breathed, her eyes filling with tears. "Oh, Mrs. McAllister. You're so good to me...so wonderful..."

"Now then, that's quite enough of that," Barbara said briskly. "I'm no saint, Julia. I'm just a selfish old woman who's trying to hang on to a good cook and housekeeper, that's all. Let's get back to work, shall we?"

Barbara started toward the door, then paused. "Oh, Julia..."

"Yes, ma'am?"

"I'm expecting a visitor this afternoon."

"A visitor?" Julia asked, still dazed with happiness.

"Yes. She'll be arriving any moment now. I'll speak to her in the morning room. I have tea in the carafe, and a plate of cookies. You won't need to bring us anything."

Julia nodded, surprised at this unusual behavior. She'd never known Barbara to make tea for herself and a guest. That was a job that was always left for Julia.

"And I'd like to answer the door myself, if you don't mind," Barbara went on, her voice elaborately casual. "If I should happen to be upstairs when the bell rings, just give me a call, would you?"

Julia stared, at a loss for words. Just then, there was the unmistakable sound of a vehicle pulling to the curb in front of the house.

Barbara's head lifted and her face grew tense, but her voice was calm and firm when she spoke.

"Julia, would you run downstairs and check to see if the pilot light is on in the furnace? Sometimes in the autumn the air currents tend to blow it out."

"But..."

"Please don't argue, Julia!" Barbara said, in a voice that allowed no opposition. "I'm extremely worried about the furnace."

"Yes, ma'am," Julia murmured, getting to her feet and hurrying toward the basement door. She looked at the cleaning rag in her hand, and set it on the top step before she ran downstairs.

She glanced at the furnace, which was working perfectly as she knew it would be. Then, consumed with curiosity, she crept over to the window and stood on a wooden apple crate to peer out into the front yard. A cab was parked in the driveway. While Julia watched, the driver bent to assist someone from the back seat.

Julia held her breath and strained upward to get a better look, then gaped in astonishment. The person coming up the walk on the arm of the cabdriver was an elderly woman, small and erect in her black silk dress and fine woolen coat. She looked elegant, calm, prosperous and well-groomed.

And she was Japanese.

CHAPTER NINE

BARBARA HURRIED to answer the door, watching while the cabdriver took leave of his customer as if she were royalty.

"Come back at three o'clock, please," the woman told him with a gracious smile. "I'll be waiting for you."

The driver, who must have received a handsome tip, grinned happily and promised to be waiting by the curb. Barbara watched while he strolled back toward his cab, then led her visitor into the house.

"My housemaid is busy at the moment," she said with distant courtesy. She took the woman's coat, noticing the fineness of the fabric and cut.

But then, what had she expected? A brightly colored kimono? Barbara shook her head, annoyed by her own silliness. She'd known from Todd's comments that Masako Tanaka was a prosperous, well-educated woman, and had lived in America for fifty years.

Still, she hadn't been quite prepared for the woman's designer clothes, the expensive fragrance she wore and the sparkling diamond and emerald brooch on her black silk lapel.

Despite her confusion, Barbara's training and instincts served her well. She hung the coat with a polite smile and led the way to the morning room, where she'd placed the tea service on a low table between two flowered armchairs.

Suddenly, Barbara found herself wishing she'd used the Spode china instead of her second-best set, but there was nothing to be done about it now. And, judging from the purposeful look on her guest's face as she seated herself, Masako Tanaka wasn't at all interested in the merits of Barbara's china.

"Please sit down, Madame Tanaka," Barbara said, indicating one of the armchairs.

"Mrs. McAllister," the elderly Japanese woman said, sitting down, folding her hands in her lap and looking directly at her hostess. "It was kind of you to receive me."

The woman would never know how kind it was, Barbara thought, keeping her face impassive as she poured their tea.

In fact, this was the first time in her entire life that Barbara McAllister had entertained a person of Japanese heritage within the walls of her house. She could still remember the shock she'd felt when the woman had telephoned and asked to call on her. Even now, it was all Barbara could do to control the flood of ancient bitterness as she looked at the wizened face and shrewd dark eyes of Kim Tanaka's grandmother.

"You said on the phone that you had something important to discuss with me," she said, doing her best to conceal her emotions. "You suggested that it involved my grandson's welfare."

"They're sleeping together," Masako said bluntly. "It has to stop."

Barbara gaped at her, and the teacup rattled in its saucer as she set it down. "*Sleeping* together?" she whispered in horror. "How do you know?"

"My granddaughter has never been able to hide anything from me," the woman said calmly. "I can tell by looking at her face."

Barbara, who had always felt much the same about Todd, nodded.

"I'm sure you would agree that this relationship is most unsuitable," Masako went on. "It will bring them nothing but sorrow."

Barbara considered these words in blank surprise. It had never occurred to her that Kim Tanaka's family might be as strongly opposed to the relationship as she was.

"Yes," she said at last. "I feel exactly the same way, Madame Tanaka. I don't think there can be any possibility for happiness in a…in a thing like this. I think it's very foolish," she concluded.

Masako Tanaka was clearly not offended by the frankness of her hostess's words. "You're quite correct," she said. "I have always wanted Kimiko to marry within her race and heritage, because I believe marriage is difficult enough without racial differences between the partners. Despite any feelings she may think she has for your grandson, she will not find happiness with him."

"And your family...her parents...do they feel the same way?"

Masako waved her hand impatiently. "Their views are of no consequence. They don't understand life, nor do they consider the future. I don't believe they really have Kimiko's welfare in mind as I do."

Barbara nodded, trying to visualize Lillian giving any kind of wise counsel to Todd about something like this. The thought was almost laughable. Todd had nobody to guide and advise him except for his grandmother, who loved him. And Barbara had no intention of failing him in this responsibility.

She looked directly at her visitor. "What can we do?" she asked simply.

Masako leaned forward. "There are a number of things we can do," she said. "You and I will never be friends, Mrs. McAllister," she added quietly. "Kim has told me how you feel. But nobody knows these two young people as well as you and I do, and nobody has as much influence over them. Do you agree?"

"Yes," Barbara said. "I agree."

"Good." Masako settled back in her chair, looking quietly at her hostess. "Then we can make some intelligent plans. Now, here is what I propose..."

The old woman continued outlining her plans while the autumn wind sighed around the eaves of the old house, and the dying chrysanthemums nodded against the window.

ON A WARM afternoon in late fall, Todd and Kim abandoned their studio to spend a rare afternoon in the park, drawn by the sunlight and the vivid autumn foliage. Todd sat with his back resting comfortably against the trunk of a stately maple, his sketch pad open on his knee. Kim lay on the blanket at his feet, writing a press release describing the upcoming exhibit of watercolors at the gallery.

Todd looked up from his sketch pad and smiled at her as she frowned and nibbled her pen, unaware of his scrutiny.

No matter how much time they spent together, Todd thought fondly, it was never enough. He never tired of being with her. Kim was a woman of mystery, different all the time. Sometimes her mood was playful and childlike, sometimes stormy and intense or thoughtfully withdrawn. She was by turns a sprite, an angel and an executive with attaché case. When they met after the briefest absence, Todd didn't know which Kim was going to emerge, but it didn't matter because he found all of them fascinating.

Suddenly, he frowned, staring at his sketch pad without seeing any of the penciled figures.

Despite his enchantment with the woman on the blanket, Todd was growing a little troubled by the intensity of their relationship. He'd never experienced such passion, such drowning, blinding floods of emotion. In the past, he'd always managed to remain in control, no matter how heavy the situation had become.

But he couldn't seem to protect himself that way any longer. The minute she was out of his sight, he missed her and wanted her with him again. When she was away, he thought about her constantly, even dreamed about her. He was obsessed with her hair and eyes, the sweetness of her mouth, the soft ripple of her laughter...

Todd shifted awkwardly on the grass, then looked up with an absent smile as Kim pressed close to him.

"May I look?" she asked.

"Sure. I'm just putting down some ideas for the next canvas. It's a Cheyenne family group moving to their summer camp."

She leaned against his arm to look at the drawing, then drew in her breath sharply, pointing at one of the figures.

"Todd, that's *me!*"

He looked in surprise at the shapely Cheyenne maiden on her spotted pony. The prairie wind whipped her long black hair across her face as she sat proudly on the horse, her slim legs wrapped in buckskin moccasins.

"I guess it does look a little like you, doesn't it?" he admitted, feeling both embarrassed and dismayed.

He'd had no intention of using Kim's face and body for the woman on the horse, but apparently, his hands had created her likeness without conscious thought on his part. It was, he thought in despair, more evidence of the way the woman was beginning to permeate every part of his life, even his work.

"You seem to be on my mind these days," he told her with an awkward smile.

"Well, I'm not sure I like being in your paintings. You're not even paying me a modeling fee."

"Okay," he said. "I'll make her less pretty, all right? Then she won't look like you."

Kim rewarded this with a smile, then lay back on the blanket with her hands behind her head and looked at him thoughtfully. "When will you be starting the new painting?"

"Pretty soon. My agent's coming to pick up the one that's finished, and as soon as it's out of the studio, I can get to work on the next one. The whole project's going really well. You're an inspiration, Kimiko."

"Well, *you're* certainly not. You're just a big distraction. I never get any work done when you're around.... Like this press release, for example. Todd, what can I possibly say about Randall's watercolors that hasn't already been said a hundred times before?"

Todd grinned. "Say that they're robust, but mischievous."

Kim laughed, then sobered and rolled over to study her half-written newspaper copy. "Do *you* like his watercolors?"

"They're okay," Todd said, frowning at the sketch pad again.

"Good." Kim began writing busily. "Then I'll say that the show is highly recommended by a local artist with an international reputation."

"You media people," Todd said, reaching over to pat her behind. "You're all the same."

"Keep your hands off me," Kim warned, "unless you mean business."

Todd chuckled. "Have you talked to Julia lately?"

"I called her last night. She's so excited about Roberto coming here, she's barely coherent.... You know what she's worried about now?"

"What?" Todd asked.

"She's afraid that something will happen to her before he gets here. She's actually reluctant to leave the house for fear of being run over by a bus, or getting in some kind of terrible accident. I'm a little worried about how intense she is, Todd."

"I know. Maybe you should see if you can talk her into going out to a movie, or something, Kim. She really loves you."

"But she won't even come down to the studio anymore. I'd have to go to your grandmother's house."

"What's wrong with that? I'd love to have you visit at my grandmother's house."

"Todd, the woman hates me. You know she does. The few times I've seen her, the atmosphere was chilly enough to make icicles in my hair."

Todd sighed, acknowledging the truth of this statement. "Nana can be so obstinate and narrow-minded, and it's not just because of her age. After all, *your* grandmother isn't like that."

"But," Kim said, looking at the river with a troubled frown, "she's not exactly warm toward you, is she? My grandmother, I mean."

"No," Todd admitted. "You couldn't say that she was warm."

"My grandmother's been acting strange lately," Kim said, still gazing at the sparkling water.

"Strange? How?"

"I don't know. Like she's got something up her sleeve but she won't talk about it. There's something really ominous about her attitude these days. She makes me nervous."

"Mine, too," Todd said in surprise. "You know, Nana seems exactly the same."

Kim rolled her head to look at him. "Todd, do you think there's something going on? Do you think they're... conspiring against us?"

"Our *grandmothers?*" he asked in disbelief. "That's the craziest idea I ever heard. You're getting as paranoid as Julia. I can hardly imagine our grandmothers existing on the same planet, let alone getting together to hatch a plot."

"Neither of them is very happy about us."

"I know, but they can't hurt us, sweetheart. The rest of your family is really supportive. They all just want you to be happy. And as for Nana, well, she's so busy getting ready for my mother's visit that she's not even paying any attention to me."

"Is your mother really coming this time?"

"I guess so," Todd said, his mood darkening. "Apparently, she and her friend are supposed to be here for Thanksgiving. They're driving up through Nevada, but my mother probably won't get past Reno. She loves to gamble."

"So she's traveling with her boyfriend and gambling with her husband's money?"

"She's just a real sweetheart, Kim. A lovely little rocking-chair and apple-pie kind of mom."

"You sound so bitter," Kim said, looking at him inquiringly.

"Bitter?" he said, keeping his voice deliberately light. "Do I sound bitter? Actually, the whole topic is just really boring. I got over being bitter a long time ago."

"I wonder."

"What do you wonder?"

"If you ever got over it. I wonder if all those harsh feelings aren't still churning around inside you, making you unhappy and suspicious of women in general."

"Don't keep trying to analyze me, Kim," he said tightly. "Okay? Just leave it alone. I don't want to discuss my mother, or how she's affected me, or whether her neglect has scarred me for life, like all those people on damned television talk shows."

"All right, Todd," she said quietly. "We won't talk about it."

Todd gave her a quick glance but she didn't seem upset by his sharpness. She was lying with her chin on her hands, watching a young couple wheel a baby stroller through the park.

As the group came nearer, Todd could see the baby, dressed all in white and propped up against a nest of pillows, waving a rattle with great energy. The child was blond, like her young parents, with pink cheeks and laughing blue eyes.

Kim smiled at the couple as they passed, then turned to watch them trundle up the leafy path. Todd returned to a thoughtful examination of the sketch on his knee, reaching out automatically to stroke the sweet curve of Kim's hip and thigh under the faded denim jeans.

"Todd . . ."

"Hmm?" He erased the Cheyenne maiden's face and started again, trying to make her less like Kim.

"Todd, what would our baby look like, do you think?"

His mouth went suddenly dry. "Baby? What baby?" he asked, looking at her.

Kim rolled onto her back and shaded her eyes. "If we had a baby," she said, "what do you think it would look like?"

"I guess," he said, going back to his drawing, "it would look like us."

"I know *that*. But would it look blue-eyed and Scottish like you, or more Japanese?"

Todd pondered. "According to Mendel's laws of heredity, our offspring would look more Japanese. At least for the first generation."

She studied his face with interest. "They would? Why is that?"

"Because darker genes are dominant. Your parents are both pure Japanese, aren't they? There's no Caucasian blood on either side?"

Kim shook her head. "Not a drop."

"Then you don't carry any recessive genes for blue eyes or blond hair, so our child probably wouldn't have those characteristics. He'd look more like you. But he'd still inherit the recessive genes from me, and could pass those characteristics to his children if he married someone who also had that background."

Kim looked pensively in the direction the young couple had disappeared with their baby. "Wouldn't he look like you at all?"

"Sure he would. After all, he'd be half-Caucasian, as well as half-Japanese. His coloring would be a little fairer than yours, and he'd likely have a different body shape. Usually," Todd added, "Eurasian children are really attractive. Caucasian and Japanese seems to be a terrific genetic combination."

"I know," Kim said with a faraway look. "I often think about it. Just wondering," she added hastily. "About what our baby would be like, I mean."

"Kim..." Todd gave her a cautious glance. "Why would we have a baby?"

"Well, it's been known to happen," Kim said dryly. "Especially if two healthy adults sleep together on a fairly regular basis."

He felt another jolt of fear, and shifted awkwardly on the blanket. "Kim, you haven't...you're still taking the pills, aren't you?"

"Yes," she said impatiently. "I'm still taking my pills."

"And you wouldn't stop taking them without telling me?"

"What kind of person do you think I am?" she asked with a sudden edge to her voice. "Do you think I want to trap you into marriage, or something? Don't flatter yourself, Todd."

"That's not what I mean," he said, alarmed by her anger. "I just think...I guess you'd probably like to have a baby sometime."

"I'm thirty-three years old, you know. If I'm going to do it, I should be getting around to it before too many years go by."

Todd looked down at her beautiful face, feeling a rising tide of panic. "Kim," he began slowly, "I've told you that I don't want children."

"Never?"

"Never. We've had this discussion before."

"I know, but I thought perhaps you weren't ready for the responsibility at this point. I didn't think you meant *never*."

"Well, I did. I'm just not cut out for parenthood, Kim."

"Why not?"

Todd shrugged. "Because I'm not, that's all. I don't think I'd be a good father. And I sure don't want to bring some poor kid into the world as an experiment to see if I'm right."

"But don't you think you'd love your baby once it was here?"

"I don't know. Everybody thinks that's the solution, don't they? Just have the baby, and the parenting instincts will automatically follow. But I'm living proof that it's not always true."

"What do you mean?"

"I don't know who my father is, Kim. My mother didn't know, so she couldn't tell me. Can you even begin to imagine what that's like? And she had no feelings for me at all when I was born, and never developed them."

"No feelings? None at all?" Kim asked, looking skeptical. "I really can't believe that, Todd."

"That's because you've never had the dubious pleasure of meeting my mother."

"So, do you think you shouldn't have been born?"

"That's impossible to answer. I just know that some people aren't equipped to be parents. There's some vital ingredient that's missing from their emotional makeup, and it can't be manufactured or imitated. I believe I'm one of those people."

"You know what I think, Todd?" she said at last. "I believe you're completely wrong about yourself. You're a loving, happy, warmhearted person. You're pretty much like a kid yourself, most of the time. I think you'd be a wonderful father."

Again he felt that cold twist of panic. "You think so? If that's true, why do I have such a different opinion?"

"Because you were so terribly hurt by the way your mother treated you when you were a small child. Your own feelings of abandonment made you afraid of love and commitment, for fear you'd just wind up being abandoned all over again. But, Todd, at some point, you really have to—"

"Stop it!" he snapped, unable to bear any more. "I've told you before, quit analyzing me! Just leave it alone."

"All right," she said quietly. Todd wished he hadn't been so short with her. He reached out and unfastened her ponytail, letting the long hair fall around her body in a shining curtain. Tossing his sketch pad aside, he moved closer and drew her into his arms, kissing her face and neck while his hands roamed over her body.

"Todd," she protested, pulling away. "Todd, not *here.*"

He could hardly hear her voice. All his feelings of fear and tension suddenly melted away in a hot surge of sexual need. He continued to caress her, his hands molding automatically to the sweet curve of her breasts, his tongue dipping into the fragrant hollow of her throat as if he were tasting the sweetness of a flower.

"Kim," he whispered in despair. "Oh, God, how can I ever get enough of you, sweetheart? I want you all the time."

But there was a chill in her manner, and suddenly she sat up and gathered her hair back into its usual ponytail, avoiding his eyes. "Let's go home," she suggested. "It's getting cold."

"Home?"

"Let's go over to your apartment. Have you got something to eat?"

Feeling numb and sick with frustrated desire, he got to his feet obediently, watching as she folded the blanket and gathered up their working supplies.

They walked across the grass to his truck in awkward silence while the park's antique carousel spilled its bright music into the afternoon stillness. But despite his pounding sexual need, Todd heard the tinkling carousel and the merry laughter of the children, and felt as though he were being taunted.

MASAKO SAT by the darkened window in a pool of lamplight, stitching quietly at her scroll. She was working on a strutting peacock, outlining the tail with a frost of iridescent green while her granddaughter sat on the stool and watched.

"I don't know how you make all those tiny stitches, Grandmother," Kim said. "It doesn't seem humanly possible for anyone to work with that kind of precision."

"All kinds of things are humanly possible," Masako said dryly. "Some much more amazing than simple embroidery, my dear."

"I suppose you're right. I feel the same way," Kim added, "when I watch Todd working on his painting. I've never seen anyone who can bring things to life so vividly. He has a wonderful talent."

Masako's eyes flashed briefly when Kim praised her lover, but she didn't say anything.

Kim glanced at the old lady curiously, wondering what was happening behind that impassive face. She'd noted this unusual self-discipline in her grandmother a number of times during recent weeks. In fact, it was part of the puzzling behavior she'd reported to Todd. Masako no longer criticized Kim's choice, or made dry sarcastic comments about him. She was either silent when Kim spoke of Todd, or gently supportive and interested.

Kim found her grandmother's attitude unsettling. She would have liked a more direct approach, something she could deal with openly. There were times when she even longed for Masako to say harsh things about Todd the way she used to so Kim could defend him. But Madame Tanaka's impassive silence continued, and the new undercurrents in their relationship were beginning to unnerve Kim.

"Todd and I spent the afternoon in the park today," Kim volunteered, getting up and wandering across the room to study her reflection in the mirror. It was past ten o'clock, almost bedtime, and she wore a pair of pale blue silk pajamas and embroidered slippers.

Todd would love these pajamas, Kim thought wistfully, yearning for him with sudden fierceness. In her loneliness, she forgot how hurt she'd been that afternoon, and how troubled she was beginning to feel at Todd's stubborn reluctance to make any kind of serious emotional commitment.

All she could think of was how much she missed him. If they were together, surely he'd realize that he could trust her, and that children were a joy, not a burden.

It would be so wonderful to be with him all the time. Kim wanted to build a life with him, go to bed with him at night and wake up in his arms every morning. If only...

"That's nice," Masako said. "The autumn is a lovely time, *n'est-ce pas?*"

"Hmm?" Kim asked, still gazing absently into the mirror, consumed with stormy passion and a vision of herself and Todd sharing a home, enjoying all the simple pleasures of life together. "Oh, the park," she added, turning and padding back toward her grandmother. "Yes, it was really beautiful."

"Where did you have dinner?"

"At Todd's place." Kim perched on the stool again and picked up a spool of orange embroidery silk. "We made a mushroom omelet and bought a loaf of onion bread."

"What's his apartment like?" Masako asked with calm interest.

Kim cast her a suspicious glance but the old lady was stitching diligently.

"Well," Kim said after a brief hesitation, "it's certainly not the most comfortable place in the world. He uses it mainly for sleeping and storing his art supplies. The poor man has hardly any furniture," she went on, warming to her topic as she always did when she spoke of Todd. "And he has no plants or pictures on the walls, or anything. But he *did* go out and buy—"

She stopped herself in time and looked down at her hands in confusion, her cheeks turning warm. She'd been about to tell her grandmother that Todd had recently purchased a huge four-poster bed with a solid oak headboard, lavishly equipped with the finest sheets and feather duvet.

"Because I'm sleeping with a princess," he'd told her solemnly. "And princesses should always sleep in beautiful beds."

"Yes?" Masako prompted, giving her a bright glance. "What did he buy, Kimiko?"

"He..." Kim floundered awkwardly. Masako had an uncanny ability to tell what Kim was thinking, no matter how hard she tried to keep things secret.

"He bought a set of dishes for the kitchen," she said with sudden inspiration, then smiled when she recalled Todd's boyish pride in his new domesticity. "I think he's getting a lot more settled these days, Grandmother."

"That's good. Perhaps soon, he'll decide to stop all his wandering and settle down to raise a family," Masako said, her eyes fixed on the work in her hands.

Kim shot her another quick glance, but again the old lady appeared to be serenely unaware of her granddaughter's suspicions.

"Won't he?" Masako snipped the thread with her silver scissors and reached for the spool of orange silk in Kim's hands.

"Want to raise a family? I don't know."

"I'm sure he will," Masako said calmly. "Any man who is responsible and worthwhile yearns to have children. Both your father and your brother were overjoyed when their babies were born."

Kim looked wistfully at her grandmother, wondering if Masako's words were true. Would Todd be delighted with the idea of fatherhood once he was presented with the reality of it? Surely he wouldn't keep being unreasonable forever, and continue to oppose any suggestion of having children.

Because if he did...

"Perhaps if he feels strongly about it, you'll love him enough to sacrifice the idea of having children," Masako suggested, her face still impassive as she threaded the needle. "After all, there is more to life than the bearing and rearing of children."

"Grandmother, are you trying to make trouble between Todd and me by pointing out all these conflicts?"

Masako gazed at the younger woman in surprise, her face a mask of innocence. "Trouble?" she echoed. "My darling, I'm merely chatting. If there's some kind of conflict, it exists in your mind, I'm afraid. I have no desire to come between you and this man. I can see how much you love him."

"Good," Kim said. "Because your opposition isn't going to accomplish anything. Nothing at all. Everybody else approves of the relationship, you know. In fact, Dad and Mom are very supportive. They really like Todd."

"I know they do," Masako said in a soothing voice, pausing in her work to stroke Kim's head with a tender hand. "He's a very personable young man. By the way, how does his mother feel about all this?" she added in the same mild tone. "Is she equally support-ive?"

"His mother?" Kim asked. "What about his mother?"

"She's coming to visit soon, *n'est-ce pas?* I won-dered if you've spoken to her on the phone, or possi-bly corresponded with her since you and Todd began this ... relationship."

Kim looked at the serene face above her. "Grand-mother, how did you know that his mother's coming to visit?"

"Why, you mentioned it to me, dear. How else would I know?"

Kim nodded slowly, still puzzled. She couldn't re-call saying anything to Masako about Lillian Mc-Allister's visit. She must have mentioned it without being aware of doing so. After all, it was certainly on her mind a lot of the time.

Kim was apprehensive about the arrival of Todd's mother, without even knowing exactly what she feared. Maybe his tension was beginning to infect her.

"So, what's happening with Julia and her child?" Masako asked, changing the subject.

"Apparently everything's going really well. They hope to get him here in December, just before Christ-mas." Kim smiled with relief, her mood lifting as she thought about Julia's little boy.

"That's good news. It's very nice of Mrs. Mc-Allister," Masako added neutrally, "to be doing all this for her housemaid. It seems rather out of char-acter, perhaps?"

"How do you know? You've never met Todd's grandmother."

Masako looked up briefly. "I'm merely making an observation. I suppose Julia is very happy?"

"Ecstatic. She can hardly contain herself. I've never known anyone to be so radiantly happy about anything."

"Motherhood is an instinct of awesome strength. One day, my sweet, you will experience it for yourself," Masako observed, stitching at her scroll. "Perhaps," she added softly.

Kim tensed again, wondering what the old lady was up to.

But Madame Tanaka's face remained calm and remote, her smile placid.

"Tell me what you're working on at your studio," she asked.

Kim nestled closer and leaned against her grandmother's knee, talking quietly about the new series of watercolors she was doing, while the darkness gathered and the night wind began to sigh through the courtyard.

CHAPTER TEN

THE GLOWING WARMTH of October drifted into a golden-bronze November. The breeze freshened, and the mornings were silvered with frost. Julia made a fire in the living room on cool evenings and the dogs spent hours in their baskets, muzzles resting on folded paws, long ears drooping over the bright tartan.

Even Hugo was getting more placid now, able to rest quietly in his basket when commanded, though he still chewed up slippers and hid partly eaten bones in unlikely places around the house.

Barbara sat in the velvet wing chair by the hearth, watching as a cold autumn rain slashed against the windows. She smiled at her two sleeping dogs while Julia moved around the dining table with her usual quiet efficiency.

"Is everything all right out there?" Barbara asked, glancing over her shoulder at Julia.

"Yes, ma'am. I'm almost ready to mash the potatoes."

Barbara nodded in satisfaction. Julia was roasting a Thanksgiving turkey, and the smell of sage stuffing drifted through the house in appetizing waves.

"Don't mash the potatoes until my daughter arrives, Julia," she said. "Just leave them simmering in the hot water. They're nicest when they're freshly mashed.''

''Yes, ma'am.''

''Did you put the wine out?''

''An hour ago.''

''Good. It's supposed to be served at room temperature. Open one of the bottles now, would you, Julia? We'll let it breathe for a while. You can bring in a tray with some of the small crystal goblets as soon as our guests arrive.''

''Yes, ma'am.''

''Julia...''

The woman paused by the door and gave her employer a sparkling glance.

Barbara smiled back at her. ''I was just thinking that we have a great deal to be thankful for, don't we, Julia? The holiday seems to have a particular significance this year.''

''I wonder if he'll really be here in time for Christmas,'' Julia murmured. ''It seems too good to be true, Mrs. McAllister. I keep waiting for something awful to happen.''

''Nothing is going to happen,'' Barbara said firmly. ''Although we can't be sure about Christmas, you know. Government moves very slowly, Julia. In fact,'' she added, making a wry face, ''the word *move* is hardly accurate. Unless you're talking about moving backward.''

Julia sighed. ''Yes, ma'am.''

Barbara glanced at her watch. "That turkey should come out soon, shouldn't it? Do you need help with anything?"

Julia shook her head and vanished, leaving Barbara gazing at the empty doorway with an absent smile. She thought about the masses of paperwork that had already been filed, and the solemn little dark-eyed boy in Julia's photograph album.

Barbara didn't even like to admit to herself how much she looked forward to having a child in the house again. It had been so long since boyish laughter had echoed through this house, and toys littered the upstairs hallway.

Her smile faded when she thought about Todd, who was such a worry to her these days. If he insisted on continuing his unsuitable relationship with the Japanese girl, Barbara was going to lose him. The prospect of that was almost more than she could bear.

Her thoughts were interrupted by the opening of the front door and a rainy gust of wind that swirled into the foyer.

"Hi, Nana," a voice called. "Something sure smells good in here."

Both dogs pricked up their ears and looked at the entryway. Barbara watched while Todd hung his jacket in the hall closet, then strolled into the parlor and dropped a kiss on her cheek.

The room came alive when he entered, Barbara thought fondly.

Todd spread sunshine wherever he went. She smiled at him, loving the sturdy masculine look of her grandson, his lithe powerful walk, the sunny gold of his hair and the way the firelight glimmered on his hard cheeks when he settled in the opposite chair and leaned forward to pat the dogs.

"I knew you'd come," she told him.

"I didn't want to disappoint you, Nana. That's the only reason I'm here."

Barbara refrained from arguing, though she'd always suspected that Todd's feelings about his mother were more complicated than he let on.

He claimed to despise the woman and regard her as being of absolutely no consequence, but he couldn't seem to resist dropping in when Lillian came to visit. Even though he was usually badly disappointed by his mother's behavior, it was as if he never quite lost hope that when he saw her, she would be different.

In fact, Todd always seemed, at some deep level, to cherish a wistful dream that one day Lillian would really look at him, reach out to her son with love and understanding and give him some of the maternal tenderness he'd always craved and never received from anyone but his grandmother.

Barbara knew, with sorrow, that Todd was doomed to disappointment. She couldn't stop loving her daughter, but the years had made Barbara realistic. She understood from a lifetime of observation that people didn't change very much.

In many ways, Lillian McAllister was essentially the same person at fifty that she'd been at five. Barbara was saddened by this knowledge, partly for her daughter's sake, but mostly for Todd's.

Still, she didn't intend to protect her beloved
grandson from disappointment in his mother. Not tonight, at least.

In earlier years, Barbara had done her best to soften
the hurt Lillian inflicted on the boy with her carelessness and self-absorption. But now, a little pain was
just what Todd needed, in Barbara's opinion. A little
pain tonight could prevent him from making a life-
long mistake. It was worth the cost, she thought, her
resolve strengthening.

Her face was tranquil and composed when she
smiled at him.

"Julia says the meal is almost ready. I hope for her
sake that Lillian's not late, as usual. I'm afraid your
mother is entirely capable of stopping at some hamburger place and eating before she gets here, if she's
too hungry to wait."

Todd's face tightened. "I know she is. She's the
most inconsiderate person in the world. God, I
shouldn't even be here," he added restlessly, stroking
Homer's back absently. "I should leave right now,
Nana, before they come. She's just going to make me
crazy like she always does."

"You've always had so little faith in people," Barbara observed, though privately she agreed with him.
"I thought your attitude might be changing. Especially now," she added, keeping her face carefully expressionless.

"Now? What do you mean?"

Barbara got up and walked gracefully across the
room to prod the bright flames on the hearth, her silk

dress whispering as she moved. "You've fallen in love," she said. "I thought maybe you were beginning to trust women a little more."

"How I feel about Kim," Todd said, watching as his grandmother set a fresh log on the grate, "doesn't mean I've changed my feelings about my mother."

"Why not? All women are much the same, after all." Barbara closed the glass doors on the fireplace, adjusted the damper and returned to her chair.

Todd stared at her in disbelief. "*All* women?" he asked. "Nana, that's such a ridiculous, empirical statement. I couldn't imagine two women more different than Kim and my mother. Or you and my mother, for that matter."

The words were hardly out of his mouth when Todd realized he'd berated his grandmother for simply repeating what he himself had always said. How many times had he shied away from a relationship before he could be hurt, believing that in the end, no woman could be trusted? So when had he changed his mind?

Barbara saw her grandson's confusion. But she had her own agenda. "Perhaps, we're not exactly the same, but most women want to look after themselves. We're like these fellows here," she added, smiling at the sleeping dogs in their padded baskets. "We're looking for a warm hearth and a secure household, and we'll do what we have to in order to get them, regardless of how unscrupulous it might be."

"Even you, Nana?"

"Even me," Barbara agreed. "I think men have to be really careful, because a woman may present one image of herself in order to get what she wants, then show quite a different side when she's got her man safely hooked."

She felt guilty about telling such a bald-faced lie, and playing so cruelly on Todd's deep-seated fears and anxieties. It seemed a brutal thing to do to the person she loved best on earth, but Barbara truly believed it was for his own good.

Even Kim Tanaka's grandmother, who had impressed Barbara more than she cared to admit... even that formidable lady had agreed that this was the wisest course of action, and the surest way of keeping the two young people apart.

"So what are you saying, Nana?" Todd asked, interrupting her guilty thoughts. "You're telling me that Kim isn't a strong, independent, honest woman at all? She's just another manipulative selfish person like my mother, pretending to be something that she isn't in order to catch me?"

Barbara shrugged. "I'm not saying anything. Your Kim might be a perfectly wonderful person. I wouldn't know. But you—"

"Well, you'd have a lot better idea," Todd interrupted with some heat, "if you'd ever let yourself get to know her, Nana. I don't see how you can make all these judgments without even spending time with her."

"Perhaps I know more than you realize," Barbara told him sharply. "And I'm not passing judgment on her. I'm just suggesting that you take a good look at your mother tonight, Todd, and think carefully about what you see."

Todd opened his mouth to protest but was interrupted by the jangling of the telephone.

He and Barbara turned to each other with something close to panic. At last Barbara sighed and got up to answer the phone. Todd looked at her face when she came back in, and understood immediately. "She's not coming," he said flatly.

Barbara sank into the chair, looking disappointed and old. "She says the weather's too bad. It's been snowing in the mountain passes, so they decided not to risk the drive to Reno."

Todd stared at his grandmother in disbelief. "You mean she's still in California, Nana?"

Barbara nodded miserably.

"God," he muttered, so disgusted that he could barely speak. "Three or four days' drive from here, and she doesn't bother to call until now."

"They thought until this morning that they might fly out, but it's Thanksgiving weekend. There are no flights available."

"Of course there aren't. So why didn't she call earlier?"

"She's just unreliable, Todd," Barbara said wearily, beginning to recover her composure. "She always has been. She's not likely to change now."

Todd clenched his hands into fists, pounding the arm of his chair. "But how can she keep hurting people like this? She's done it to me all my life. How can she keep getting away with it?"

"How can she be stopped? Do you think if there had been some way to change her, I wouldn't have tried it while she was growing up?"

He got up and moved restlessly around the room. Hugo lifted his head, whimpering, obviously aware of the tension in the room. Todd stooped to fondle the dog's ears while Julia appeared in the doorway, looking at them inquiringly.

"It seems there's been a change in plans," Barbara told her. "My daughter and her friend won't be coming for dinner, after all. It will just be Todd and me. I'm very sorry, Julia," she added gently. "I know how hard you've worked on this meal."

Julia looked with sympathy at Todd's angry face, then turned away quickly. "It's all right," she said in her soft voice. "It's always a pleasure to make a nice meal for the two of you. Shall I serve it now?"

"If you don't mind, Julia," Barbara said. "I'm sure Todd's hungry, aren't you, dear?"

Todd leaned against the mantel in silence, staring at the fire and thinking about the afternoon in the park with Kim, when he'd told her he didn't ever want to have children.

He'd been right. No child should have to suffer the kind of coldness and rejection that he'd known since babyhood. What did he know of parenting, except how to cause hurt?

"Todd?" Barbara asked. "Are you ready for dinner?"

He squared his shoulders, then looked up at the two women and tried to smile.

"Sure," he said. "Bring it on, Julia. I'm starved, and that turkey smells delicious."

JULIA ARRANGED the china carefully in the dishwasher, listening to the halting conversation from the living room.

She washed the silverware and the crystal and put them away, frowning as she closed the cupboard doors, wondering how people could be so different. Lillian McAllister had a fine son who'd hungered for her affection all his life, and she couldn't give him anything. Julia, on the other hand, had a son she adored, and a heart so full of love for him that she felt she would die if she couldn't hold him soon.

If Roberto were close to her, he wouldn't be looking angry and disappointed like Todd McAllister. Julia would give him so much love...

She sighed and took a last look around the tidy kitchen, then paused in the living-room archway. "Anything else, ma'am?"

Barbara, who was sitting with her needlework in the velvet wing chair, turned with a smile. "No, thank you, Julia. The meal was delicious."

"Perfect, as usual," Todd agreed, with a ghost of his old sparkle.

"Thank you. I'll be in my room, then, if you need me," Julia said.

She walked softly down the hall to her room, slipping inside and closing the door with relief. But the silence was soon oppressive, and the rain, slashing against the window, seemed to emphasize her loneliness. She turned the small television set on and went into the adjoining bathroom to wash her hands and face, staring with unseeing eyes at her reflection in the mirror.

Suddenly, a voice from the television penetrated her consciousness. She paused, her hands wrapped in a towel, and hurried back into her bedroom, then stood transfixed by the bright flickering images on the screen.

"The Philippines is a cluster of large and small islands," the announcer was saying, "altogether about the size of Arizona. But these rugged islands are home to almost fifty million people."

Julia swallowed painfully, practically drowning in homesickness as a collage of familiar landscapes played across the screen—tilled rice fields, lush rain forests and surf pounding the rocky coastline.

"There are at least fifty volcanoes in the Philippine archipelago," the announcer went on, "and ten of them are known to be active. This latest eruption is just one in a series of catastrophic natural disasters for the people of this small island nation."

Julia put her hand over her mouth, watching in horror as the newscast relayed scenes of devastation, of fleeing villagers and burning forests and ruined homes. She shivered and wrung the towel in her hands, remembering the time in her girlhood when a volcanic eruption had brushed close to their village. There was nothing on earth to compare with that horror. She could still feel the searing heat, the gritty ashes in her hair and clothes, the creeping fingers of lava that glowed orange in the night, whispering through the darkness toward their home like some malignant giant bent on destruction.

And the confusion, she thought with a little moan of sympathy as she watched the people running, clutching their clothes and their children, and whatever possessions they could carry in their haste to flee the flames and mud slides.

As Julia watched, an old woman carrying a ragged bundle and two chickens stumbled and was almost trampled beneath a cart.

"Believe it or not, the people you see on your television screen are the lucky ones," the announcer said, his voice heavy with professional sadness. "At the village, in the direct path of the lava flow, no survivors have been found. The devastation is unbelievable, and many thousands are feared dead. All that's left standing is the stone church on the edge of town, somehow spared when the lava overflowed the mountainside."

Julia gasped and swayed on her feet. She crumpled to the floor and huddled there, staring at the blackened stone building on the television screen.

Julia knew that church. She'd been baptized there, and so had Roberto. All the family weddings had taken place in that church, and the funerals, as well. The destroyed village was the place where she'd grown up, the town where her family still lived.

The town where Roberto lived, and played with his red ball....

THE NEXT DAY, early in the afternoon, Kim drove over to Barbara McAllister's house and rang the doorbell, then stood waiting tensely on the doorstep, shivering as she looked around at the barren yard. Overnight the temperature had plummeted, and the driving rain had changed to snow. Drifts lay across the empty flower beds and piled around the sides of the house, sculpted into ridges and channels by the bitter wind.

Todd came to the door and Kim looked up at him with silent appeal.

"How is she?" she said softly.

"About the same. Come in, Kim."

Kim followed him into the house and down the hall to the kitchen. Julia and Barbara were both there, sitting at the table with cups of tea in front of them.

"Oh, Julia," Kim whispered when she saw the woman's ravaged face. "I'm so sorry."

She sank into the chair next to Julia. Barbara watched in silence as Kim drew Julia into her arms and held her close, patting her back gently.

"Have you heard anything else?" Kim asked, looking over Julia's dark head at Todd. He stood by the counter, making a fresh pot of tea. He gave a warning shake of his head and touched his finger to his lips. Kim nodded and looked down at Julia, who was whispering something.

"Julia, what did you say? I didn't hear you, dear."

"I kept telling you I was so afraid that something might happen to me before he came. I never thought...I never thought of something happening to *him,"* Julia said brokenly, holding a tissue to her swollen eyes.

"But we don't know for sure that anything's happened to him," Barbara said firmly. "Do we, Kim?"

Kim looked up at the older woman, startled to be addressed directly by Todd's grandmother. She shook her head. "No, we don't. Apparently, it's all a terribly confusing situation over there, Julia. Nobody knows anything for sure."

Again, Todd gave her a warning glance and carried the teapot to the table. He filled their cups and edged toward the other room, motioning for her to follow. Kim exchanged a brief glance with Barbara, then released Julia.

"You know, I think I left my keys in my car," she said. "I'll be right back, Julia."

She followed Todd down the hallway and into the living room, where the dogs lay placidly in their baskets by the hearth as if nothing had happened.

"Todd, what is it?" Kim whispered.

"We got a call this morning," Todd murmured. "About midnight Philippines time, I guess. Things are really crazy over there."

Kim tensed. "A call? Who was it?"

"Some kind of official. He said none of Julia's family were among the survivors."

"Oh, God..."

"But that doesn't definitely mean they're among the casualties, either, Kim. They're officially listed as missing."

"Does Julia know about the phone call?"

"We had to let her speak with him. His English wasn't all that good, and neither of us could understand him."

"How did she react?"

Todd shook his head. "She just seems sort of numb. She refuses to discuss the call, as if it never happened. That's why we phoned you, Kim. Nana's really worried about her. We thought maybe you could get her talking and ease some of the pressure."

"She's probably still in shock. Oh, Todd..." Kim moved close to him, clinging to him for comfort.

But as soon as his arms closed around her, Kim realized that something had happened since she'd seen him last, something beyond the trauma of Julia's loss. There was no warmth in his embrace, no comfort or intimacy in his body as he held her. They might have been a pair of strangers holding each other for security during a crisis.

Kim remembered that Todd's mother was supposed to have come yesterday for Thanksgiving, but there was no sign of the woman here at Barbara's house. She drew away, suddenly chilled, and looked up at him.

Todd's face was still, his eyes remote and guarded. The engaging cowboy who'd loved her with such abandon seemed to have vanished. And this man, the one who held her, was almost a stranger.

Kim pulled away from him and moved toward the door.

"I'll go and sit with her for a while," she said. "Your grandmother could probably use some rest."

"That's good," Todd said quietly. "Thanks, Kim."

She looked at him a moment longer, then nodded and went into the kitchen.

JULIA WATCHED the moonlight on the snow, standing by her window and staring with haunted eyes at its glowing silver brightness. Several days had passed since the devastating volcano. She wondered if the same moon shone on her ravaged village, and if somewhere Roberto was looking at it just as she was now.

Of course not, she thought mechanically. It's daytime at home. He's playing somewhere, bouncing his new red ball....

She clung fiercely to the image of Roberto playing with his ball. It was necessary to hold this picture in her mind and never let it go. Otherwise, her grief would carry her down into madness.

Since that one brief phone call the day after the disaster—the call she refused to think about—Julia had learned nothing about her family's situation. There was a great deal of news from the stricken country, including the rising death toll and the terrible devastation. New villages were threatened almost daily by the creeping lava flow.

But there was no word for Julia, who was just one of many thousands affected by the tragedy. For the first few days, she'd waited in terror, feeling cold and sick every time the phone rang. But the long hours had passed with no new information.

Julia knew that Barbara and Todd and Kim all believed the worst. She was sure they thought that if any of her family had survived, someone would have contacted her by now to assure her of their safety, and that the continuing silence meant all of them had perished in the first eruption.

Julia, though, held stubbornly to the opposite belief. If all her family had been lost, there would be official word by now. The silence proved to her that somehow, miraculously, they had survived and weren't counted among the dead.

She couldn't imagine Roberto lost and dying in terror while his mother lived in this comfortable place halfway around the world. It was unthinkable, so Julia simply refused to entertain the thought. She believed that he was safe, and soon she would be contacted.

All she could do was wait.

Finally, Julia turned away from the window. She climbed into her bed and lay staring at the ceiling, longing for sleep that never seemed to come, no matter how exhausted she was. Briefly, she found herself wishing Hugo were still a puppy, wriggling and whimpering in her bed. At least then, she would have something to hold.

Her arms felt so terribly empty. . . .

"Roberto," she whispered aloud to the fading moonlight, her face streaked with tears. "Oh, my darling. My little darling."

She sobbed harshly, then caught herself and lay in rigid silence, waiting with all of her being for the phone call that never came.

CHAPTER ELEVEN

TODD STOOD by the window of the studio, looking down at the street where Christmas decorations glittered on lampposts and in storefronts. Since the storm on Thanksgiving weekend, a dusting of snow had remained on the ground, making the candy canes and silver bells look less incongruous than they had two weeks ago when they were first put up.

It still didn't feel much like Christmas, but Todd knew that the lack of holiday cheer was more in his mind than in the scene beyond the windows. He wandered back to his easel and picked up a brush, squinting critically at the huge canvas.

The second painting in the series was virtually complete, depicting the Cheyenne family on their way to their summer camp. Todd had grown so attached to these people over the past couple of months that he almost regretted having to finish the painting and let them go.

He liked the dark, hawk-nosed father and his plump wife under her burden of cooking pots, the laughing children, the solemn uncle and the proud young daughter, who still looked a bit like Kim despite his best efforts to change that.

Todd swallowed hard at the sight of the girl's slim buckskin-clad body and beautiful face, and forced himself to concentrate on the rest of the painting.

All the detail was historically accurate and rendered with loving care, from the trailing neck ropes and painted brands on the ponies to the ragged dogs following the leather travois. He touched a glossy highlight to one of the dogs, then stood back and frowned, wondering if the foreground needed a little more attention.

The door opened behind him. Kim hurried in, laden with packages, her cheeks pink with cold. Todd's heart pounded with excitement as it always did at first sight of her, but he kept his face carefully noncommittal.

"Hi, sweetheart," he said. "Get all your shopping done?"

"Almost." She peeled off her coat and hung it on a peg by the door. "I know it's necessary, but I have absolutely no desire to do Christmas shopping right now. It's just such an effort. How's Julia today?" she asked, her voice softening with concern. "Have you spoken to your grandmother?"

"It's all pretty frustrating. The embassy's now saying that a few people survived from one of the villages in the path of the lava flow, but they can't verify that it was Julia's. The survivors were apparently taken to one of the temporary aid stations on the other side of the island, but nobody's been able to track any of them down."

"Oh, Todd..."

"Don't get excited. Tomorrow they'll announce that it was all a mistake and there were no survivors, after all. We've already been through this kind of thing three or four times. Meanwhile, the cycle of hope and disappointment is driving poor Julia out of her mind."

Kim poured boiling water onto the tea leaves and set the pot to steep. "Do you want some?" she asked over her shoulder.

"Sure," Todd said absently, still brooding over the foreground of his painting. "Thanks, Kim."

"With honey, or plain?"

"Better sweeten it a bit. I've been working for hours, and I think maybe I forgot to eat."

Kim frowned and poured tea into the cups. She stirred honey into Todd's and carried it over to him, then brought her own cup and sat on a tall stool near his easel.

"You know, I still can't believe it," she said slowly. "Julia had a little boy and never talked about him for all those months. How could she do that?"

Todd dabbed the brush in his palette and outlined some tall grass around a boulder. "She was afraid of Nana, mostly. I guess they really stressed at the immigration office that American employers wanted single women without dependents. Julia was convinced she'd lose her job if she confessed to having a little boy."

"Poor Julia. It must have been so hard and lonely for her." Kim stared moodily into the depths of her cup. "And now she doesn't even know if he's alive. I can hardly imagine how she must be suffering."

"'Hostages to fortune,'" Todd muttered, adding more grass to his painting.

Kim looked up at him, startled. "What did you say?"

"It's a quote from John Buchan," Todd said, turning briefly to look down at her. "'He who hath a wife and children hath given hostages to fortune.' Children make you so vulnerable."

"I guess they do. Is that why you don't ever want to have any, Todd?"

He tensed, recognizing that quiet tone in her voice. Since the onset of Julia's trouble, they'd tried to continue as if nothing had changed, but the relationship was under increasing strain and both of them were aware of it. Sooner or later, all the hidden emotions and conflicts would have to be brought out into the open.

"Yeah," he said, concentrating on the rough outlines of the boulder. "I guess that's why I don't want to have any."

"Don't you think that's a pretty cowardly attitude?"

"What's cowardly? Choosing not to suffer the way Julia's suffering right now? I think that's just simple intelligence."

Kim set her cup down on the table behind her stool and looked at him steadily. "Do you? Well, I don't think it has anything to do with intelligence, Todd. I think you had an unhappy childhood, so you don't believe there can be any other kind. You're terrified of intimacy and responsibility."

"I might not be crazy about responsibility," he said, "but you of all people should know that I'm not afraid of intimacy. After all, we've been pretty intimate a time or two, haven't we, Kim?"

"You know what I mean," she said, sipping her tea with a frown of impatience. "There's a whole part of you that never gets shown to anybody."

"And, being a woman, you want to haul all my secrets out into the light where they can be examined and analyzed, right?" His voice was still casual, but he felt growing tension.

"I don't think people should keep secrets when they love each other," Kim said quietly. "Is that so bad, Todd?"

"There's a difference between keeping secrets and being allowed a little privacy."

She watched him for a moment, her face unreadable. At last, she drew a deep breath and began to speak.

"Todd, I know how much you value your privacy and I've tried to respect it, but I can't leave this alone anymore. I can't face the prospect of a future on your terms. I love you, but I don't want to be a footloose wanderer with no encumbrances. I want a home and children."

Finally, after months of skirmishing, the challenge had been issued. The words hung between them, clear and irrevocable. Todd had no idea how to respond. All he knew was that losing this woman would be the most terrible thing he'd ever have to endure.

"Kim," he began helplessly, "you know I can't promise you anything like that. You were aware going into this that we had different views on things. Why can't we find some kind of compromise?"

"Like what?" she asked bitterly. "We'll have a dog instead of children? We'll have a home for part of the year, and you'll try not to be so frightened of stability if I'll try to be a little more of a vagabond? Come on, Todd. There's just no way it's ever going to work, and you know it."

The dark waters began to close over his head, and his breath caught painfully in his throat. Todd set the brush down carefully on the shelf of his easel and turned to look at her. "What are you saying, Kim?"

Her eyes were black and enormous, her face pale with emotion, but her voice was calm and tightly controlled. "I guess," she said quietly, "I'm saying goodbye, Todd. Let's part on friendly terms before one of us gets really hurt."

He laughed abruptly and walked over to look out the window, wiping his hands furiously on the paint rag. "Before one of us gets hurt," he said. "You mean you won't be hurt if we split up, Kim?"

"Of course I will," she said behind him. "But not as much as I'd get hurt if we keep on with this, and I let myself become more involved in something that was impossible right from the start. I can't go into a future that's based on lies and fear. Look, Todd—" she held out her hand, ticking items off on her fingers "—you don't want children, and I do. I love family life, and you want to live on the road. Your grandmother hates me because I'm Japanese, and my grandmother doesn't think you'd make a good husband. With all that against us, how can we possibly expect to be happy together, no matter how great we are in bed?"

His heart began to thud dully in his chest. "So, what are you saying? You really want me to leave?"

"No, of course I don't. I really want you to stay and live with me forever. But not if you're always going to be so afraid of commitment and responsibility. Not if you'll never trust any woman because your mother's hurt you so badly. Under those circumstances, I guess you're right. I want you to leave."

Todd stared at her beautiful remote face, wondering how he could reach her and draw her back to him. But he could tell that she'd been thinking about this for a long time, and the decision she'd reached went all the way into her soul.

He knew, as well, that he'd never loved her as much as he did at this moment.

He hesitated, struggling for a brief desperate moment to picture himself living the life she wanted. He thought of himself as a husband and father, paying a mortgage and taking kids to weekend soccer games.

Part of him clung wistfully to the vision, but he knew it was impossible.

"All right," he said at last, dipping the brush carefully in turpentine and cleaning it with a paint-stained rag. "If that's what you want, Kim, that's how it'll be. My agent will collect this canvas later in the week when it's dry, and I'll send someone over to get the rest of my stuff."

She nodded woodenly.

"Goodbye, Kim," he said, looking back at her as he moved to the door and put on his jacket.

She gave another jerky nod, then sat watching with fathomless dark eyes while he opened the door and stepped out into the musty hallway. Todd closed the studio door behind him and wandered down the stairs and into the windswept street with its garish Christmas decorations. He couldn't believe the final break had actually happened with so little warning. He kept expecting to hear her voice calling him back, but it didn't come.

At last, he plunged his hands into his pockets and trudged into the bitter wind, feeling more alone than he'd ever been in his life.

SEVERAL DAYS LATER, Julia was in the kitchen making Christmas fruitcakes from Barbara's old family recipe. Christmas was now only a few weeks away, and the fruitcakes had to be baked and wrapped in linen soaked with rum, stored away to mellow in the back of the pantry.

The big house was spicy with the fragrance of baking, with almonds and candied fruit, cinnamon and cloves. Julia threw herself into the task, mixing and chopping with fierce energy, trying to hold the dreadful thoughts at bay.

She wasn't even aware that the front doorbell had rung until she heard Barbara's voice out in the foyer, speaking to somebody, and then the muffled sound of footsteps approaching the kitchen. Julia straightened and looked up guiltily at the doorway, wiping her hands on her apron.

She should have heard the bell. It was her job to answer the door, not Barbara's. But her employer's face was gentle with sympathy when she appeared in the doorway.

"Julia?" Barbara asked quietly. "Can you spare a minute, my dear? There's somebody here to see you."

Wide-eyed and trembling with sudden fear, Julia stared at the older woman. "Yes," she whispered. "Yes, I'm ... I can spare some time."

Barbara nodded and stepped aside, gesturing to someone behind her before disappearing down the hallway. Julia watched the doorway, her terror deepening as a man appeared and stood looking at her.

But the man in the kitchen doorway wasn't a government official with bad news to tell. It was Todd, looking so quiet and concerned that tears formed in Julia's eyes again.

She brushed at her eyes and smiled mechanically. "Would you ... like some coffee, Todd?" she offered. "There's a fresh pot on the—"

"Julia, I came by to see how you're doing." He came into the room and paused at the table next to her. "Sit down, Julia, and visit with me for a minute," he said gently, holding out a chair, which she sank into gratefully.

"Have you heard any more news?" Todd asked.

"None." She gripped the dishcloth and began twisting it nervously in her hands. "I haven't heard anything."

"Julia, exactly what members of your family lived in that village, besides Roberto? Please try to talk about them. You might feel better if you told me."

"There's my mother," Julia whispered, "and...and my brother, Cesar, and his wife and two children. That's... all my family."

"And the man who called that first day...he didn't mention any of those people?"

She shook her head. "No," she whispered. "None of them."

"Julia, if one of those adult family members had survived, they would have called you by now. You know that," Todd said gently. "They'd have found a way to contact you, knowing how terribly you'd be suffering. I think if you'd accept it, you might feel able to start dealing with this."

Julia forced herself to look at him.

"I know what you're saying. I know," she muttered tonelessly, struggling to find the courage to say the words for the first time, "that my mother and brother probably didn't survive. I know what it's like when one of these disasters happens at home. All the houses are so...so flimsy, and they don't ever..."

Her voice broke and she fell silent. Todd moved close to her, and put his arms around her while she choked back her sobs.

"It's all right, Julia," he murmured. "It's all right to cry. You need to accept this and let yourself feel it. We'll help."

"You don't...you don't understand!" Julia turned away, still twisting the dishcloth in her hands. "You don't understand," she repeated. "There's something I haven't told anybody."

"Then tell me. You can trust us, Julia. We'll do anything we can to help you."

"I know you will," Julia said. She paused and took a deep, ragged breath. "Todd, Roberto is alive. I'm not sure about the others, but I *know* my little boy is not dead. He's all alone somewhere..."

She began to sob harshly. Todd held her, stroking her back with soothing motions as if she were a child. "Oh, Julia," he whispered. "My dear, I'm so sorry."

"But he's not dead!" she said a little wildly, pulling away and staring at the man next to her. "I tell you, Roberto's not dead. I know he's not!"

"How do you know, Julia?"

"Roberto is part of myself," Julia whispered hoarsely. "Even so far away, he's tied to me, like this." She held up the strings of her apron. "If Roberto were gone from the world," she concluded simply, "I would know."

Todd studied her face in grave silence, then nodded. "Maybe you're right," he said at last.

Julia felt a warm flood of gratitude. "You believe me," she said in wonder. "You understand."

"I think I do. God knows, I don't have much experience of the relationship between parents and children," he said with a sad attempt at a smile, "but I think I can understand the bond of love you're talking about."

"If Roberto were gone, I wouldn't feel this way," Julia repeated. "I can accept that perhaps my mother and brother are gone. It's a terrible thing to have to live with, Todd. But our people know that death is part of life, and after the grief, we can still go on living. I just can't accept," Julia concluded, "that Roberto is dead. If I believed that, my heart would die, too."

Todd watched her for a moment, searching for words. But he didn't argue with her. "Maybe you should go to the Philippines and make some inquiries," he said at last. "If the little boy survived and the adults didn't, would he be able to tell people where you are?"

Julia hugged her arms. "I don't know," she whispered. "I'm afraid to go there, Todd. I couldn't get anywhere close to where the village was. It's all destroyed."

"I know. But Julia—"

"Besides," she went on, "what if I leave, and then they try to call me and I'm not here? What if Roberto needs me and I'm in an airplane somewhere? What if he tells them his mother is in America and they bring him over here, and then I'm...I'm gone when he comes? He must be so afraid... Roberto is so little..."

Her words jumbled together and she began to cry again, big hot tears rolling silently down her cheeks.

Todd picked up the dishtowel and wiped her face, then squared his shoulders with determination.

"Julia," he said gently. "I think you're right. I think you should stay here and wait with people who care about you."

"But I have no one here."

"Yes, you do. My grandmother depends on you, Julia. She looks on you almost as a daughter, and you've got a much better relationship with her than her own daughter ever had. I know it's difficult, but I'm asking you to stay with her and be a friend to her. Can you do that, Julia?"

"What about you?" Julia asked. "Won't you be here?"

He shook his head. "I'm afraid not. I'm going away."

"Where . . . where are you going?"

"I'm leaving, Julia. Kim and I aren't getting along very well," he said quietly. "I'm not a good enough man for her. I think we both realize it. So it's time for me to leave."

"Where are you going?"

"Back to Hawaii. I plan to finish my last two paintings there. I really miss the tropics."

"Oh," Julia said. "But that's so sad! I can't believe that you and Kim—"

She saw the look on his face and stopped mid-sentence.

"When will you leave?"

"In a day or two. As soon as I can pack and get a flight. But I want you to know that my grandmother will keep calling the embassy and doing everything she can to get information about Roberto. And so will Kim. Everybody will keep trying every day until they've either located him or you tell them to stop. All right?"

"All right," Julia whispered in a shaky voice. "Thank you, Todd."

Julia could hardly understand all the things he said after that. She knew only that he was offering comfort and help, and that he was going to convince all of them that Roberto wasn't dead.

It was enough.

"WELL," Barbara said later that evening, glancing cautiously at her grandson who sprawled in the opposite chair with Hugo on his lap, "at least you got your second canvas finished before you...had to move from the studio."

"Yeah," Todd said without expression, idly lifting Hugo's ears like little flags and letting them drop. "That's great, Nana. Getting that painting done was the most important thing in my life."

Barbara was dismayed by the sarcasm in his voice. She'd never seen him like this, her happy-go-lucky golden boy. Even his mother's carelessness hadn't had this effect on him.

"How's...everything else?" Barbara asked gently, aching for him.

"Kim, you mean?" Todd looked up sharply. "You want to know how Kim is, Nana? Well, I wouldn't have the slightest idea. I haven't talked to her for days. She won't take my calls."

"Oh, Todd..." Barbara lifted her hands as if to reach out to him, then let them drop helplessly into her lap.

"I never knew what it was to miss somebody like this, Nana," he said, staring into the flames on the hearth and stroking Hugo perfunctorily. "Love 'em and leave 'em, that was the way I lived. Be careful not to get too serious, because you'll want out pretty soon. But this time..." He looked at her soberly. "This time I didn't want out. I love that woman. Life without her is a pure living hell. Every day, I feel like half my body's been torn away and I don't know where to find it. I can't imagine laughing or being happy again."

"Todd," Barbara said, terrified by the emptiness in his eyes and voice. "Todd, it really wasn't a suitable match at all, you know. I'm sure that in time you'll realize—"

"Not a suitable match!" He slammed his hand on the arm of the chair, suddenly furious. "For God's sake, Nana, what's so unsuitable about it? The fact that Kim is Japanese, and fifty years ago my grandfather fought against the Japanese?"

Barbara sat straighter in her chair. Two angry red spots began to burn on her cheeks, but she made no response.

"Well, let me tell you a little secret, Nana. This is really hilarious, you know that? *Kim's* grandfather fought against the Japanese, too! What do you think of that?"

Barbara stared at him, wondering if grief had driven him out of his mind.

"You don't believe me?" Todd got up, spilling Hugo from his lap and striding restlessly around the room. "Well, it's true. Yoshio Tanaka was a patriotic American. He was a Boy Scout and a Little League baseball player. He died in the Philippines, fighting for his country, and the American administration awarded him the Medal of Honor. Posthumously, of course. You weren't the only one who lost a husband to that war, Nana. Kim's grandmother lost hers, too."

Barbara twisted her hands together, thinking about the prim little lady in her back silk dress, sipping tea from Barbara's second-best cup.

"But why didn't you tell me . . ."

"Because it shouldn't make any difference!" Todd shouted at her. "It doesn't *matter* what side he fought on, Nana! It's all in the past."

Barbara stared at him, her mind whirling as she tried to absorb all this. "But," she began haltingly, "my . . . my feelings about all that . . . they weren't the major problem between you and Kim. Were they?"

"Oh, no, Nana. My differences with Kim go a lot deeper than your prejudice. All the way back to my crippled childhood and my mother's stubborn refusal to contemplate any way of life except the one she wanted. It's not your fault. None of it is your fault."

Remembering how she'd conspired with Masako Tanaka to play on Todd's worst doubts and fears, Barbara wasn't so sure.

"And this sudden decision to go back to Hawaii," she said. "Are you sure that's really wise? Perhaps if you were to..."

"I'm not going to Hawaii, Nana. At least not right away. I'm going to the Philippines."

"To the..."

"Don't let anybody know," Todd whispered, leaning forward and fixing her with an intent look. "Please, Nana, it's important not to let Julia know I'm over there. She's suffering so cruelly from false hope as it is. She'd only be more disappointed if she decided I'd be able to accomplish some kind of miracle."

"You don't really believe there's a chance of finding any of her family, do you?"

"Not a hope in hell. But I still want to go. I'll take copies of all those papers you filed in case I need to present some kind of documentation. And I want you to tell Julia and Kim and anybody who might ask that I've gone back to work in Hawaii for an indefinite period of time."

"How long will you be in the Philippines?"

"As long as it takes to get some kind of definite answers. In the meantime, Nana..."

"Yes?"

"I promised Julia you'd keep calling the embassy every day to try to find something out about the boy. She refuses to believe that he's dead until someone tells her outright."

"Of course I'll keep calling. What about you, Todd? What will you do when we have some definite word?"

"I'll likely fly directly from the Philippines to Hawaii and stay there, so you won't be seeing me again for quite a while, Nana."

"Todd, I'm really not sure if that's wise."

"I have to find a way to live without her," he said simply. "I don't even know if it's possible."

"Have you told her that?"

"She doesn't care. She thinks I'm afraid of life, and she doesn't want to tie herself to a man like that."

"And is she right? Are you afraid?"

"Yes." Todd shifted on the chair, looking down at his hands. "I think I'm a coward, afraid to risk my feelings. Just a bloody coward."

"If you're able to admit to them now," Barbara asked, "then what's the problem?"

"It's too late!" Todd said in despair. "She doesn't want me anymore."

"Not even if you tell her how you feel?"

"I can't tell her. She won't give me the chance. I've hurt her so much that she doesn't even want to risk seeing me again, and I don't blame her. It's too late," Todd repeated helplessly.

Barbara sat looking at him in silence, her face wretched with sympathy. "Oh, Todd," she whispered at last, reaching out to take his hands. "Oh, my darling, I'm sorry. I'm so very, very sorry."

After a moment, she picked up her needlework and began stitching again, looking tired and unhappy.

Todd watched her in surprise, puzzled by her words and manner.

But the distress in her voice prevented him from asking questions.

CHAPTER TWELVE

MASAKO PLACED tiny white stitches in the silk, mounded and shadowed into gentle banks of snow. Above the snow on the embroidered scroll, withered stalks swayed and cast blue shadows, waiting for spring to bring them back to life.

We all wait for spring, she thought sadly. We spend our lives waiting for spring, all of us....

The old lady looked down at Kim, who sat in her usual place on the ottoman, rolling tangled lengths of embroidery silk into neat skeins. The girl was as lovely as ever, possibly even more beautiful these days as she wrestled with her pain. Her eyes were darkly shadowed, her cheeks as pale and translucent as fine pearl, her mouth soft and drooping with sadness.

"Do you want to talk about it, *chérie?*" Masako asked gently.

Kim looked up, startled. "About what?"

"About your sorrow. It breaks my heart to see you so sad."

"I thought you'd be happy about this, Grandmother. You wanted Todd out of my life, and now he's gone. I haven't seen him for over a week."

"Has he taken all his things from the studio?"

Kim nodded, biting her lip. "He sent some work-men over to collect them. I never thought I could be this lonely," she added, her voice so low that Masako could hardly hear her. "That big studio just echoes, Grandmother. I can't bear to work there anymore."

"So how do you spend your afternoons?"

Kim shrugged. "Sometimes I stay late at the gallery and work with the children, or just... wander around the streets, looking at all the Christmas things and the people shopping..."

Her voice broke and she got to her feet, moving restlessly across the room to stare at her reflection in the mirror.

Masako turned stiffly in her chair to look at the girl's slim back. "Why did he leave you, my darling?" she asked gently.

"He didn't leave." Kim spoke to her grandmother's reflection as she toyed nervously with the silver brushes on the dresser top. "I sent him away. I gave him an ultimatum, and he made the choice."

"So calmly?"

"Well, it's been coming for a long time. We just finally agreed that our views of the future were completely different. You were right, Grandmother. He's not the man for me. He's never going to settle down and have a real home. When I forced him to make a choice, he chose his freedom over... over me."

Masako nodded thoughtfully and returned to her stitching.

It had all happened exactly as she'd hoped, then. Her own careful manipulation, added to that of the other grandmother, had achieved the desired result.

So why did she feel no triumph? In fact, all she felt was a hollow sense of guilt when she looked at her granddaughter's pale unhappy face.

How complicated everything was. Masako had acted only out of love, and so had Barbara McAllister. They'd done what, in their experience and wisdom, they knew was necessary to ensure the future happiness of these beloved young people. Sometimes, Masako told herself firmly, people needed to suffer in order to find the best path for their lives. Better a little suffering right now than a lifetime of misery in the future.

But when she met Kim's dark tragic eyes in the big mirror, Masako couldn't escape a nagging, uneasy sense that something was wrong. Terribly wrong.

Even worse, she was afraid that she, Masako, was to blame.

"Where is he now?" she asked.

Kim turned away restlessly. "Julia says he's gone back to Hawaii."

"Hawaii!"

"That's where he was working before he came to Spokane. I guess he wanted to get as far away as he could. Sometimes," Kim added, "I think about Christmas coming, and think I'll die of loneliness without him. And then I remember Julia and feel ashamed."

"How is Julia these days?" Masako asked, grateful for the change of subject.

"Not very good. I mean, she's brave on the outside, but her heart is slowly breaking. Especially since day after day goes by without any news. It almost makes me want to go to the Philippines myself and turn some of those government offices upside down."

"Nobody could accomplish anything in the midst of that chaos," Masako said. "There is nothing that anyone can do, except wait."

"But it's the waiting that kills your soul, Grandmother."

Masako nodded. "Is Mrs. McAllister being kind to Julia?"

"She's been wonderful," Kim said. "She's as gentle and loving as if Julia were her own daughter. Since Todd left," she added, "she's even being nice to me. She actually treats me like a friend."

"Does she, dear?"

"Yes. I guess," Kim said quietly, "she feels I'm not a threat anymore."

"Or perhaps she recognizes that she was mistaken, and wishes to make amends."

"You think so? Well, I'm afraid it's a little too late for that. And it's too late for me to be happy, ever again."

Kim turned and left the room abruptly, leaving Masako to brood over her needlework.

Too late, Masako thought wearily. Please, God, let it not be too late!

CAR HORNS BLARED, people wheeled by on bicycles and jammed into one another on the crumbling sidewalks, and street vendors shouted raucously, hawking their wares in the burning sunshine. Todd wandered through the teeming city of Manila, looking around with growing desperation.

He shouldn't even be here. If he wanted to help, he could have stayed at home on the other side of the world, comforting Julia and maintaining regular contact with the embassy. That would have been the rational thing to do. Coming to the Philippines all alone to search for her child had been an insane idea.

The vast city of Manila, far from the scene of the volcano was confusing enough. He shuddered to think what he might encounter if he gained permission to venture onto the island where Julia's village used to be.

The crowd closed in around him like a wave. He had to fight a claustrophobic urge to rush to the airport and take the first flight home to the United States.

He'd recovered soon enough from his jet lag, learned what he needed to know about the country's customs and finances and set out in a businesslike manner to get information about Julia's family. But from the beginning, Todd had battled a constant tide of red tape and frustration.

Now that he was in Manila, nothing was as simple as it had seemed in Spokane when he'd conceived this secret plan. For one thing, everybody here apparently expected to be bribed, from office boys to high-ranking government officials. There was such widespread corruption in the country's bureaucracy that he never knew what to make of the information he was given. And learning the fate of one small boy in this massive confusion was much more difficult than finding a needle in a haystack. At least a haystack would be stationary. It wouldn't keep moving and shifting, seething with the restless activities of millions of people.

Todd peered at a smudged address on a sheet of paper, examined the front of a sagging building, then fought his way up the stairs, edging past a woman laden with ripe melons and a father shepherding three small children. In a stuffy office on the third floor, he waited with twenty other people, almost faint from the heat, wondering again just what he thought he was doing.

This address was his last chance. He'd been passed along from agency to agency, from one overworked government official to another, trying to find somebody who could help. If this last course failed, he was doomed to go back home without any shred of hope to offer Julia.

At least he hadn't told her the truth about where he was going and what he was planning to do. Todd couldn't bear the thought of her sustaining another disappointment, and this one at his hands. He sat on the rickety chair remembering her shy whispered words, and her passionate conviction when she'd told him her son was still alive.

He knew this mission was somehow all tied up with his feelings about Kim. If he could help Julia, maybe in some way that would prove to Kim that he wasn't a selfish, uncaring man who refused to get involved. Maybe then, she'd smile at him again, touch him with love and gentleness . . .

He squared his shoulders, waiting patiently for his turn behind the glass partition.

Finally, his name was called and he confronted yet another official, a small dark man in shirtsleeves with rings of sweat under his arms. The man looked almost unbearably tired. Todd presented his photograph of Roberto and his information about Julia's family, in what had by now become a familiar routine. He watched while the official studied the papers in silence.

"What relationship are you to these people?" the man asked.

"The boy's mother is a domestic in my grandmother's home. My grandmother has made application to sponsor the child. All the paperwork is on file, and you have copies there. We were waiting for ratification of the visa when the volcano erupted."

"And you, too, are American?"

"Yes, I am. The boy's mother has been in America for a year. She's been saving money to send for him. My grandmother has a large, comfortable home," Todd added. "She's prepared to give shelter indefinitely to the mother and the boy."

"I see. Not much point in that now, is there? Not if the boy's dead."

"No," Todd said curtly. "I suppose there isn't."

The man looked up for a moment, his eyes shrewd and appraising. Then he consulted the paper again.

"And the child...Roberto...he lived in this village with his uncle? Cesar Adolpho, is that right?"

"That's right."

"How old was the boy?"

"Six years old," Todd said patiently. "It's all on the form there. Look, all I want is permission to go to the island and examine the casualty lists. If we know for sure, we can start to deal with the loss. Is that too much to ask? It's very difficult for Mrs. Adolpho, living on the other side of the world and having no word about the fate of her family."

The official frowned at the paper. At last he nodded and looked up at Todd.

"We learned recently that four children from the village weren't present during the first eruption," he said. "They'd been taken by bus to a neighboring town to visit the immunization clinic. Apparently, when the mountain erupted, the bus driver left the children and hurried back to his home in an attempt to reach his family members."

"He abandoned the kids?"

The official nodded. "Not very responsible of him, I'm afraid. But, ironically, it turned out to be the thing that saved their lives."

"They weren't killed?"

"No. The driver never returned, and nobody else from the village survived. We're having difficulty tracing the families of the abandoned children. All four of them are quite young."

Todd's heart began to hammer painfully in his chest. He stared at the agent. "How young?"

The man shrugged. "Very small. Four, five years old. They are being cared for, but you must understand that they are quite deeply disturbed. They can't tell us much about their families."

Todd swallowed painfully. "Do you think...do you think one of them might be this boy?" he asked, pointing to the photograph.

Again the man gave a weary shrug. "I have no idea. I haven't seen any of the children. What I'll do," he added, reaching into one of his file drawers, "is give you a permit to travel to the island. Nobody's being allowed in without a permit, you know."

"Oh, yes, I know," Todd said bitterly. "I've been refused a dozen times, in at least five languages and eleven government offices."

"Well, I'll give you a letter of entry so you can go to the aid station and check for yourself."

"Thank you," Todd whispered, pocketing the forms and shaking the man's hand. "Thank you so much."

"Mr. McAllister?"

"Yes?"

"I hope you find him," the official said, with a tired smile that made him look much younger. "I truly hope you do."

MASAKO TANAKA sat in her chair by the window, gazing out at the courtyard where her great-grandchildren were busy making a snowman. In the stillness of the winter afternoon, she could hear their merry shouts through the heavy plate glass, and enjoy the brightness of their knit hats and mittens, their laughing eyes and rosy cheeks.

Masako smiled tenderly at the little ones, thinking how pleasant it would be to have all the family together at Christmastime. Then, abruptly, her face saddened when she remembered Kim, who had begun to spend her days working alone in her studio and never came home until late in the evening.

"I can't stand to be there with the family, Grandmother," she'd said quietly. "Not when everybody's feeling happy and festive and I'm still so miserable. Please give them my apologies and tell them I'll be coming later."

"But, my dear..."

"Please," Kim had said, and Masako had fallen silent, stabbed to the heart by the misery in her darling's pale face.

She heard a knock on her door and turned away from the happy scene beyond the window.

"Mother?" Midori said. "There's a visitor for you. Are you feeling up to some company?"

"For me?" Masako asked blankly. "My dear, I'm not expecting anybody. Who is it?"

Her daughter-in-law gave a little warning shake of her head, then stood aside to admit a tall woman in a gray tweed suit.

Masako extended her hand with her usual courtesy, though her head whirled in confusion. "Mrs. McAllister," she murmured. "How pleasant to see you again. Please, won't you have a seat?"

Midori hovered nearby while Barbara McAllister seated herself in one of the lacquered chairs.

"Would the two of you care for a pot of tea, Mother, or some coffee? I can..."

"No, thank you, dear," Masako said, waving her hand in a gesture of gentle dismissal. "Perhaps I'll make some tea a little later, after Mrs. McAllister and I have talked."

Midori nodded, smiled politely at the guest and withdrew, leaving the two older women alone.

Barbara sat for a moment gazing out the window at the children, who had finished their snowman and were decorating it with holly wreaths and sprigs of mistletoe.

"Do you celebrate Christmas?" she asked Masako abruptly. "I mean, is your religion..."

"Yes, we're Christians, Mrs. McAllister," Masako said with a smile. "My family has been Christian for more than two centuries. There was a time," she added thoughtfully, "when our religion caused us to be discriminated against in Japan. In fact, I believe that was why I was allowed to go to Paris for my education."

Barbara nodded, and Masako was surprised to see that there was no longer any animosity in the other woman's eyes. She seemed troubled, but her anger had vanished.

"Why have you come to see me today?" Masako asked gently.

Barbara hesitated, twisting the straps on her leather handbag. "You and I...we've done a terrible thing," she said at last. "We've caused pain to the people we love most in the world."

Masako nodded sadly. "Yes," she said without argument. "You're right. We have."

Barbara looked up, her eyes full of anguish. "Madame Tanaka, I'd do anything in the world to take back what I've done. I played on Todd's fears, just the way we planned. I told him all women were the same, that he couldn't trust anybody and Kim would turn out to be as cruel and manipulative as his mother. My behavior was unforgivable. He's so unhappy now, and he doesn't deserve to be."

"I did the same. I told Kimiko she'd have to sacrifice her dreams if she wanted this man. I kept drawing her attention to those deep-seated fears of his and she believed me and acted on my words."

"How is she now? Deep down, I mean. She's pleasant enough when she speaks to me, but is she as unhappy as Todd?"

Masako's face creased with sorrow. "I've never seen her so miserable. The poor child, she can hardly eat or sleep. She yearns for him all the time, and she doesn't seem able to be comforted by the family or anything else. If this keeps up, I'm going to become very concerned about her health."

"I was afraid that might be the case. Madame Tanaka," Barbara asked simply, "what can we do? Is there any way to repair the wrong we've done?"

"I don't know."

Both women were silent for a moment, looking out at the merry group of children in the snow-covered courtyard.

"If we could only get them together," Barbara ventured at last. "They're still so much in love with each other, maybe just being forced into the same room would be enough at least to get them talking again. Do you think so?"

Masako inclined her silvery head with grave courtesy. "But Todd is in Hawaii, isn't he? Will he come home for Christmas?"

Barbara hesitated, then shook her head. "No, I...I don't expect him home for some time."

"Kim would never go to Hawaii, even if I begged her to take me there for a holiday. I'm afraid she's very bitter, Mrs. McAllister, and deeply hurt."

"She has every right to be. Todd treated her badly, and he's aware of it. You know, Madame Tanaka, except for his disappointments with his mother, he was always such a happy little boy. The way he is now...it just breaks my heart."

"I know," Masako said softly. "I know."

There was a long silence while both women looked out at the children again.

"And you, Mrs. McAllister?" Masako asked with gentle courtesy. "What are you doing these days?"

"I'm just doing my best to comfort Julia, and support her through this crisis."

"Still no word?"

"None at all. It's...very distressing."

"Kim tells me you've been kind to Julia, Mrs. McAllister. I wonder what that poor girl would have done without you."

"I care for her a great deal," Barbara said quietly. "Julia is a dear, sweet person, Madame Tanaka."

"Please, call me Masako."

"Masako," Barbara said, testing the unfamiliar name cautiously, almost shyly. "And my name is Barbara."

Masako inclined her head gravely.

"Todd told me," Barbara began in a hesitant voice, "he told me recently that your husband was an American, and that he fought on our side during the war."

"Yes, that's true. Yoshio was American to the core."

"I didn't know that."

"Does it make any difference?"

"No," Barbara said softly. "No, it really doesn't. For a lot of years, I thought it did, but now I recognize that it doesn't matter anymore. It's all in the past."

"Yes." Masako gave her a sober look of approval. "It's all in the past. And we, my dear Barbara, are in the present. And those little ones—" she waved at the laughing group beyond the window "—they are the future. I hope they manage things better than our generation did."

"I hope so, too," Barbara said. She looked at the woman sitting opposite her. "I was so angry with him," she whispered suddenly. "Sometimes I almost hated him."

"Your husband?"

Barbara nodded, her head lowered. "I know that it must have been terrible for Alex, and that he suffered and was lonely and afraid, but so was I, Masako. You must understand what I mean because you lived through the same thing, didn't you?"

"Yes, Barbara. I lived through it, too."

"I think I never really forgave Alex for going off and leaving me alone to raise my child. But I couldn't allow myself to think that, not when he was away fighting a war. It would have been far too selfish of me."

Masako nodded, looking shrewdly at her guest.

"I've never told this to anybody," Barbara murmured. "Never in all my life."

"Perhaps it's time you did," Masako suggested. "After all, you had every right to be angry."

"I did?"

"Of course you did. All of us did. War is a hideous thing. I believe women have been terribly angry about it for centuries, and rightly so. There's nothing at all for you to feel guilty about."

Barbara sat in silence for a moment, her eyes glistening with tears. Then she reached over and took Masako's hand.

BACK IN HIS HOTEL ROOM, Todd gripped his precious permit and sank onto the sagging bed with its serviceable gray blanket, and stared at the telephone. He forgot what time it was in America, and how difficult it was to get a call through at the best of times. He even forgot how angry Kim had been the last time they'd spoken.

All he knew was that right now, this instant, he needed to hear her voice or he would die. Without thinking any further, he took a deep nervous breath and reached for the telephone like a drowning man grasping a lifeline. He was afraid that her voice would sound strange and distant, but it didn't. It was as clear and sweet as he remembered, and so close that she was almost in the room with him.

Todd clutched the receiver, swallowing hard as he tried to speak.

"Hi, Kim," he said at last, hoping he sounded easy and casual. "How are you?"

"I'm fine," she said, instantly cautious. "Did you really go to Hawaii?"

"Yeah," he said, assuring himself that at least this was partially true. His plane had, after all, stopped in Hawaii to refuel before flying on to the Philippines....

"I suppose it's pretty cold back there in Washington," he said wistfully.

"Yes, it is. But," she added, "not in Hawaii, I guess."

Todd looked out the window at the hot copper sun. "It's pretty warm here," he said.

"Did you have a good trip?"

"It was okay. Just long, that's all. Kim..."

Todd bit his lip nervously. It was wonderful to hear her voice, but the conversation was so strained and difficult when she wouldn't help.

"How is your family?" he said at last.

"They're all fine," Kim said. "Everybody's getting excited about Christmas," she added after a moment's silence. "Personally, I wish they'd cancel the whole thing this year."

Todd hesitated, drawing a deep breath. "Kim..."

"Yes?"

"I haven't been able to get through to my grandmother since I got here. How are she and Julia?"

"Pretty much the same. I've been dropping over there most afternoons for a visit. Julia's getting very pale and thin, but otherwise she seems to be bearing up. And your grandmother keeps calling the embassy, demanding to be told the latest news. Not that any of this matters to *you,*" Kim said bitterly.

"What do you mean?"

"Isn't it obvious? As soon as the going gets difficult, or there's some kind of emotional need, you're gone. It must be very pleasant, Todd, basking in the sun in Hawaii and being far away from all these problems. I really envy you."

"God, Kim..."

"I should go," she said at last. "I have a class at the gallery this morning."

"All right. I just wanted to make sure you were all right."

"I see. Well, thank you very much."

"Kim, please give my regards to Julia, and tell my grandmother I'm fine. Tell her I'll be calling soon. Would you do that?"

"All right. Goodbye, Todd."

"Kim," he said hastily, panicking at the note of dismissal in her voice. "Could I see you sometime? Could we just go out for coffee, or something?"

"Todd, don't be ridiculous. You're in *Hawaii*."

"I mean, if I were to... come home for Christmas, say. Would you be willing to see me?"

"No, I don't think so."

Todd drew another deep breath to steady himself. "Look, I'm dying without you, girl. I can't live this way. I need to see you. I promise I won't try to touch you, or anything. I just need to see you and be sure that you're all right."

"You don't have to worry, Todd. I'm just fine. Now, if you don't mind..."

"Kim, don't hang up! Please, Kim, I'm begging you. Is that what you want? Then I'll be glad to beg. Please have a cup of coffee with me during the Christmas holidays, all right? Just fifteen minutes, that's all I'm asking."

"Todd, you don't seem to recall that it was your decision to end this. You packed your things and walked out of my life. I was prepared to make a future with you, but you couldn't stand the idea of commitment."

"People change, you know, Kim. Maybe I can learn to look at things differently if you'll just give me a chance."

"I don't think so. You may want this relationship, but on your terms alone. And I can't accept those terms."

"Why not?"

"Because they're based on cowardice, Todd. Your fear of commitment comes from fear and anxiety. You're like the little boy who's afraid of the dark and refuses to confront that fear. I can't tie myself to someone who's afraid of all those shadows."

"What if the shadows have always felt terribly real to me, Kim?" he asked softly.

"Then you'll just have to deal with them on your own," she told him, sounding gentle but detached. "I'm really sorry. I don't want to be harsh, but I don't think you have any idea how much you hurt me when you walked out. I'm starting to feel a little better now, and I can't risk another hurt like that. I'd really prefer not to see you again."

"Kim," he pleaded, "give me a chance. Don't shut me out. At least let me try to be the man you want."

There was a brief charged silence. Todd could almost feel her wavering, measuring his words as she struggled to decide. He waited. But when she finally spoke, her voice was coldly withdrawn once more. "I'm really sorry. I just can't," she said. "Stay in Hawaii, Todd. I hope you have all kinds of success and happiness, but I don't want to see you again."

There was a soft click, then silence. It took him a moment to realize that she'd hung up.

Todd sank onto the stained bedspread and hid his face in his hands, not even conscious of the muggy heat in the room, the stale smell of cooking wafting up from the restaurant below, and the ceaseless din of traffic pouring through the crowded streets.

CHAPTER THIRTEEN

IT WAS DAYS before Todd could arrange a chartered flight to the devastated island. By the time he got there, he was almost sick with heat and weariness.

He jolted from the airstrip in a rickety cab through scenes of incredible desolation. Most of the lush countryside had been laid waste and a fine gray ash lay over everything, several feet thick in places. People labored with carts and wheelbarrows, scooping up the sticky ash and hauling it away, dumping it in huge central piles where, Todd had been told, it would be stored and used later to fertilize the crops. On these impoverished islands, nothing was ever wasted.

He left the cab, covering his mouth with the paper mask he'd been given on the plane. In crowded Manila, many people wore these masks as a matter of course, because the pollution made the air dangerous to breathe. And here, on a remote island where the atmosphere should have been sparkling clean, volcanic ash filled the air with tiny particles that burned in his throat and lungs like fire.

Inside the makeshift government offices, Todd showed his forms and repeated his story. "I'm an American. My grandmother is sponsoring the child. I've come here on her behalf."

At last he was taken to a bare compound ringed with stark barbed wire, where a crowd of young children were doing vigorous exercises in spite of the heat, chanting a song in noisy unison. A flock of chickens pecked the ground among their dancing feet, and a couple of goats wandered near the fence.

Todd looked briefly at the children, then quickened his steps to follow his guide, a silent little old man who stopped at the door of a metal hut on the edge of the compound. The hut was surrounded by ragged bushes and some dusty flowers that Todd couldn't recognize.

"Wait," the man said, indicating a shadowed veranda made of plastic strips propped up on two shaky wooden poles. "You wait here." Then he vanished, carrying a sheaf of Todd's papers.

Todd leaned against the wall, watching the children. Most of them appeared to be girls. None of them looked anything like his picture of Roberto.

"Mr. McAllister?" a woman's voice said, nearby. "Would you come in, please?"

Todd straightened and peered into the shadowy interior of the hut while his guide emerged, bowed silently and then walked away. Todd entered the hut, blinking at the sudden dimness. A fan whirred somewhere, creating an impression of coolness. When his eyes adjusted to the light, he was even more astonished.

Except for a couple of exotic touches, like a folding bamboo screen in one corner and a solemn little monkey who sat on the back of a chair grooming himself with fierce concentration, the place might have been a modest apartment in any American city.

Todd saw a plain tweed couch, a small television set, some ornamental glassware on crocheted doilies, a cheap coffee table and an armchair containing a folded crossword puzzle and a pair of reading glasses. Everything was neat and clean, with no trace of the volcanic dust that covered most of the island.

"It's a nice place you have here," he said to his hostess, a plump, smooth-faced woman, perhaps in her early sixties. She wore a bright flowered sundress that left her dark shoulders bare. Her black hair was heavily frosted with gray, and her eyes, when she turned a thoughtful gaze upon him, were small, black and very intelligent.

"Thank you. I try hard to keep it this way," she said calmly, moving into an adjoining room and gesturing him to follow. The room, though tiny, was an efficient office with an ancient but serviceable-looking manual typewriter and rows of metal filing cabinets.

Todd sank onto a hard vinyl chair, studying the woman as she seated herself behind the desk.

"My name is Mrs. Madeleine Virata," she said. "I'm the school administrator."

He extended his hand, surprised by the firmness of her grip. "You have a beautiful voice, Mrs. Virata. I assume your accent is British?"

She nodded gravely. "I was educated in England and took my degree at Oxford. I studied modern history," she added with a smile that contained a trace of irony.

"Very impressive. That makes you pretty highly qualified, doesn't it?"

Madeleine Virata shrugged and looked at the papers on her desk, reaching for another pair of reading glasses in a desk drawer. "I suppose it does. I've never given it much thought. Now, Mr. McAllister, I understand that you are searching for this child...Roberto Adolpho is his name?"

She peered at Todd over the rims of her glasses.

"Yes. The boy lived here on this island with his uncle. His mother works for my grandmother in America. It's all there in the file."

"I see. And the officials in Manila thought your missing child might be one of the four abandoned little ones who were brought to the orphanage after the eruption?"

Todd shifted wearily in the chair. "They thought it was a lead I might want to follow. But they didn't think there was much likelihood that Roberto survived."

"Well, they're quite right. You must realize that your chances of success in this mission are extremely remote."

"I realize it more and more every day I spend here, Mrs. Virata. When I look around at all this devastation, it seems almost presumptuous to think that the little boy we're interested in might somehow have survived, when there were so many others who didn't."

Mrs. Virata studied his face for a moment, then returned to the file.

"Well," she said at last, "I'm really not sure if I can help you. Some of these new arrivals haven't even been able to tell us their names. They're extremely upset, and we aren't staffed to handle additional small children."

"Of course. It must be very difficult for you," Todd hesitated. "Could I at least . . . look at the kids?" he asked. "Since I've come this far."

Madeleine Virata pursed her lips. "Perhaps," she said.

"Perhaps? What do you mean?" Todd said with growing impatience. "Can I see them, or can't I?"

"I said perhaps," she repeated, looking directly at him.

Todd stared at her for a moment, then sank back in his chair. "Oh, hell," he muttered. "Even *here.*"

She smiled, seeming not at all troubled by his reaction. "This distresses you, Mr. McAllister? You are offended?"

"I've been handing out bribes at every turn, so I'm pretty much used to it by now," Todd said. "It's just that somehow I didn't expect that it was going to happen in an orphanage. My mistake, I guess," he added bitterly.

Mrs. Virata gave him a tranquil smile. "The widespread bribery in the Philippines is upsetting to you, Mr. McAllister?"

Todd shifted nervously in the chair. He realized that he couldn't afford to antagonize the woman, not when he'd come this far. "I'm not accustomed to it," he said. "Not on this scale."

"I see. The officialdom of America is a much purer system, I suppose?"

"I know that there's corruption everywhere in the world, Mrs. Virata. It just seems that over here, it's so much more...overt."

"Ah, yes. But you see, Mr. McAllister, our officials in the Philippines do not use the money obtained by their bribery to buy themselves big cars, or season tickets to sporting events. In fact, every official you've encountered here is probably supporting a dozen or so members of his extended family. He needs the extra money to keep a roof over their heads, and food in all those stomachs."

Todd looked straight at her. "You already have a roof over your head, Mrs. Virata. And you don't seem to share the place with a lot of other people. Why do you need to bribe me?"

Unexpectedly, she smiled. "Don't be so angry and self-righteous, young man. It won't cost you very much to get a look at these children."

"How much will it cost?"

"Thirty American dollars."

That was pretty steep, but still not as much as he'd been required to hand over a couple of times in Manila. Todd sighed and reached for his wallet.

"A month," Madeleine Virata added.

Todd stopped with his hand in the pocket of his jeans and stared at her. "A *month?* For how long?"

"Forever," she said with a placid smile.

The little monkey hopped into the room and picked its way daintily across the desk, then climbed the woman's arm and settled on her plump shoulder, nestling against her and closing its eyes with a comical look of bliss.

Mrs. Virata stroked the monkey gently and kept her eyes fixed on Todd.

"You've got to be kidding," he said with rising anger. "I'm supposed to pay you thirty dollars a month for the rest of my life, just so you can take me out there and show me some orphans?"

The monkey opened its eyes to glare at Todd, looking like an indignant old man. Todd glared back and the little animal subsided, whimpering.

"That's not all you'll get," Mrs. Virata told him calmly. "I'm proposing to sell you one of these children. Thirty dollars a month will buy you a child."

Todd looked at her blankly. "What would I do with a little kid? I don't understand."

She chuckled. The monkey opened its eyes again, reaching up to touch her ear. "You won't take the child away, Mr. McAllister. Your thirty dollars will support her here until she's completed her education. Then it will begin supporting another child."

"Thirty dollars a month will support a kid?"

Mrs. Virata nodded gravely. "It buys a child's food, clothing, textbooks and medical treatment as long as she's here."

"I can't believe it. In America, thirty dollars won't buy a pair of running shoes."

"We're much more sparing with our resources, Mr. McAllister. In addition," she added briskly, "you'll get a letter every month from your child, written in English, as well as regular reports on her academic progress. I will expect you to answer the letters," she added sternly.

Todd smiled, thinking how much Kim was going to love that correspondence. Then he remembered and the pain struck him like a physical blow. He sagged in his chair.

"Is something the matter?" the administrator asked gently.

Todd looked into her wise dark eyes. "My...the woman I love," he said awkwardly, "she left me, Mrs. Virata. I was just thinking how much she'd enjoy getting those letters from our foster child, and then I remembered that she doesn't want to see me again."

"And this hurts you a great deal?"

"Yes, it does."

Mrs. Virata folded her hands on her desk, as calm and professional as if they were discussing the problems of one of her students. "Why did she leave you?"

With a sad smile, Todd looked at the woman. "Because I was afraid of the responsibility of having children."

She examined him in thoughtful silence. "Well, well. Fate is such an odd thing, is it not?" she said unexpectedly.

Todd waited for her to continue, but she didn't. Instead, she got to her feet, dislodging the monkey, who tumbled onto the desk with an injured look, then picked itself up and scampered away into the other room.

"You can sign the papers for your foster child later," Mrs. Virata said. "Perhaps we'll go now and look at the children."

Todd got up and left the metal hut, following her out into the stifling afternoon heat. They walked across the compound where the girls were finishing their exercise class and a number of smaller children had appeared, carrying tin cups and plates heaped with rice and something that looked like spinach.

Todd turned to Mrs. Virata, feeling bitterly disappointed. There were only three little boys in the compound, and none of them was the child he was looking for.

"Are these all of them?" he asked.

She nodded. "They're having their lunch and playtime. They're all here."

"I see." Again Todd looked at the laughing group, then drew in his breath sharply. One of the taller girls had moved aside, revealing a little boy who squatted by the opposite fence, solitary and withdrawn.

The child was staring at his dirty bare feet and bouncing a red ball listlessly on the baked earth.

"That one," Todd whispered. "The one with the ball. Who is he?"

"We don't know his name," Mrs. Virata said. "We can't get him to tell us much of anything. But I'm not sure," she added, giving Todd a warning glance, "that he understands any English. He never responds to a word I say in English."

She crossed the dusty ground to speak to the little boy in one of the island dialects. He listened without expression, then got up obediently and followed her to the fence where Todd waited.

Todd stood in the blazing sunlight, gazing into the boy's haunted dark eyes. His heart turned over and his breath caught painfully in his throat.

He knew at once that this was Julia's little boy. This sad, dirty-faced waif was the smiling child whose picture Todd had shown to a hundred weary government officials over the past weeks.

"Roberto," Todd whispered when he was able to speak. "Roberto, your mother sent me to find you."

The child's eyes widened. He held himself tightly in check, staring up at Todd, then shrinking against Mrs. Virata's sturdy body. She reached gently down to stroke his dark hair, but he kept his eyes fixed on Todd.

"Julia, your mother," Todd repeated, kneeling beside the boy and taking the small body into his arms. Roberto felt thin and frail under Todd's hands, like a captive bird. He could sense the child's heart beating frantically with alarm. Tenderness flooded him, deep and warm.

"My . . . my mama?" Roberto whispered hoarsely against Todd's shoulder.

Mrs. Virata looked at Todd. Tears shone in her eyes, and she brushed them away. "I've never heard him speak English," she repeated. "But still, you know, I wondered . . ."

Todd hugged the child, his throat choked with emotion. "Yes, son," he whispered. "Your mama knew you were here, and so I came to get you. She's going to be so happy, Roberto. We'll phone her right away and tell her about you."

"I'm afraid not," Mrs. Virata murmured. "Phone service to the island has been knocked out since the disaster. You won't be able to contact America until you return to Manila."

Todd frowned, still holding the little boy. "I'll probably be leaving as soon as I get back to Manila," he said. "I have a flight booked to Spokane two days before Christmas, but I was planning to get off in Hawaii if I didn't find Roberto."

"Do you have a seat booked for him, as well?"

"Of course," Todd said calmly.

Mrs. Virata threw back her head and laughed, causing several of the children to look over at them with shy smiles. "You Americans!" she said. "Always so optimistic."

"Why not?" Todd said with rising jubilation and a touch of his old sunny arrogance. "I found him, didn't I?"

"Yes, you certainly did." Mrs. Virata sobered and shook her head. "But the paperwork!" she muttered with a gloomy frown. "Always so much paperwork. It won't be easy, Mr. McAllister."

Todd smiled at her over the little boy's head.

"Paperwork's the easy part," he said, hugging Roberto.

THE SEASON MARCHED on toward Christmas, filled with crisp golden days of sunlight on glistening snow and starry evenings that sparkled with colored lights and music. Barbara McAllister's house was decorated for the holidays with pine boughs and holly, and rich with the smell of baking. Even the dogs had festive red bows attached to their collars. But there was no feeling of celebration in the occupants of the house. Barbara and Julia went quietly about their days, wrapped in their private thoughts, both of them waiting and bracing themselves for whatever lay ahead.

Kim visited for dinner two nights before Christmas, drawn by her sympathy for Julia and her own loneliness. She forced herself to deal with the emptiness and the silence in the studio. But the evenings were still difficult for her.

Julia and Barbara sat with her quietly. By now, it was accepted as a matter of course that Julia took her evening meals in the dining room like a member of the family.

And in a way, she'd really become family. Kim shook her head, thinking about the vagaries of fate and the infinite strangeness of human nature. Barbara McAllister had changed to an astonishing degree in these past weeks. It was, perhaps, the only positive thing to have come out of all their suffering.

No longer did Kim sense coldness and hostility from Todd's grandmother. Barbara, though subdued, welcomed her with genuine warmth whenever Kim came to visit.

And as if that weren't astonishing enough, Barbara McAllister also seemed to have developed a friendship with Kim's grandmother. In fact, she'd called a couple of times at Kim's home. The two old ladies sat together and talked about the past, entertaining themselves over cakes and tea and laughing at their reminiscences.

It was almost too strange too grasp, all of it....

"Will you be able to drop in for a visit on Christmas Day?" Barbara asked gently, interrupting Kim's thoughts. "You know that Julia and I would both be grateful for the company."

Kim looked at her vaguely. "I...I'm not sure," she said after a moment. "I think I told you that I spoke with Todd a few days ago," she ventured. "He called me from Hawaii."

Barbara gave her a startled glance, then looked quickly down at her plate. "Yes, dear. You told me that he called."

"Well, he mentioned that he might be...coming home for Christmas. Do you think he will?"

Barbara hesitated, looking nervous. "I don't think so," she said at last. "If he were going to be home for Christmas, I'm sure he would have called by now to let me know."

Kim nodded, feeling both relieved and disappointed. "In that case, I might drop in for a while," she said. "I'd really hate to...to bump into him unexpectedly," she added with an apologetic glance at Barbara, "considering how strained things are between us right now. But I'm afraid Christmas is going to be a lonely day for me, too, even though my family will all be there."

Barbara patted her hand. "It's possible to be loneliest in a crowd," she said quietly. "I know that feeling."

Kim smiled at the older woman gratefully. "So if it's all right with you, I could come by for a few hours in the afternoon and maybe take the two of you out for a drive if the weather's nice."

"That would be very pleasant," Barbara said.

Kim fell silent. She wondered a little desperately if it was ever going to leave her, this feeling of loss and pain. *I love him,* she thought, remembering his strong jaw, the clean powerful line of his neck and shoulders. *I love him so much...*

Julia gave her a look of gentle sympathy and passed her a shallow dish filled with cabbage rolls.

"Thanks, Julia," Kim said, smiling at her. "I think this is my second helping, isn't it? I shouldn't be such a glutton."

"It's nice to see you enjoying them," Julia said quietly. "I crumbled bacon into the meat the way you like it."

"They're delicious," Kim said. "Like everything you make."

Julia gave her a brief smile and returned to her own meal. She was much thinner these days, strung as fine as wire, with a taut frightened look, as if she could hear far-off sounds that nobody else recognized. Kim and Barbara both worried about her, wondering how much more her gentle nature could endure.

Julia spent all her time waiting for the phone to ring, for something to come in the mail, for word to arrive from the devastated islands on the other side of the world.

We're all spending our lives waiting, Kim thought.

EVENTUALLY, Todd found himself back in the same office in Manila, up on the third floor among the crowds of people patiently waiting with their children and animals and crates of vegetables. He looked at the weary little man in shirtsleeves, who gazed back at him impassively.

"Come on, Emilio," Todd said, having long since progressed to a first-name basis with the official. "Most of this work was done long ago, when my grandmother started proceedings in America. All I need are a couple more papers, and one government stamp, and we're out of here. Please, can't you do this for me?"

Emilio shook his head, frowning at the bulky file on his desk. "You've done an amazing amount of work on this, Mr. McAllister, and so has your family. But I still need proper clearance on the child's exit visa. And I'm afraid all the departments will soon close for the Christmas holiday."

"I know that!" Todd said with passion, leaning across the desk.

Roberto looked over at them, smiling shyly. The little boy sat at a table in the corner of the office, his feet dangling, working industriously in a coloring book that Emilio's secretary had found in an old cabinet. The crayons were mostly blunt fragments but Roberto handled them as reverently as if they were made of gold.

He was neatly dressed in new khaki shorts, recently purchased by Todd, along with a striped T-shirt and a small pair of gleaming athletic shoes. Occasionally, Roberto dipped his head and checked under the table to make sure the shoes were still there.

"He's such a good little kid," Todd said quietly, turning back to the man behind the desk. "He plays in the hotel room for hours while I make calls and fill out papers. He eats whatever I put in front of him. He never complains about anything, or fools around, or fusses when I bathe him and wash his hair. He doesn't make any trouble at all."

Emilio nodded, gazing thoughtfully at the boy's dark head.

"Look, Emilio, I've got two seats booked on a plane that's leaving Manila tomorrow afternoon," Todd went on. "We'd arrive in Spokane the morning of Christmas Eve. He could actually be with his mother for Christmas, if you'd just get these last few papers processed for me."

"Mr. McAllister, you must understand that I can't..." Emilio passed his hand over his hair with a weary sigh. "Does his mother know you've found him?"

Todd shook his head. "I couldn't get through on the phone at first. Then when things were going so well, I started hoping maybe we'd still be able to make the flight, and we could...sort of surprise her," he finished lamely.

"Well, I'll do what I can."

Todd got up and turned to look at the little boy. "We have to go now, Roberto."

Roberto packed his crayons neatly in the box, set it on the edge of the desk and closed the book regretfully. He slid down from the chair and crossed the room to lean against Todd's leg, putting two fingers in his mouth and looking solemnly at the other man.

"You may take the crayons and the book, Roberto," Emilio said gently. Then, as the boy ran to get the crayons, the young Filipino turned to Todd. "I'll do my best," he said again. "I can't promise anything."

Todd smiled his gratitude. "You know where I'm staying if you should hear any good news, right?"

"Oh, yes, I know where you're staying," Emilio said with a faint smile. "I'm sorry," he added, looking genuinely regretful. "I wish I could have done more for you."

"Thanks, Emilio. You've been good to us. I know you've done all you can."

Todd paused by the door with Roberto close at his heels. "Hey, Emilio," he said softly.

"Yes?" The man glanced up, already absorbed in his files.

"Merry Christmas, Emilio. Regardless of how all this turns out, buy something nice for your kids and tell them it's a present from America."

Todd strode back across the room and placed a bulging envelope on the man's desk, then grabbed Roberto's hand and walked down the three flights of dingy stairs, out into the street.

Roberto trotted beside him, clutching the coloring book and crayons.

"Todd, where are we going now?" he asked in his soft musical voice, craning his neck to see the tall man's face. "Are we going to the store again? Are we having supper soon? If we go back to the hotel, can I do more coloring before bedtime?"

Todd grinned down at him. "I thought you never talked."

"I didn't talk at that place. I didn't like it." Roberto stopped to examine a large blue-green beetle scurrying along the curb.

"Why not?"

"The girls pulled my hair, and I missed my uncle and my grandmother."

Todd was silent, wondering what went on inside that little head. Roberto never spoke of the horrors he'd seen, or the loss of his family.

Even more strangely, he never questioned Todd's presence in his life. The little boy seemed to accept as a matter of course the fact that this smiling, curly-haired giant had arrived to whisk him out of the orphanage and carry him through the sky to the place where his mother waited. Abruptly, with startling vividness, Todd found himself remembering the afternoon he'd spent with Kim in the park, when she'd asked him what their child would look like. He even remembered the crispness of the autumn air, the brilliantly colored leaves and Kim's slender body on the blanket as she looked wistfully at the baby in the stroller.

He remembered, too, his dread when she'd mentioned the possibility of a child. Now he wondered what had frightened him so much.

A child born to the two of them would probably be a little like Roberto, Todd thought. He'd have big dark eyes and a bright smile and fine, regular features, and artistic hands like both his parents....

Roberto slipped his hand into Todd's and squeezed his fingers. Todd held the small hand, overwhelmed by sudden emotion. He blinked his eyes to hold back embarrassing tears, and tried to smile at the boy.

"Well, it's getting late, kiddo. What do you want to eat?"

"A hamburger, like yesterday?" Roberto said after sober consideration.

Todd chuckled and swung the boy's arm, trying not to think about Kim.

"Well, I gave most of my cash to Emilio," he said. "But I suppose I can still manage a couple of hamburgers."

Roberto gave a delighted little skip, then took himself in hand and strode gravely at Todd's side, trying to look manly and big like his companion.

They dined on hamburgers and fries, and afterward they wandered back toward the hotel, stopping in the park to feed scraps of bread to the pigeons, a daily ritual that Roberto loved. Todd paused by the lake, his hands in his pockets, watching the child at the water's edge and thinking how bleak his own life was going to be when he'd passed Roberto into Julia's care and was on his own again.

All the things that had once been so absorbing, like his work and travels, his friends and parties and good times...they all seemed strangely hollow and empty when he looked at them from the other side of the world. Only this little boy—and Kim—were real.

"Will you tell me a story at bedtime?" Roberto asked shyly as they walked.

"Sure. Which one do you want to hear?"

"About the cowboy," Roberto said. "When he rode the bucking bull and got thrown right over the fence."

"Okay. You know, that cowboy was a real person, Roberto."

"Was it you?"

Todd smiled down at him. "Yeah, son. It was me."

Roberto sighed with pleasure and gripped Todd's hand tightly. "I knew it was you."

Todd smiled again. Together they walked up the sidewalk to the shabby hotel that was beginning to feel almost like home.

In the deserted lobby, a teenage boy scrutinized them with dark eyes, then moved forward quickly, reaching in his jacket pocket as he approached. Todd tensed and moved Roberto behind him, into the shelter of his leg. "What do you want?" he asked sharply.

The boy smiled and held out an open envelope full of stamped papers and official-looking documents. "Emilio says Merry Christmas," he murmured in broken English.

Then he was gone, melting into the crowded street while Todd stood gazing after him and clutched the envelope in shaking hands.

CHAPTER FOURTEEN

THE MORNING of Christmas Eve dawned gray and gloomy, with an icy wind howling and dark clouds that brooded over the western plains, threatening snow. Barbara woke and looked out her window, then hurried to dress in woolen slacks and a cashmere sweater, shivering in the early-morning chill.

She went downstairs to find Julia already in the kitchen.

"Good morning, my dear," Barbara said. "The holiday has finally arrived, hasn't it? Although I suppose it's not officially Christmas until tomorrow."

"At home, we always had our biggest celebration on Christmas Eve," Julia said softly from the counter, where she was squeezing orange juice. "We had a huge breakfast together and then visited all day, went to church in the evening and opened our presents before we went to bed. Christmas Day was mostly for resting and recuperating."

Barbara smiled. "You know, that sounds like an extremely sensible plan."

Julia didn't respond, and Barbara looked with sympathy at her thin back, the rigid line of her neck and shoulders.

"Julia..."

"Yes, ma'am?"

"Let's have our breakfast in the dining room this morning, shall we? It seems a little more festive in there, and besides, it's a shame to waste that lovely Christmas centerpiece."

Julia looked around and smiled. "Shall I light the candles, ma'am?"

"Of course!" Barbara said briskly. "If we don't enjoy them, who will? Here, I'll set the table, and you bring in the food."

Trying hard to keep both of them cheerful, and to create a semblance of a holiday mood, Barbara set the table with her best china and her heavily engraved flatware, then lit the candles on the centerpiece and stood back to admire the glowing table. She nodded in satisfaction when Julia arrived, bearing a silver tray with fresh coffee, poached eggs, toasted English muffins and strawberry jam.

"This is beautiful," Julia said, looking with a sigh at the cozy scene in the dining room, which contrasted so sharply with the gloomy winter morning beyond the windows. "Oh, I wish..." Her voice trailed off as she twisted her hands together.

Barbara reached out to touch the younger woman's arm gently.

"I wish," Julia went on with an effort, "that I'd remembered the honeydew melon. I think there's still some in the fridge. I'll bring it, shall I?"

"Would you like me to get it?"

"No," Julia whispered, turning away to hide her tears. "That's all right, ma'am. I'll just run and cut a few slices, and be right back."

Then she was gone, hurrying into the kitchen before she broke down and sobbed. Barbara poured a cup of coffee and reached for a muffin, gazing out the window with unseeing eyes.

The doorbell jangled harshly through the morning stillness. Barbara tensed, wondering who could be calling so early.

Surely not, she thought, glancing cautiously at the closed kitchen door. Not more bad news for Julia. That would be just too cruel . . .

She set her cup on the table and went to answer the door.

"It's likely the paperboy," she told herself, speaking aloud for courage. "He forgot to collect his Christmas tips, I suppose. Well, young man . . ."

Barbara opened the door and gaped in amazement.

Todd was standing on the front step, his hair and shoulders lightly dusted with big soft flakes of snow. Beside him a small boy with solemn dark eyes stood clutching his hand. The child wore stiff new jeans and a cherry-red ski jacket, and gripped a bright paper sack under his free arm. He was silent, but trembling visibly with emotion.

"Hi, Nana," Todd said with an easy smile. "Merry Christmas."

"*Todd!* Is this . . . could it possibly be . . ."

"It sure is," Todd said, leading the little boy into the foyer and closing the door behind them.

Barbara sank to her knees and looked directly into the child's face. "Well, hello, Roberto," she murmured through her tears. "You can't imagine how happy I am to see you."

"This is the grandmother I told you about," Todd said when Roberto gave him a cautious look. "She's very, very nice. And she just loves little boys."

Roberto nodded gravely, apparently satisfied that it was all right if Todd said so.

"Hello, Grandmother," the boy said politely, holding up his paper sack while Todd helped him remove his coat. "I have a present for you. It's wrapped in pretty paper and it has a big gold bow."

"Is that right, sweetheart? Well, we'll just have to go inside and put that present under the Christmas tree, won't we? Because today is only Christmas Eve, you know. We'll have to wait until tomorrow to open our presents."

Todd smiled down at them. "We sure will," he said. "Roberto and I have been traveling for thirty hours. We both need a bite to eat, and a few hours of sleep, and then we'll be good as new. Where's Julia, Nana? Is she around?"

Barbara got to her feet and reached down to stroke the little boy's shining head.

He stood quietly in the foyer, clutching his sack of Christmas presents and looking with wide eyes at the luxurious house, clearly unlike anything he'd ever seen.

"Why didn't you *call?*" Barbara asked Todd in a fierce whisper. "You should have given us a chance to prepare!"

"There was no phone service at all from the island where I found him, Nana. And even in Manila, international service is pretty sporadic this time of year.

Finally, I just gave up and decided it was quicker to fly here than try to phone."

"I'll bet you did," Barbara said dryly. "Poor Julia, she's probably going to have a heart attack. I almost had one myself. Todd, how on earth did you ever..."

"It's a long story, Nana. And I'm too tired to tell any of it now. I want a meal and a nap, and then I'll tell you all about my travels. Go," he urged her gently. "Go tell Julia I've got a little surprise for her."

Todd bent and lifted the boy, presents and all, cuddling him tenderly in his arms. He kissed the child's flushed cheek and his shining black hair, and patted his back. With the ease of perfect trust, Roberto nestled against the big man's chest and lay his head down. Still holding the bright sack of gifts in one hand, he put two fingers in his mouth and his eyelids began to flutter.

"Oh, the sweet darling," Barbara murmured. "*Both* of you are darlings," she added with a misty smile, standing on tiptoe to kiss her grandson's cheek.

"Go," Todd repeated. "You don't know long how I've looked forward to this moment, Nana."

Barbara nodded and moved back into the dining room, walking uncertainly as if there were clouds under her feet instead of thick Persian carpets.

Julia stood at the table arranging slices of honeydew melon on a crystal tray with kiwi fruit and strawberries. She seemed to have recovered her composure, though her eyes were still suspiciously red.

"Was there someone at the door just now?" she asked. "I thought I heard voices."

"Yes, dear. We've had an early-morning visitor."

Julia grew pale, and her face took on the tense, frightened expression she always had when people called or rang the doorbell.

Barbara chose her next words with caution, trying not to shock the woman too terribly. "Actually, it's Todd," she said in a casual voice. "He's decided to come home for Christmas, after all."

"He's come all the way from Hawaii?" Julia asked in surprise. "He must be so tired."

"Julia," Barbara said gently, "Todd hasn't been in Hawaii. When he left here, he flew directly to the Philippines."

"The...the..." Julia stood silent and wide-eyed, her hand covering her mouth. She stared wildly at the doorway where Todd had appeared and stood alone, smiling at her.

"It's a nice country you've got over there, Julia," he said. "The islands are incredibly beautiful."

"But, Todd...did you...were you able to..."

"It was a real rushed trip," Todd said. "I didn't do much shopping, or anything. In fact, I only brought back one little souvenir."

He reached behind him and drew Roberto into view. The child stood tensely next to Todd, staring at his mother. Julia gasped and swayed on her feet, clutching the table for support. Her eyes shone with tears as she leaned down toward the solemn little boy in the doorway.

"Roberto," she whispered at last. "Oh, darling, is it really you? Is it you?"

The boy dropped his parcel and released Todd's hand. He took one tentative step toward the woman by the table, then another. Finally, with a hoarse racking sob that almost broke Barbara's heart, Roberto launched himself across the dining room into his mother's arms, gripping her with small, fierce hands and pressing tightly against her.

Julia lifted the boy and held him, laughing and crying. She whispered broken endearments against his tousled hair, stroking his body tenderly.

Barbara and Todd watched in silence, not conscious of the tears streaming down their cheeks.

"Roberto," Julia whispered to the little boy. "Where did you come from? You're a miracle. You're a little Christmas angel."

"Here's another miracle," Barbara murmured, her voice husky as she moved over and put an arm around her grandson. "This man's a miracle, Julia."

Julia looked up at him with shy radiance. "Oh, thank you," she murmured. "Todd, how can I ever begin to thank you?"

Todd shifted awkwardly and brushed at his eyes. "Seeing you together like this is all the thanks I need," he told her. "I've gotten really attached to this little guy over the past few days, Julia. It's good to see him happy."

Clearly comforted and reassured by his mother's embrace, Roberto leaned back in her arms and smiled at her, then reached up to grasp a handful of her hair and tug it gently. "I bought you a present, Mama," he said. "Todd helped me. We bought it at a big store where the airplane was."

Julia smiled at him mistily. "Did you, sweetheart? Is it a Christmas present?"

"Yes!" Roberto said, bouncing with excitement. "But you have to wait until Christmas. Todd said you have to wait, because Santa Claus doesn't come until tonight."

"I'll wait," Julia promised gravely. "I think now it will be easy to wait," she added, her face luminous as she smiled at the others in the room.

"There's lots of snow, Mama," Roberto said, looking out the window. "Santa Claus can come in his sled with the reindeer, because there's snow everywhere, even up on the roof. Todd told me stories about Santa Claus on the plane."

Barbara was the first to regain her composure. She moved across the room and stroked Roberto's head. The child cuddled in his mother's arms, looking shyly at this strange tall woman.

"It's been quite a long time since there's been a little boy in this house," Barbara said. "But I think perhaps we can still find some toys in the attic, and there's a young dog over there who'd like a boy to play with."

Roberto scrambled down from Julia's arms and stood leaning against her, returning the interested scrutiny of Hugo in his basket by the hearth.

Barbara smiled at Todd. "I know you're tired, dear. But you might as well pull up a chair and have something to eat before you go to bed. You too, Roberto. Do you like jam?"

Todd shook his head, clearly amused by his grandmother's ability to take charge of any situation. He caught her eye and tipped his head with a smile, gesturing at Roberto who was venturing across the carpet toward Hugo's basket, still clinging to his mother's hand. Hugo's tail thumped on the tartan and his eyes brightened with excitement at the cautious approach of the small boy.

"He's me all over again, Nana," Todd whispered. "Isn't he?"

Barbara nodded, watching Roberto kneel by the hearth to pat the wriggling dog. "Yes, I believe he is," she murmured. "God help us all."

Eventually, Julia and Roberto, with Hugo at their heels, vanished into the kitchen, where soft voices and laughter could be heard, interspersed with the sound of many kisses.

Todd looked at his grandmother. "Nana . . ."

"Yes, dear?"

"I'm so tired, I'm almost dead on my feet. But I'm a little worried about Santa Claus."

Barbara chuckled. "It's been a long time since you and I had a discussion about Santa Claus, my boy."

"I know, but I wasn't certain that we'd be able to get here in time, and you and Julia sure weren't expecting us. I don't know if Santa's as well prepared as he should be."

Barbara nodded solemnly. "Well, son, if we could find a helper for Santa, do you think you might have a list of gift ideas that would meet with Roberto's approval?"

"I sure would. The poor little kid loves everything, and he has nothing. He's never had anything. I've got a list as long as your arm."

"Well, then, let's plan our day, shall we? You can sleep for a few hours, and I'm sure Roberto will need a nap, too. And," Barbara added with a misty smile, "I rather doubt that Julia will mind baby-sitting. So perhaps I'll go out this afternoon and see what I can do about Santa's list."

"You're wonderful, Nana."

Her face sobered. "Let's just say I'm a little better than I used to be."

"Nana, have you seen Kim? Is she all right? I should call her and let her know about Roberto. She'll be so happy."

"You can't call her," Barbara said firmly. "Her grandmother says Kim's going to be shopping all day and working in her studio this evening. We can't get hold of her until then."

"Kim's grandmother?" Todd took a long gulp of coffee and gave Barbara a startled look. "Since when do you get information from Kim's grandmother?"

"Masako and I have become good friends," Barbara said placidly, ignoring his stunned expression. "She's a delightful person. Now, have something to eat and go up to bed, and I'll look after shopping and getting hold of Kim. All right?"

He nodded and spread jam obediently on one of the muffins.

A GENTLE SNOW drifted from the sky as night flowed over the city, bringing with it the profound silence that is so common on Christmas Eve. Stores closed early, and there were few cars on the streets. People were safely at home with family and loved ones, relieved that all the frantic preparations were over and the peace of the season could at last begin to fill their hearts and homes.

Kim worked doggedly in her studio, glancing out the window from time to time at the snowy street below with its adornments of glittering lights and tinsel. Only one business was still operating, an all-night convenience store with lighted windows shining like gold beacons through the falling snow.

While she watched, a small family came hurrying along the street, laughing together. The man held a child by the boy's mittened hand, and the young mother carried a baby in a fur-trimmed snowsuit. They vanished inside the store and came out soon afterward, laden with packages. The child stumbled along beside his father, chattering with excitement, and the young man bent to lift him and swing him aloft, then kissed his cheek and held him as they disappeared around the corner.

Kim turned away from the window, feeling unbearably lonely, as if she were the only person in all the world who was by herself on this dark quiet night. But, as she'd told her grandmother, she couldn't bear to be at her father's house with her brother and sister and their families.

Especially the children, cozy in their pajamas and slippers, red-cheeked with excitement over Santa's visit....

She frowned and dipped her brush into a jar of green paint, carefully outlining the soft-veined leaf of a water lily.

The phone jangled loudly in the stillness. Kim looked up in surprise, then hurried across the room to answer.

"Hello, Kim Tanaka speaking."

"Kim, I'm sorry to bother you."

"Mrs. McAllister," Kim said in surprise.

"I hate to interrupt you at your work, dear, but I wanted to remind you about tomorrow. You are coming over, aren't you?"

Kim could hear the anxiety in the older woman's voice and she smiled. Who would have thought, only a few weeks ago, that Todd's grandmother would be so eager to see her. Or that Kim, herself, would be happy to be visiting Barbara's home.

"Yes, Mrs. McAllister, I'll be there."

"Good. Julia and I are looking forward to it. And . . . Kim . . ."

"Yes?"

"You do know that you're always welcome here. I know how difficult you're finding it to spend time with your family and their children at this time, so if you decide you don't want to be alone tonight, we'd be happy to see you."

"Thank you, Mrs. McAllister. But it's going to be quite late when I finish work. I don't think I should come out tonight, especially since it's snowing so heavily."

"As you please, dear. But the invitation still stands."

Shaking her head in disbelief, Kim hung up the phone. She looked around the studio, then made a decision. Mrs. McAllister was right. This was not a night to be alone.

She raced around the studio cleaning brushes and putting away her paints, then grabbed her jacket and keys. She hurried down the steps and out to her car, pulling it recklessly around in the falling snow and heading across the glistening city to the old tree-lined suburb where Todd's grandmother lived.

The doorbell didn't appear to be working. When nobody answered her knock, either, Kim pushed the door open cautiously and slipped inside, left her boots on the mat and ventured into the silent living room, looking around with growing alarm.

"Hello?" she called softly. "Is anybody here?"

She paused, charmed in spite of herself by the warmth and beauty of the gracious old room. A fire glowed on the hearth under a garland of pine starred with winking colored lights. In the corner, a huge tree glistened, surrounded by brightly wrapped gifts.

In fact, there seemed to be an inordinate pile of gifts for just two women. While Kim was looking at them in surprise, Homer became aware of the intruder and barked a couple of times in desultory fashion, then lowered his muzzle onto his paws and fell asleep again.

Somewhere in the distance, Kim heard the sounds of laughter, followed by approaching footsteps. The door from the kitchen opened and Barbara appeared, holding a mixing bowl against a white apron.

"Hello, dear. We mustn't have heard the doorbell. We're making popcorn balls, and it's very noisy," she added with a smile.

"Popcorn balls?" Kim asked.

"Hey, Nana? Who's there?" a familiar voice called, sending chills down Kim's spine.

Todd ambled into the room behind his grandmother, stopping abruptly when he saw Kim. His face grew taut with emotion, and his eyes blazed.

"Kim," he said softly. "Sweetheart, it's so good to see you."

Kim stared back at him, speechless. He was the same man she'd loved for so long, but somehow different. He looked thin and tired, and the hard planes of his face seemed gaunt and pale beneath his tan. But his eyes were at peace, calm and happy, resting quietly on her with a love so intense that Kim began to shiver.

Suddenly, a small boy appeared at Todd's side, edging cautiously out from behind the big man's denim-clad legs and peering at Kim with dark inquisitive eyes.

Kim felt the world spinning crazily around her.

"This little guy is Roberto, my traveling companion," Todd said, lifting the boy into his arms and kissing his cheek. "Roberto, say hello to Kim. She's one of the nicest ladies in the whole world."

"Hello, Kim," Roberto whispered. Then, overcome with shyness, he buried his head against Todd's chest. Barbara murmured something about popcorn balls and vanished into the kitchen, where she could be heard talking to Julia in a soft voice.

Kim took a couple of halting steps across the room, groping for words. "You didn't . . . you never went to Hawaii," she said. "Did you?"

"Actually, I did. The plane landed in Hawaii to refuel. But then it went on to the Philippines, and I went with it."

"So when you called me . . ."

"I was on the other side of the world. I was so tired and lonely, I thought I'd die if I couldn't hear your voice."

"Oh, Todd . . ."

She looked at the child, who had apparently recovered from his initial shyness and scrambled down from Todd's arms to examine the pile of glittering presents under the tree.

"Lots of these are for me," he told Kim solemnly.

She smiled through her tears. "I'm sure they are. Everybody is very happy to see you, darling. Did you like the plane ride?"

Roberto nodded. "Todd told me lots of stories, and when I was tired, he held me so I could sleep better."

Kim felt a lump in her throat. She was reluctant to meet Todd's eyes, afraid of what she might see there.

"How did you find him?" she whispered. "How on earth did you even know where to begin?"

"I didn't. I just waded in and got started, and made all kinds of mistakes, and eventually was lucky enough to find some people who could help."

"Oh, Todd . . . How's Julia?"

"She's radiant. Positively incandescent. We have to keep putting more cement in Mama's shoes or she'll float away like a balloon, won't she, Robbie?"

The child laughed at this, a throaty boyish chuckle that made Kim laugh, too. She looked at Todd, still dizzy with shock and a sudden fierce hunger that she was powerless to control.

He was even bigger than she remembered, more handsome and vital in person that he'd seemed in all her lonely dreams over the past month. He wore moccasins, faded jeans and an old denim shirt smeared with paint. His hand rested on Roberto's head with a gesture of instinctive protectiveness.

Roberto, too, was liberally smeared with paint. They'd obviously been doing some artwork before the popcorn-ball project had begun.

"Have you been painting, Roberto?" Kim asked.

The boy nodded eagerly and reached into a cabinet under the sideboard, extracting a rolled sheet of drawing paper. He opened it out to display a series of brownish smudges, topped by a blob of bright red. Paint had also spattered in one corner and dripped down the paper in messy red-and-brown trails.

"This part was an accident. Todd says it looks like . . . what's the name?" the boy asked, looking up at Todd.

"Jackson Pollock?" Kim suggested, smiling.

"That's right," Roberto agreed, giving her a surprised glance. "And see this?"

"Yes, it's very bright. What is it, dear?"

"It's Hugo! With his red bow on."

As if in response to his name, Hugo clattered in from the kitchen and frowned up at them with some urgency.

"I think poor Hugo needs to go outside," Todd said. "Roberto, you put on your coat and boots and take him into the backyard, okay?"

Roberto nodded, rushing toward the kitchen before Todd finished speaking, with Hugo close at his heels. "Maybe we'll see Santa out there!" he called as he ran. "Maybe Santa's coming already!"

"Oh, I don't think so, young man," Barbara's voice said from the kitchen. "I think Santa only comes after all little boys are asleep."

Beyond the door, Julia said something as well. Suddenly she laughed, a sound so joyous and infectious that Kim and Todd both smiled.

"What a great kid," Todd said softly, looking at the closed door where child and dog had vanished. "You were right, Kim. Did you know that?"

"About what?"

"I really love kids. And I'm good with them. The hours I spent with that little guy were the most enjoyable I can ever remember. I'm not careless and irresponsible like I thought I'd be, Kim. I loved looking after him, and I'd die before I'd ever let him be abandoned or hurt. I don't even know what I was always so afraid of."

"You were afraid of your past," Kim whispered, longing to reach out and touch him. "But the past doesn't have to ruin the future, Todd."

"Another thing I've learned," he went on, his voice calm and steady, "is how much I love you. It isn't just a physical attraction or some kind of superficial thing, Kim. I adore you. I love you with all my heart and soul, and I'll love you just the same when you're as old as your grandmother. I'll never stop loving you. What's more, I know I can trust you with my heart for as long as I live. I want—"

"Oh, Todd..."

"Don't interrupt. You have to let me finish, because I've been rehearsing this for weeks. I want to marry you, Kim. Do you think you can ever forgive me for being so stupid, and for hurting you the way I did?"

"Todd...I don't know what to say."

"Don't say anything, sweetheart. If you love me, just come and kiss me before I die from wanting you."

Even if she'd wanted to resist, it was too late. She was already in his arms, and there was no help for her any longer. As soon as she was folded in that familiar embrace, resting against his broad chest and feeling the softness of his mouth on hers, she was lost. She nestled in his arms and returned his kiss, sighing with pleasure.

"Oh, it feels so good," she whispered when he finally gave her a chance to speak. "It feels so good, Todd. I've missed you terribly."

"I know. Me, too. Kim?"

"Hmm?" She lifted her face to him again, her eyes closed in bliss.

"Merry Christmas, darling," he said, his voice husky. "Tell me, do you have any plans for the rest of the evening? Or the rest of your life, for that matter?"

She tried to answer but there were no words to express her joy. Besides, he was kissing her again, his lips moving hungrily over her face and throat while her heart soared in happiness and old Homer watched them sleepily from the firelit hearth with a look of grudging approval.

"Oh, yes," Kim whispered at last. "Merry Christmas. The first of many, my love. The very first Christmas of our lifetime."

"Kim, listen. Isn't that beautiful?"

In the distance, coming nearer, they heard the sound of carolers. Their silvery song echoed in the snow-filled night like a chorus of angels, then faded gradually into silence.

For a magic, fleeting moment, the stillness of perfect peace rested on all the world, as sweet and ageless as the love filling the hearts of the two people beside the glistening Christmas tree.

HARLEQUIN SUPERROMANCE®

WOMEN WHO DARE
They take chances, make changes
and follow their hearts

Abbey had never expected to find herself in hiding, living
a secret life. And she'd never expected to become an
instant mother. But she'll do *whatever* it takes to protect
her sister's children. Even if that means lying to the man
she loves...and risking her own chance at happiness.

Call Me Mom
by Sherry Lewis

Available in January, wherever Harlequin books are sold.

WWD94-4

HARLEQUIN®

A M E R I C A N ◆ R O M A N C E®

This holiday, join four hunky heroes under
the mistletoe for

Christmas
Kisses

Cuddle under a fluffy quilt, with a cup of hot chocolate and these
romances sure to warm you up:

#561 HE'S A REBEL (also a Studs title)
Linda Randall Wisdom

#562 THE BABY AND THE BODYGUARD
Jule McBride

#563 THE GIFT-WRAPPED GROOM
M.J. Rodgers

#564 A TIMELESS CHRISTMAS
Pat Chandler

Celebrate the season with all four holiday books sealed with a
Christmas kiss—coming to you in December, only from
Harlequin American Romance!

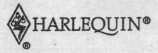 **HARLEQUIN®**

The proprietors of Weddings, Inc. hope you
have enjoyed visiting Eternity, Massachusetts.
And if you missed any of the exciting Weddings,
Inc. titles, here is your opportunity to complete
your collection:

Harlequin Superromance	#598	*Wedding Invitation* by Marisa Carroll	$3.50 U.S. ☐ $3.99 CAN. ☐
Harlequin Romance	#3319	*Expectations* by Shannon Waverly	$2.99 U.S. ☐ $3.50 CAN. ☐
Harlequin Temptation	#502	*Wedding Song* by Vicki Lewis Thompson	$2.99 U.S. ☐ $3.50 CAN. ☐
Harlequin American Romance	#549	*The Wedding Gamble* by Muriel Jensen	$3.50 U.S. ☐ $3.99 CAN. ☐
Harlequin Presents	#1692	*The Vengeful Groom* by Sara Wood	$2.99 U.S. ☐ $3.50 CAN. ☐
Harlequin Intrigue	#298	*Edge of Eternity* by Jasmine Cresswell	$2.99 U.S. ☐ $3.50 CAN. ☐
Harlequin Historical	#248	*Vows* by Margaret Moore	$3.99 U.S. ☐ $4.50 CAN. ☐

HARLEQUIN BOOKS...
NOT THE SAME OLD STORY

TOTAL AMOUNT	$
POSTAGE & HANDLING	$
($1.00 for one book, 50¢ for each additional)	
APPLICABLE TAXES*	$ _____
TOTAL PAYABLE	$ _____
(check or money order—please do not send cash)	

To order, complete this form and send it, along with a check or money order for the
total above, payable to Harlequin Books, to: **In the U.S.:** 3010 Walden Avenue,
P.O. Box 9047, Buffalo, NY 14269-9047; **In Canada:** P.O. Box 613, Fort Erie, Ontario,
L2A 5X3.

Name: _____
Address: _____ City: _____
State/Prov.: _____ Zip/Postal Code: _____

*New York residents remit applicable sales taxes.
 Canadian residents remit applicable GST and provincial taxes.

WED-F

Where do you find hot Texas nights, smooth Texas charm and dangerously sexy cowboys?

Crystal Creek reverberates with the exciting rhythm of Texas. Each story features the rugged individuals who live and love in the Lone Star state.

"...Crystal Creek wonderfully evokes the hot days and steamy nights of a small Texas community...impossible to put down until the last page is turned."
—*Romantic Times*

"With each book the characters in Crystal Creek become more endearingly familiar. This series is far from formula and a welcome addition to the category genre."
—*Affaire de Coeur*

"Altogether, it couldn't be better." —*Rendezvous*

Don't miss the next book in this exciting series. Look for
THE HEART WON'T LIE by MARGOT DALTON

Available in January wherever Harlequin books are sold.

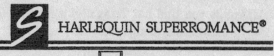

HARLEQUIN SUPERROMANCE®

A Superromance *Showcase* book.

OUT OF THE DARKNESS

by

Lynn Erickson

Miguel Rivera y Aguilar is a creature of the night. A vampire. Since 1481 he has been seeking his nemesis, Baltazar. Instead, he finds Karen Freed, a nurse who's been looking for a man like Miguel all her life. Together they attempt to outwit the forces of darkness that threaten to tear them apart. Together they seek a way to spend this lifetime forging a binding love, a human love. But will Baltazar destroy them first?

Find out in January 1995. Look for *Out of the Darkness* wherever Harlequin books are sold.